WJHC

On The Air!

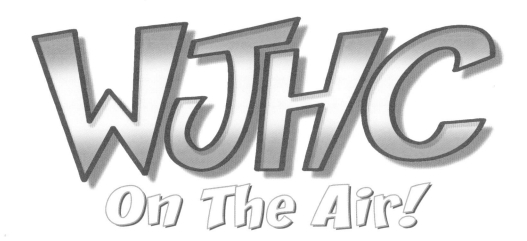

Writer
Jane Smith Fisher

Character Designer and Penciler
Kirsten Petersen

Issue 1 Inker
Phil Avelli Jr.

Issues 2 and 4 Inker
Adam Dekraker

Issue 3 Inker
Kirsten Petersen

Before the Bell and Scrapbook Inker
Ravil Lopez

Colorist and Letterer
John Green

Original Issue 1 Colorist and Letterer
Laura Chin

Original Issue 2 Colorist and Letterer
Susan Daigle-Leach

Editor
Iyna B. Caruso

Book Design and Production
John Green

Project Consultant
Alex Simmons

Print Coordination
Harold Buchholz

Inspiration
Andrew Fisher

WJHC was created by
Jane Smith Fisher

Special thanks to cover artist
Joe Staton

Wilson Place Comics, Inc.
P.O. Box 435
Oceanside, NY 11572

www.WJHC.com

ISBN: 0-9744235-0-5
Printed in Korea

For Andrew
And all our corners

Meet the cast of WJHC

Janey Wells - Watch and learn. This girl's on a fast tack to the top. When Janey's on a mission nothing can stand in her way.

Ciel (pronounced Seel) Chin-King - Now Ciel knows fashion. Just don't be fooled by her trendy girl looks. Great ideas pop out of this brightly colored mind.

Tara O'Toole - In every school there's someone who thinks they're just a little better than everyone else. Well Jackson Hill's someone is Tara O'Toole.

The Skate - "Way cool" is the only way to describe Jackson Hill's beatnik on blades. And wait 'til you see how this guy works a microphone.

Roland Drayton - You have to give this kid credit. He'll take on any challenge--even if he's the completely wrong one for the job.

Sandy Diaz - Meet Jackson Hill's electronics whiz--lifetime member of the Audio/Visual department. You know a guy like this will come in handy.

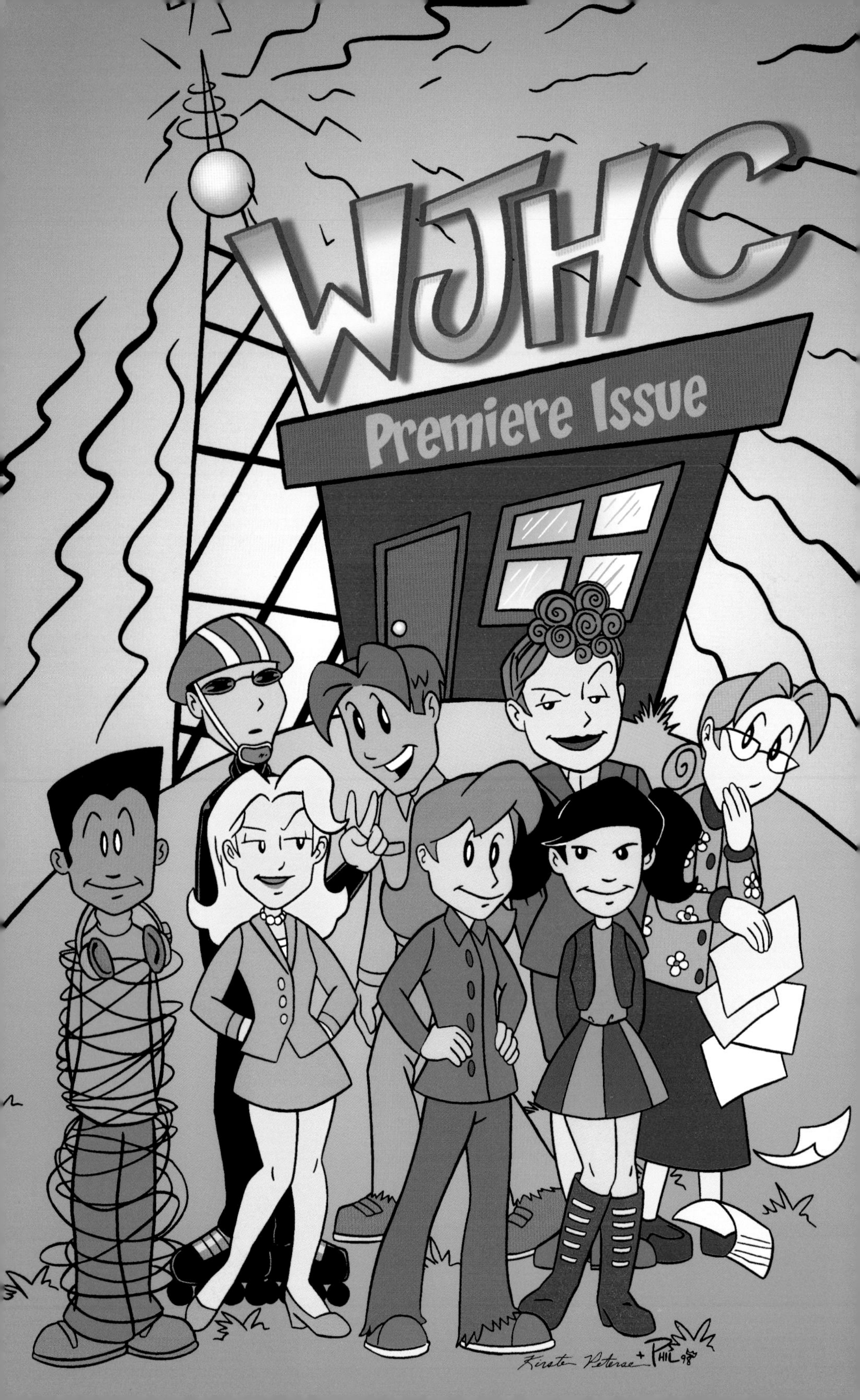

WJHC
Premiere Issue

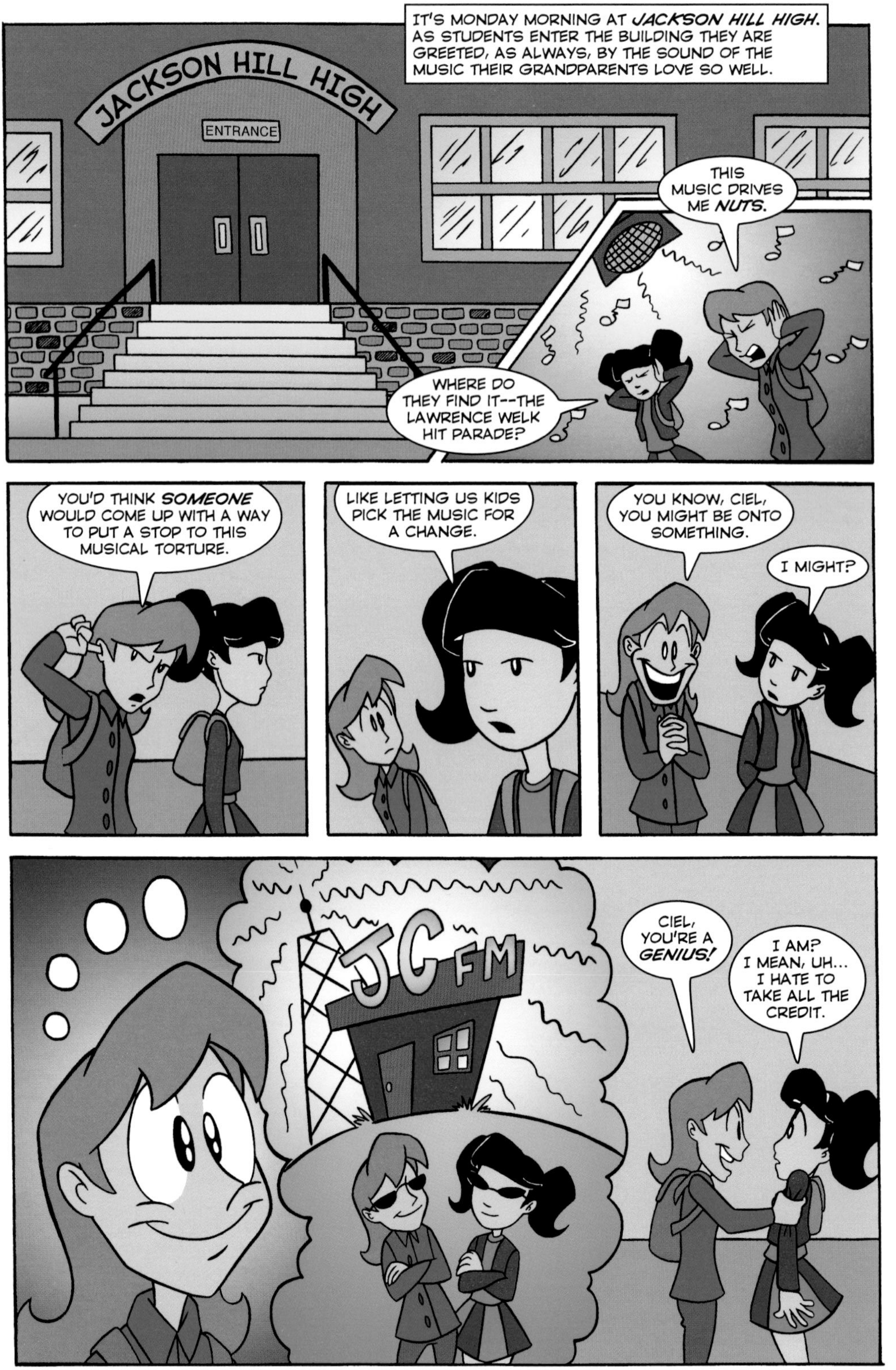
IT'S MONDAY MORNING AT JACKSON HILL HIGH. AS STUDENTS ENTER THE BUILDING THEY ARE GREETED, AS ALWAYS, BY THE SOUND OF THE MUSIC THEIR GRANDPARENTS LOVE SO WELL.
JACKSON HILL HIGH
ENTRANCE
THIS MUSIC DRIVES ME NUTS.
WHERE DO THEY FIND IT--THE LAWRENCE WELK HIT PARADE?
YOU'D THINK SOMEONE WOULD COME UP WITH A WAY TO PUT A STOP TO THIS MUSICAL TORTURE.
LIKE LETTING US KIDS PICK THE MUSIC FOR A CHANGE.
YOU KNOW, CIEL, YOU MIGHT BE ONTO SOMETHING.
I MIGHT?
JC FM
CIEL, YOU'RE A GENIUS!
I AM? I MEAN, UH... I HATE TO TAKE ALL THE CREDIT.

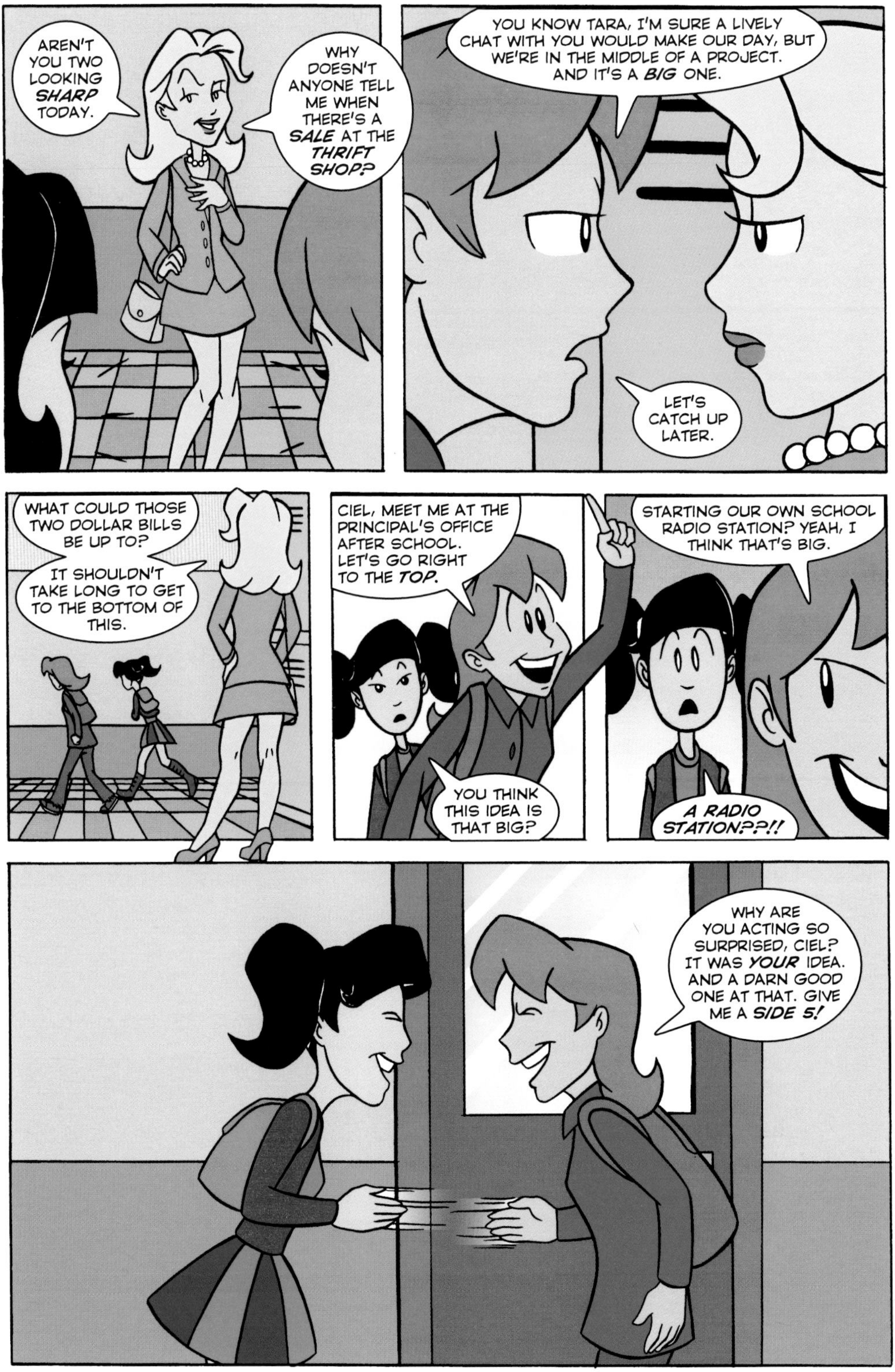
AREN'T YOU TWO LOOKING SHARP TODAY.
WHY DOESN'T ANYONE TELL ME WHEN THERE'S A SALE AT THE THRIFT SHOP?
YOU KNOW TARA, I'M SURE A LIVELY CHAT WITH YOU WOULD MAKE OUR DAY, BUT WE'RE IN THE MIDDLE OF A PROJECT. AND IT'S A BIG ONE.
LET'S CATCH UP LATER.
WHAT COULD THOSE TWO DOLLAR BILLS BE UP TO?
IT SHOULDN'T TAKE LONG TO GET TO THE BOTTOM OF THIS.
CIEL, MEET ME AT THE PRINCIPAL'S OFFICE AFTER SCHOOL. LET'S GO RIGHT TO THE TOP.
YOU THINK THIS IDEA IS THAT BIG?
STARTING OUR OWN SCHOOL RADIO STATION? YEAH, I THINK THAT'S BIG.
A RADIO STATION??!!
WHY ARE YOU ACTING SO SURPRISED, CIEL? IT WAS YOUR IDEA. AND A DARN GOOD ONE AT THAT. GIVE ME A SIDE 5!

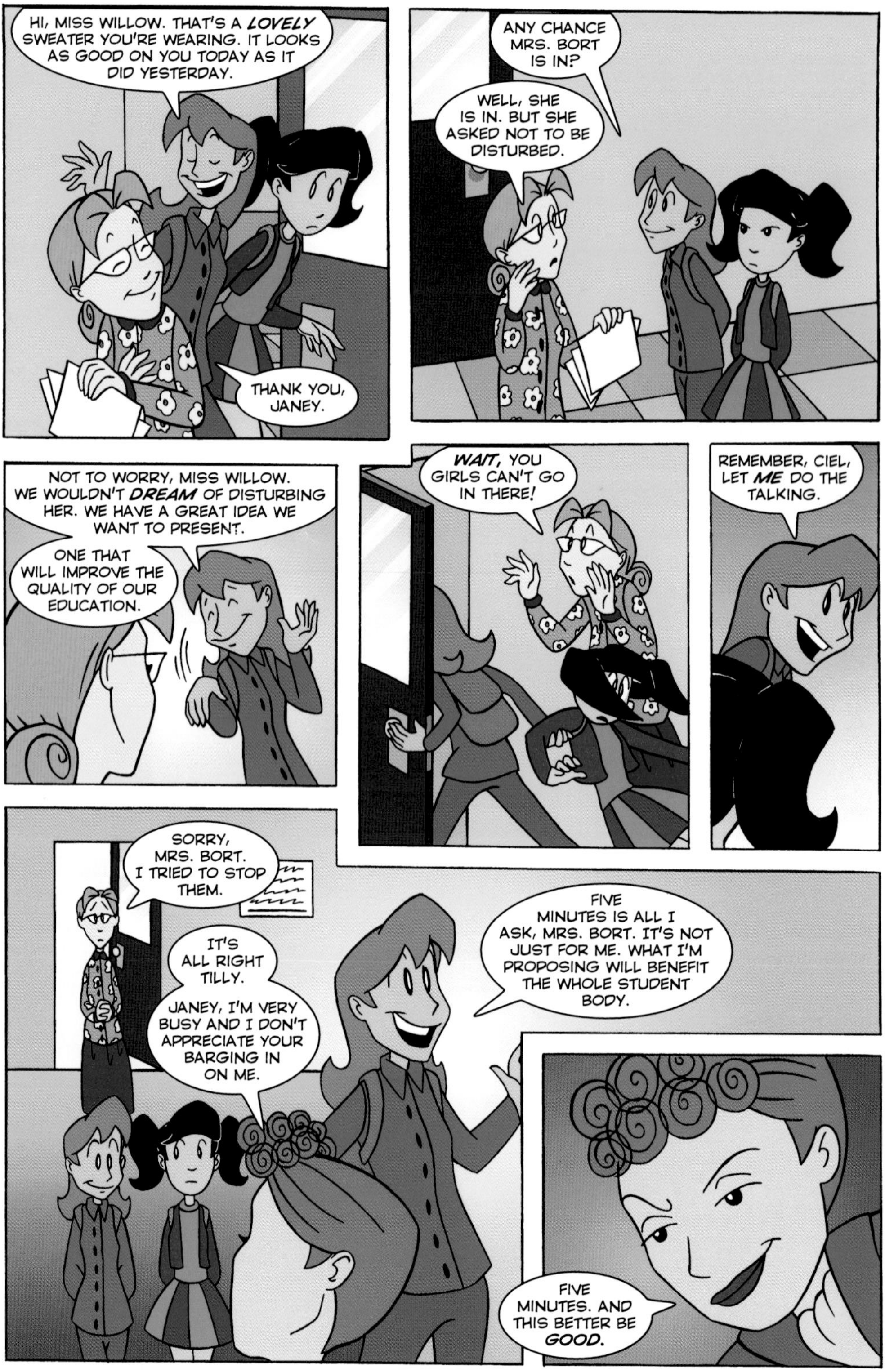
HI, MISS WILLOW. THAT'S A *LOVELY* SWEATER YOU'RE WEARING. IT LOOKS AS GOOD ON YOU TODAY AS IT DID YESTERDAY.
THANK YOU, JANEY.
ANY CHANCE MRS. BORT IS IN?
WELL, SHE IS IN. BUT SHE ASKED NOT TO BE DISTURBED.
NOT TO WORRY, MISS WILLOW. WE WOULDN'T *DREAM* OF DISTURBING HER. WE HAVE A GREAT IDEA WE WANT TO PRESENT.
ONE THAT WILL IMPROVE THE QUALITY OF OUR EDUCATION.
WAIT, YOU GIRLS CAN'T GO IN THERE!
REMEMBER, CIEL, LET *ME* DO THE TALKING.
SORRY, MRS. BORT. I TRIED TO STOP THEM.
IT'S ALL RIGHT TILLY.
JANEY, I'M VERY BUSY AND I DON'T APPRECIATE YOUR BARGING IN ON ME.
FIVE MINUTES IS ALL I ASK, MRS. BORT. IT'S NOT JUST FOR ME. WHAT I'M PROPOSING WILL BENEFIT THE WHOLE STUDENT BODY.
FIVE MINUTES. AND THIS BETTER BE *GOOD.*

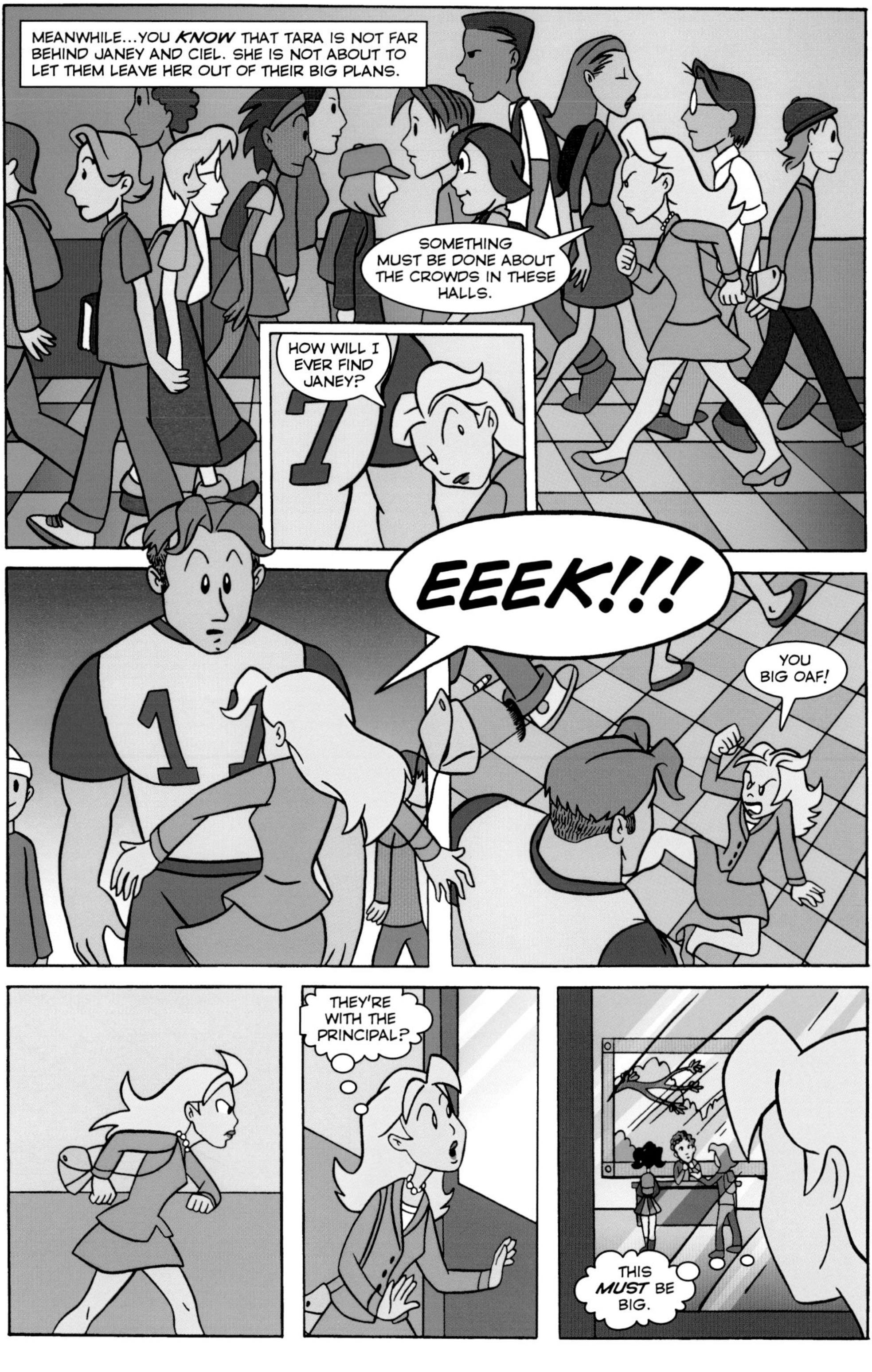
MEANWHILE...YOU KNOW THAT TARA IS NOT FAR BEHIND JANEY AND CIEL. SHE IS NOT ABOUT TO LET THEM LEAVE HER OUT OF THEIR BIG PLANS.
SOMETHING MUST BE DONE ABOUT THE CROWDS IN THESE HALLS.
HOW WILL I EVER FIND JANEY?
EEEK!!!
YOU BIG OAF!
THEY'RE WITH THE PRINCIPAL?
THIS MUST BE BIG.

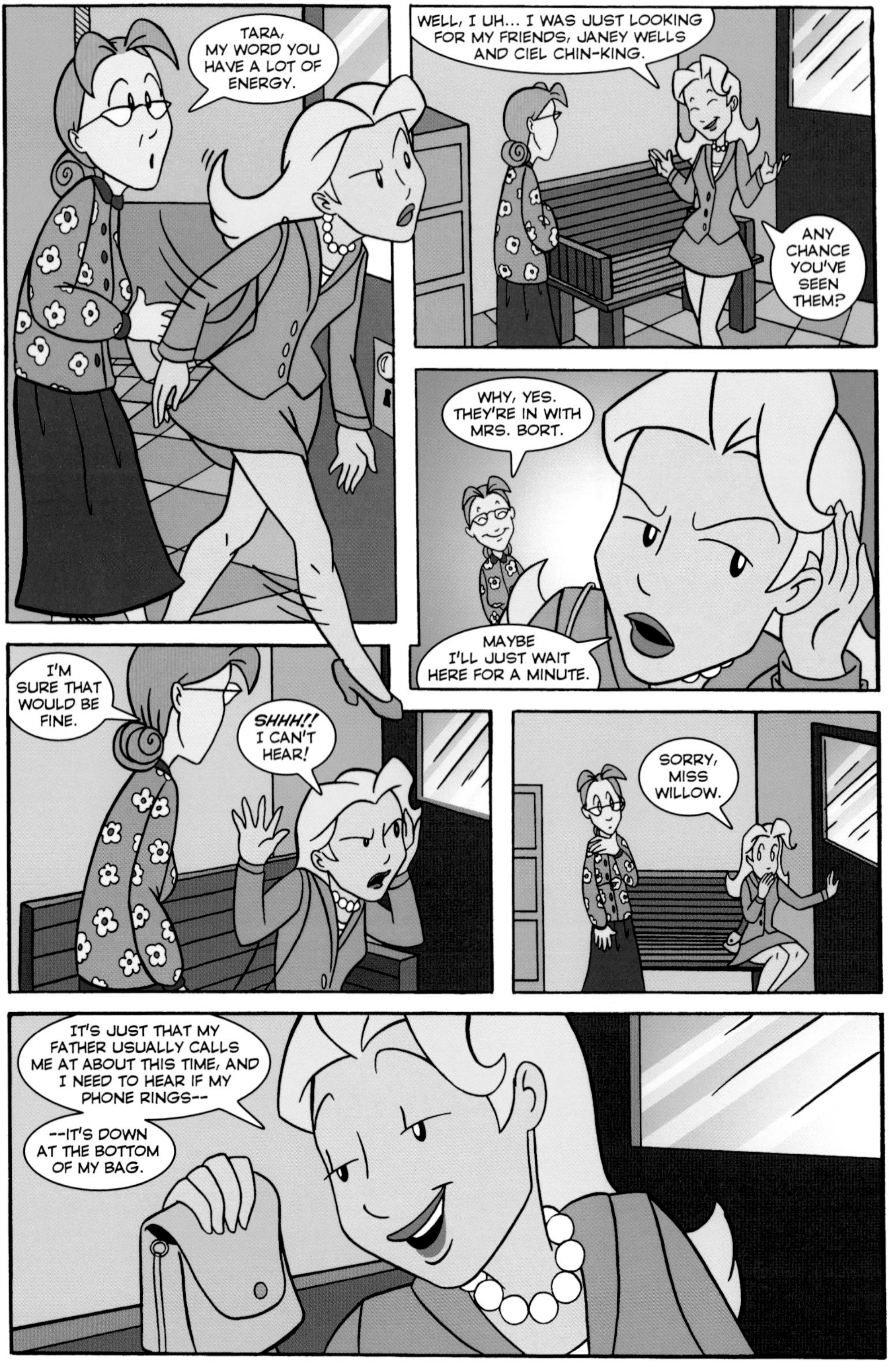
TARA, MY WORD YOU HAVE A LOT OF ENERGY.
WELL, I UH... I WAS JUST LOOKING FOR MY FRIENDS, JANEY WELLS AND CIEL CHIN-KING.
ANY CHANCE YOU'VE SEEN THEM?
WHY, YES. THEY'RE IN WITH MRS. BORT.
MAYBE I'LL JUST WAIT HERE FOR A MINUTE.
I'M SURE THAT WOULD BE FINE.
SHHH!! I CAN'T HEAR!
SORRY, MISS WILLOW.
IT'S JUST THAT MY FATHER USUALLY CALLS ME AT ABOUT THIS TIME, AND I NEED TO HEAR IF MY PHONE RINGS--
--IT'S DOWN AT THE BOTTOM OF MY BAG.

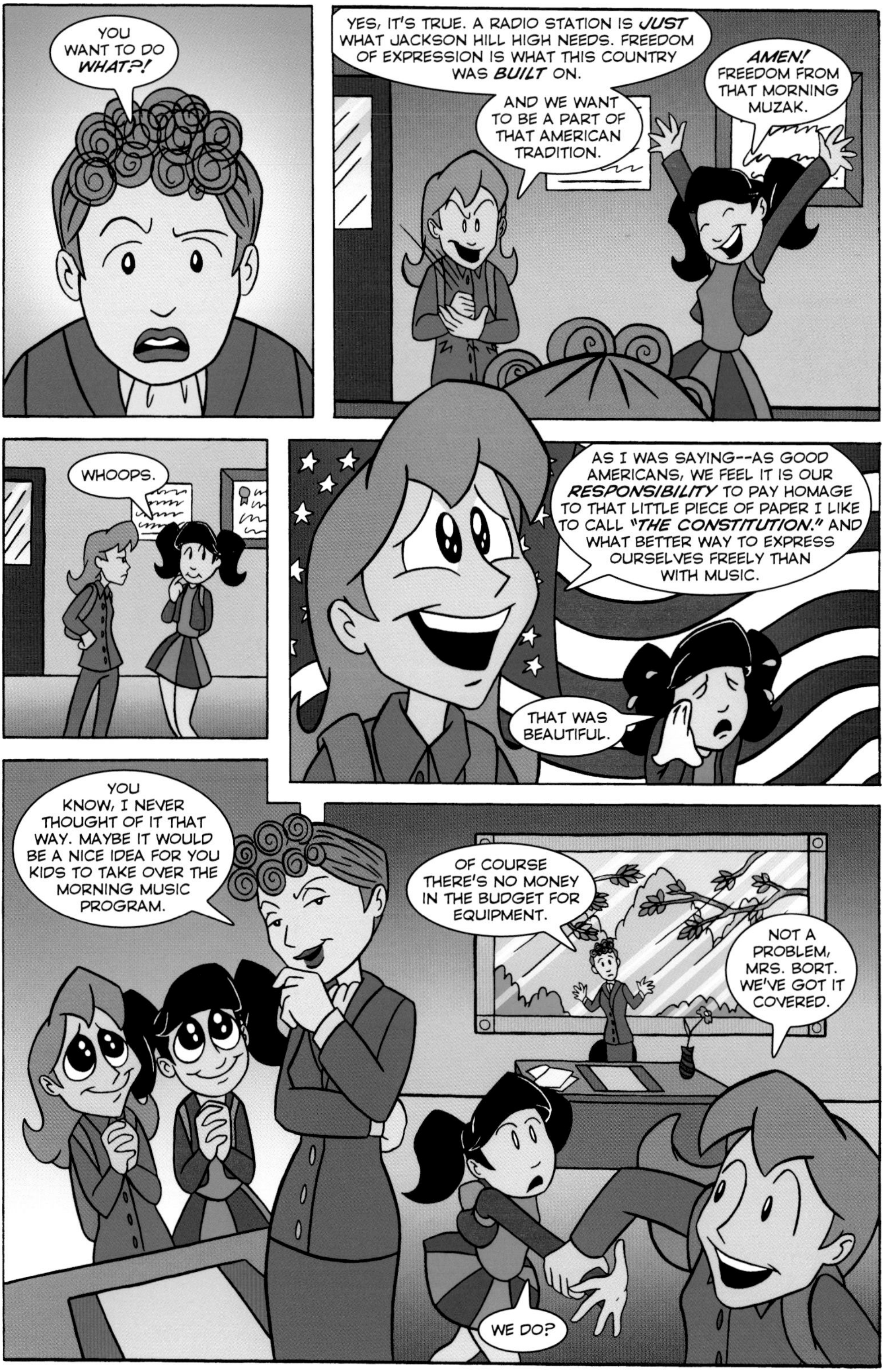
YOU WANT TO DO WHAT?!
YES, IT'S TRUE. A RADIO STATION IS JUST WHAT JACKSON HILL HIGH NEEDS. FREEDOM OF EXPRESSION IS WHAT THIS COUNTRY WAS BUILT ON.
AND WE WANT TO BE A PART OF THAT AMERICAN TRADITION.
AMEN! FREEDOM FROM THAT MORNING MUZAK.
WHOOPS.
AS I WAS SAYING--AS GOOD AMERICANS, WE FEEL IT IS OUR RESPONSIBILITY TO PAY HOMAGE TO THAT LITTLE PIECE OF PAPER I LIKE TO CALL "THE CONSTITUTION." AND WHAT BETTER WAY TO EXPRESS OURSELVES FREELY THAN WITH MUSIC.
THAT WAS BEAUTIFUL.
YOU KNOW, I NEVER THOUGHT OF IT THAT WAY. MAYBE IT WOULD BE A NICE IDEA FOR YOU KIDS TO TAKE OVER THE MORNING MUSIC PROGRAM.
OF COURSE THERE'S NO MONEY IN THE BUDGET FOR EQUIPMENT.
NOT A PROBLEM, MRS. BORT. WE'VE GOT IT COVERED.
WE DO?

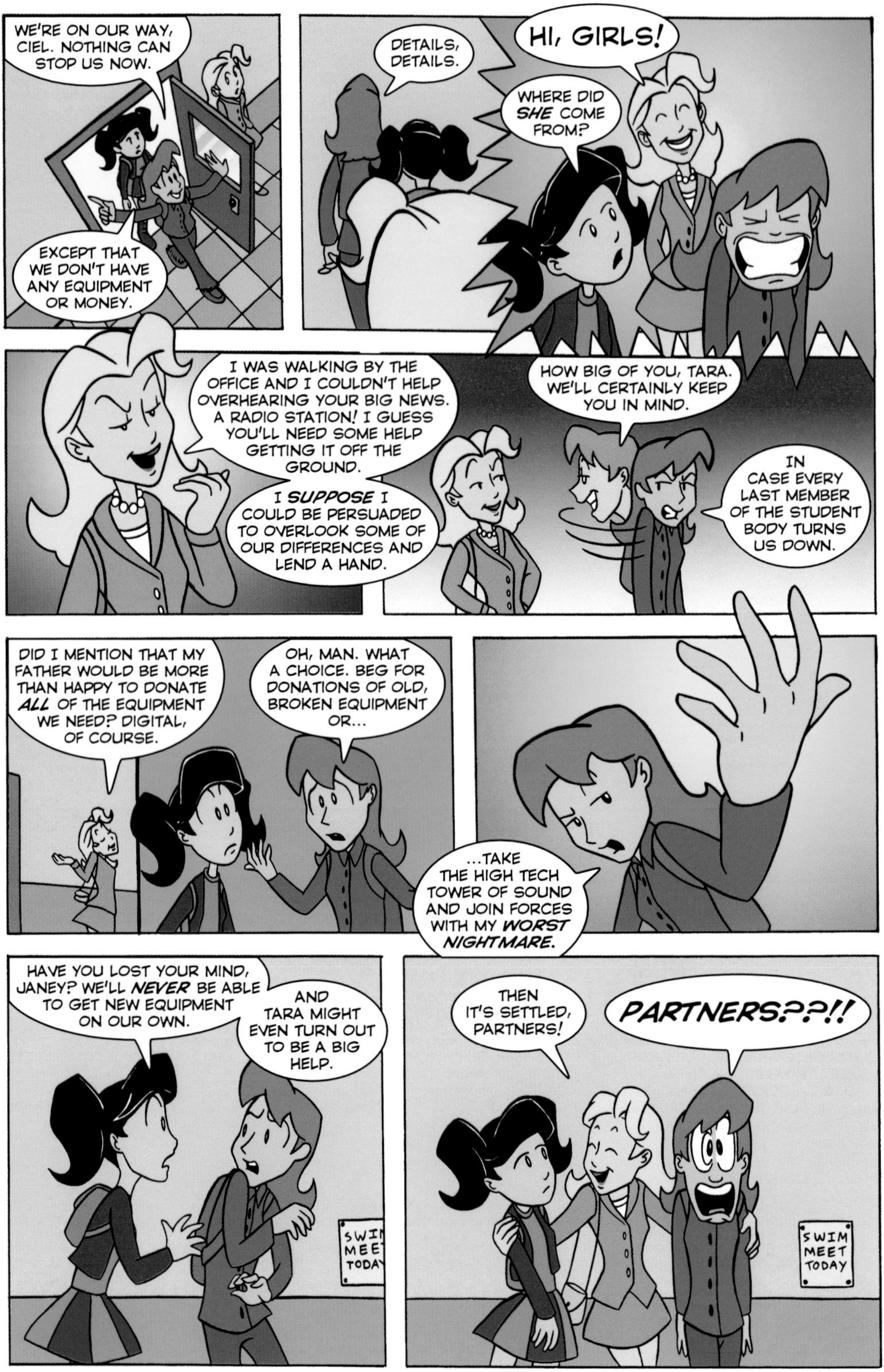
WE'RE ON OUR WAY, CIEL. NOTHING CAN STOP US NOW.
EXCEPT THAT WE DON'T HAVE ANY EQUIPMENT OR MONEY.
DETAILS, DETAILS.
HI, GIRLS!
WHERE DID SHE COME FROM?
I WAS WALKING BY THE OFFICE AND I COULDN'T HELP OVERHEARING YOUR BIG NEWS. A RADIO STATION! I GUESS YOU'LL NEED SOME HELP GETTING IT OFF THE GROUND.
I SUPPOSE I COULD BE PERSUADED TO OVERLOOK SOME OF OUR DIFFERENCES AND LEND A HAND.
HOW BIG OF YOU, TARA. WE'LL CERTAINLY KEEP YOU IN MIND.
IN CASE EVERY LAST MEMBER OF THE STUDENT BODY TURNS US DOWN.
DID I MENTION THAT MY FATHER WOULD BE MORE THAN HAPPY TO DONATE ALL OF THE EQUIPMENT WE NEED? DIGITAL, OF COURSE.
OH, MAN. WHAT A CHOICE. BEG FOR DONATIONS OF OLD, BROKEN EQUIPMENT OR...
...TAKE THE HIGH TECH TOWER OF SOUND AND JOIN FORCES WITH MY WORST NIGHTMARE.
HAVE YOU LOST YOUR MIND, JANEY? WE'LL NEVER BE ABLE TO GET NEW EQUIPMENT ON OUR OWN.
AND TARA MIGHT EVEN TURN OUT TO BE A BIG HELP.
SWIM MEET TODAY
THEN IT'S SETTLED, PARTNERS!
PARTNERS??!!
SWIM MEET TODAY

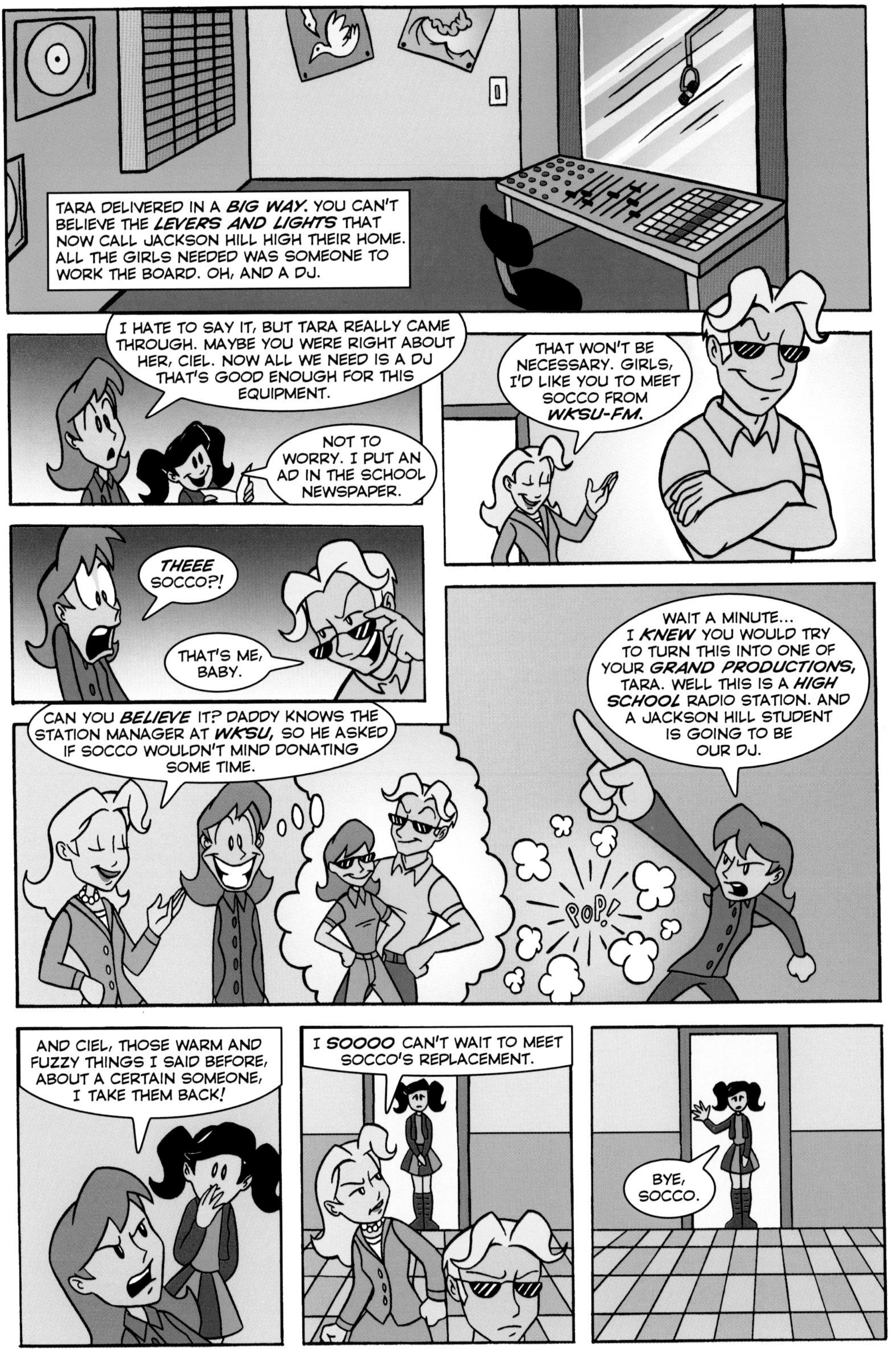
TARA DELIVERED IN A BIG WAY. YOU CAN'T BELIEVE THE LEVERS AND LIGHTS THAT NOW CALL JACKSON HILL HIGH THEIR HOME. ALL THE GIRLS NEEDED WAS SOMEONE TO WORK THE BOARD. OH, AND A DJ.
I HATE TO SAY IT, BUT TARA REALLY CAME THROUGH. MAYBE YOU WERE RIGHT ABOUT HER, CIEL. NOW ALL WE NEED IS A DJ THAT'S GOOD ENOUGH FOR THIS EQUIPMENT.
NOT TO WORRY. I PUT AN AD IN THE SCHOOL NEWSPAPER.
THAT WON'T BE NECESSARY. GIRLS, I'D LIKE YOU TO MEET SOCCO FROM WKSU-FM.
THEEE SOCCO?!
THAT'S ME, BABY.
CAN YOU BELIEVE IT? DADDY KNOWS THE STATION MANAGER AT WKSU, SO HE ASKED IF SOCCO WOULDN'T MIND DONATING SOME TIME.
POP!
WAIT A MINUTE... I KNEW YOU WOULD TRY TO TURN THIS INTO ONE OF YOUR GRAND PRODUCTIONS, TARA. WELL THIS IS A HIGH SCHOOL RADIO STATION. AND A JACKSON HILL STUDENT IS GOING TO BE OUR DJ.
AND CIEL, THOSE WARM AND FUZZY THINGS I SAID BEFORE, ABOUT A CERTAIN SOMEONE, I TAKE THEM BACK!
I SOOOO CAN'T WAIT TO MEET SOCCO'S REPLACEMENT.
BYE, SOCCO.

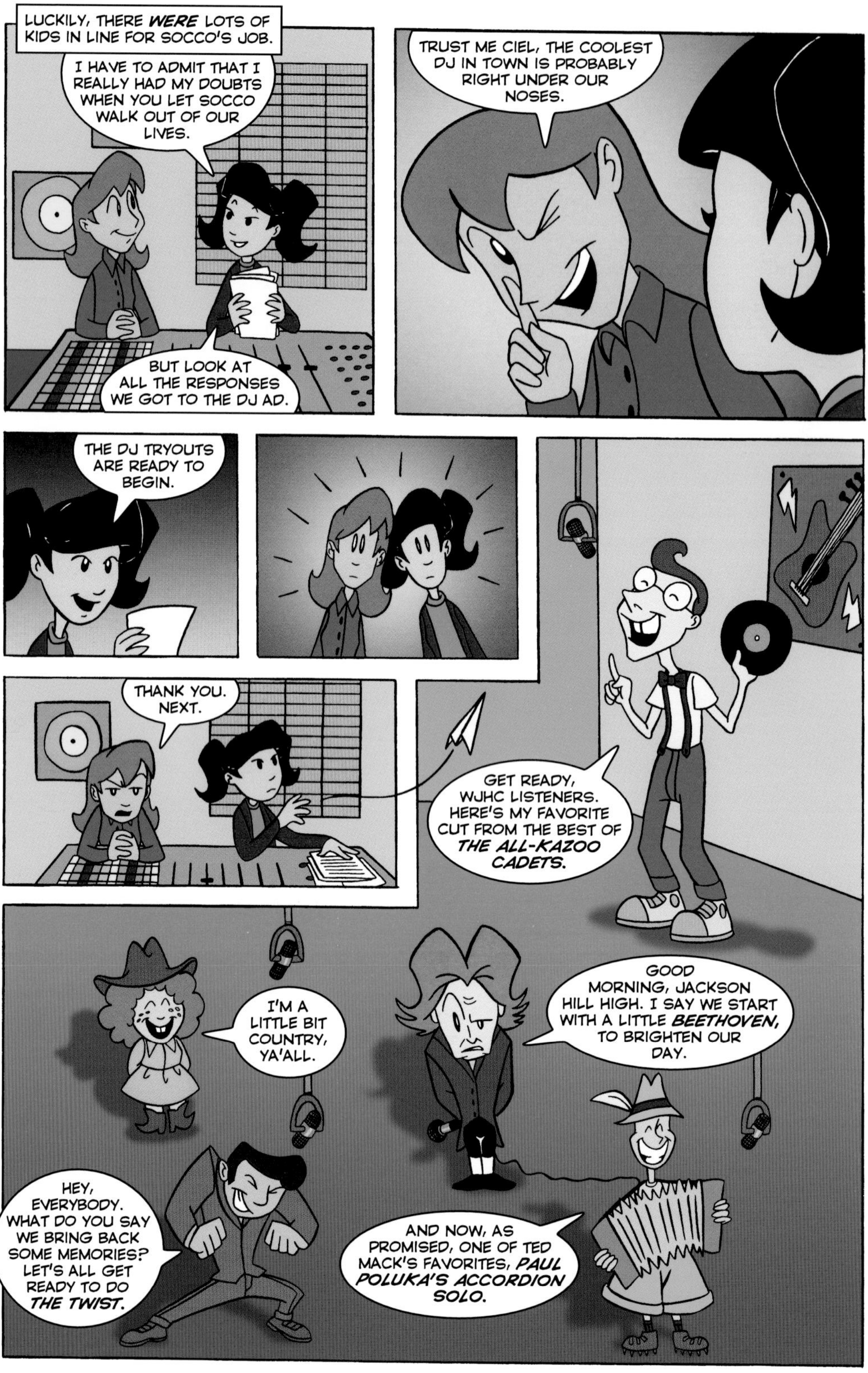
LUCKILY, THERE WERE LOTS OF KIDS IN LINE FOR SOCCO'S JOB.
I HAVE TO ADMIT THAT I REALLY HAD MY DOUBTS WHEN YOU LET SOCCO WALK OUT OF OUR LIVES.
BUT LOOK AT ALL THE RESPONSES WE GOT TO THE DJ AD.
TRUST ME CIEL, THE COOLEST DJ IN TOWN IS PROBABLY RIGHT UNDER OUR NOSES.
THE DJ TRYOUTS ARE READY TO BEGIN.
THANK YOU. NEXT.
GET READY, WJHC LISTENERS. HERE'S MY FAVORITE CUT FROM THE BEST OF THE ALL-KAZOO CADETS.
I'M A LITTLE BIT COUNTRY, YA'ALL.
GOOD MORNING, JACKSON HILL HIGH. I SAY WE START WITH A LITTLE BEETHOVEN, TO BRIGHTEN OUR DAY.
HEY, EVERYBODY. WHAT DO YOU SAY WE BRING BACK SOME MEMORIES? LET'S ALL GET READY TO DO THE TWIST.
AND NOW, AS PROMISED, ONE OF TED MACK'S FAVORITES, PAUL POLUKA'S ACCORDION SOLO.

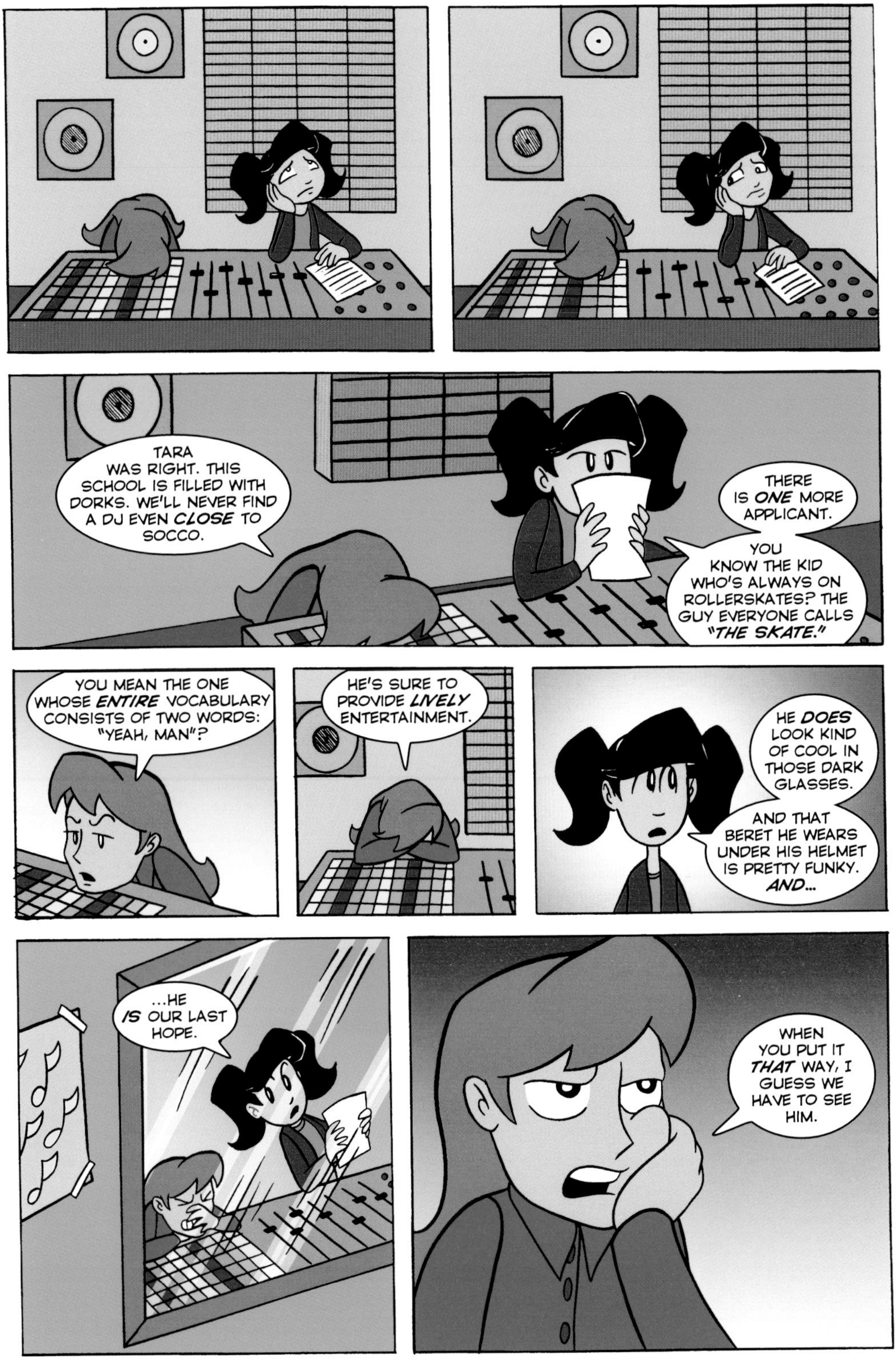
TARA WAS RIGHT. THIS SCHOOL IS FILLED WITH DORKS. WE'LL NEVER FIND A DJ EVEN *CLOSE* TO SOCCO.
THERE IS *ONE* MORE APPLICANT.
YOU KNOW THE KID WHO'S ALWAYS ON ROLLERSKATES? THE GUY EVERYONE CALLS *"THE SKATE."*
YOU MEAN THE ONE WHOSE *ENTIRE* VOCABULARY CONSISTS OF TWO WORDS: "YEAH, MAN"?
HE'S SURE TO PROVIDE *LIVELY* ENTERTAINMENT.
HE *DOES* LOOK KIND OF COOL IN THOSE DARK GLASSES.
AND THAT BERET HE WEARS UNDER HIS HELMET IS PRETTY FUNKY. *AND...*
...HE *IS* OUR LAST HOPE.
WHEN YOU PUT IT *THAT* WAY, I GUESS WE HAVE TO SEE HIM.

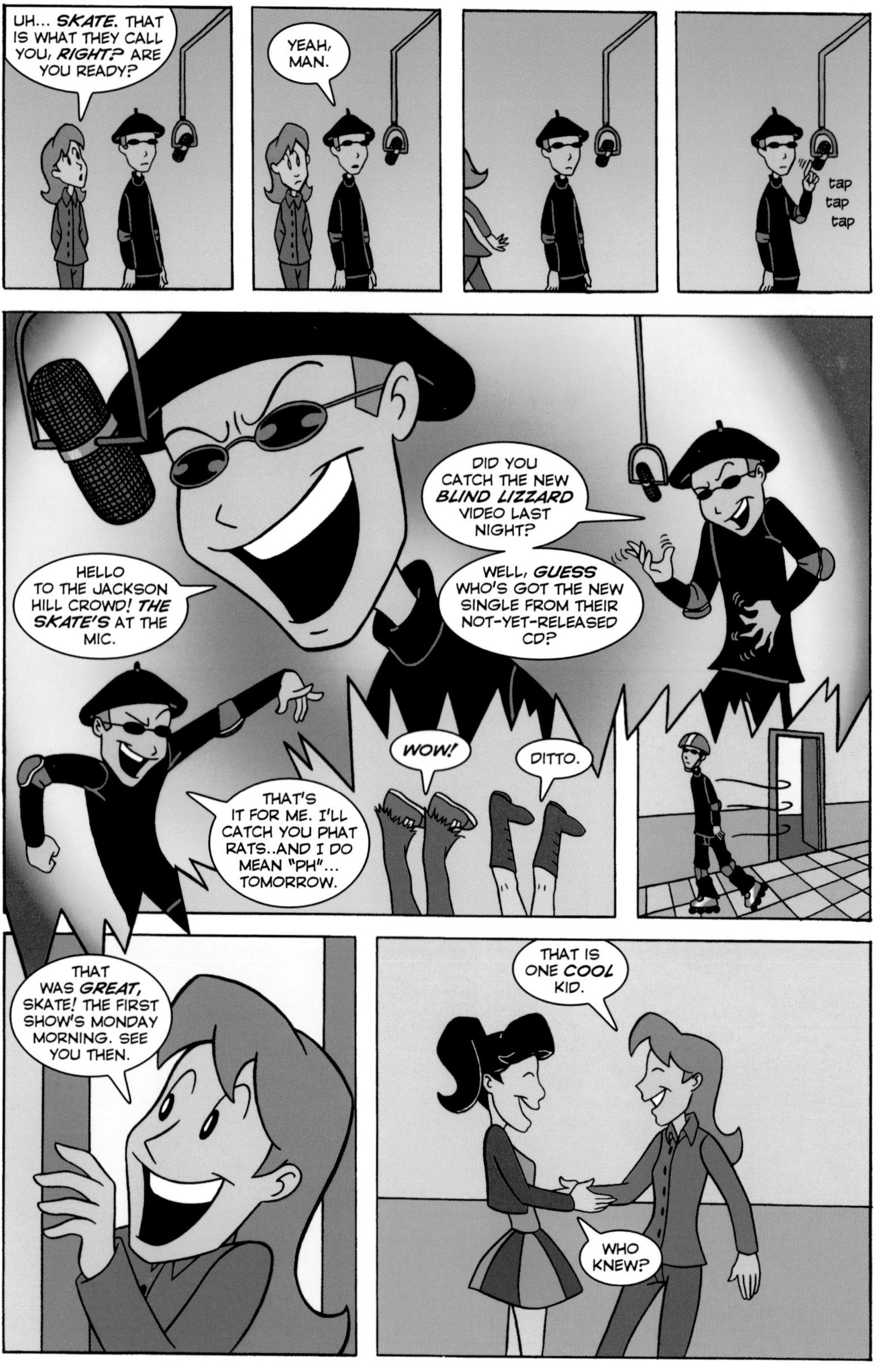

UH... SKATE. THAT IS WHAT THEY CALL YOU, RIGHT? ARE YOU READY?
YEAH, MAN.
tap tap tap
HELLO TO THE JACKSON HILL CROWD! THE SKATE'S AT THE MIC.
DID YOU CATCH THE NEW BLIND LIZZARD VIDEO LAST NIGHT?
WELL, GUESS WHO'S GOT THE NEW SINGLE FROM THEIR NOT-YET-RELEASED CD?
THAT'S IT FOR ME. I'LL CATCH YOU PHAT RATS..AND I DO MEAN "PH"... TOMORROW.
WOW!
DITTO.
THAT WAS GREAT, SKATE! THE FIRST SHOW'S MONDAY MORNING. SEE YOU THEN.
THAT IS ONE COOL KID.
WHO KNEW?

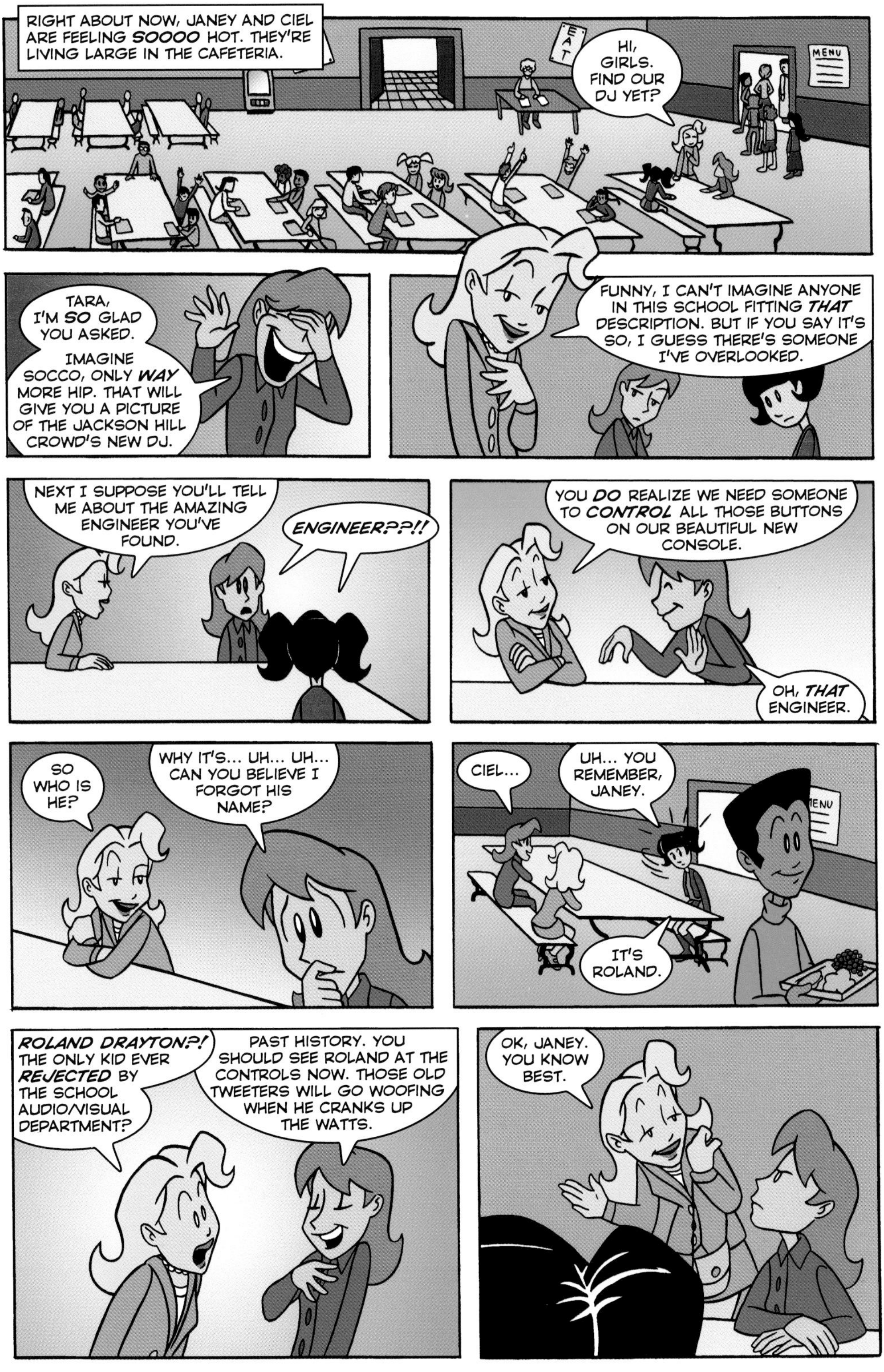
RIGHT ABOUT NOW, JANEY AND CIEL ARE FEELING SOOOO HOT. THEY'RE LIVING LARGE IN THE CAFETERIA.
EAT
MENU
HI, GIRLS. FIND OUR DJ YET?
TARA, I'M SO GLAD YOU ASKED.
IMAGINE SOCCO, ONLY WAY MORE HIP. THAT WILL GIVE YOU A PICTURE OF THE JACKSON HILL CROWD'S NEW DJ.
FUNNY, I CAN'T IMAGINE ANYONE IN THIS SCHOOL FITTING THAT DESCRIPTION. BUT IF YOU SAY IT'S SO, I GUESS THERE'S SOMEONE I'VE OVERLOOKED.
NEXT I SUPPOSE YOU'LL TELL ME ABOUT THE AMAZING ENGINEER YOU'VE FOUND.
ENGINEER??!!
YOU DO REALIZE WE NEED SOMEONE TO CONTROL ALL THOSE BUTTONS ON OUR BEAUTIFUL NEW CONSOLE.
OH, THAT ENGINEER.
SO WHO IS HE?
WHY IT'S... UH... UH... CAN YOU BELIEVE I FORGOT HIS NAME?
CIEL...
UH... YOU REMEMBER, JANEY.
IT'S ROLAND.
ROLAND DRAYTON?! THE ONLY KID EVER REJECTED BY THE SCHOOL AUDIO/VISUAL DEPARTMENT?
PAST HISTORY. YOU SHOULD SEE ROLAND AT THE CONTROLS NOW. THOSE OLD TWEETERS WILL GO WOOFING WHEN HE CRANKS UP THE WATTS.
OK, JANEY. YOU KNOW BEST.

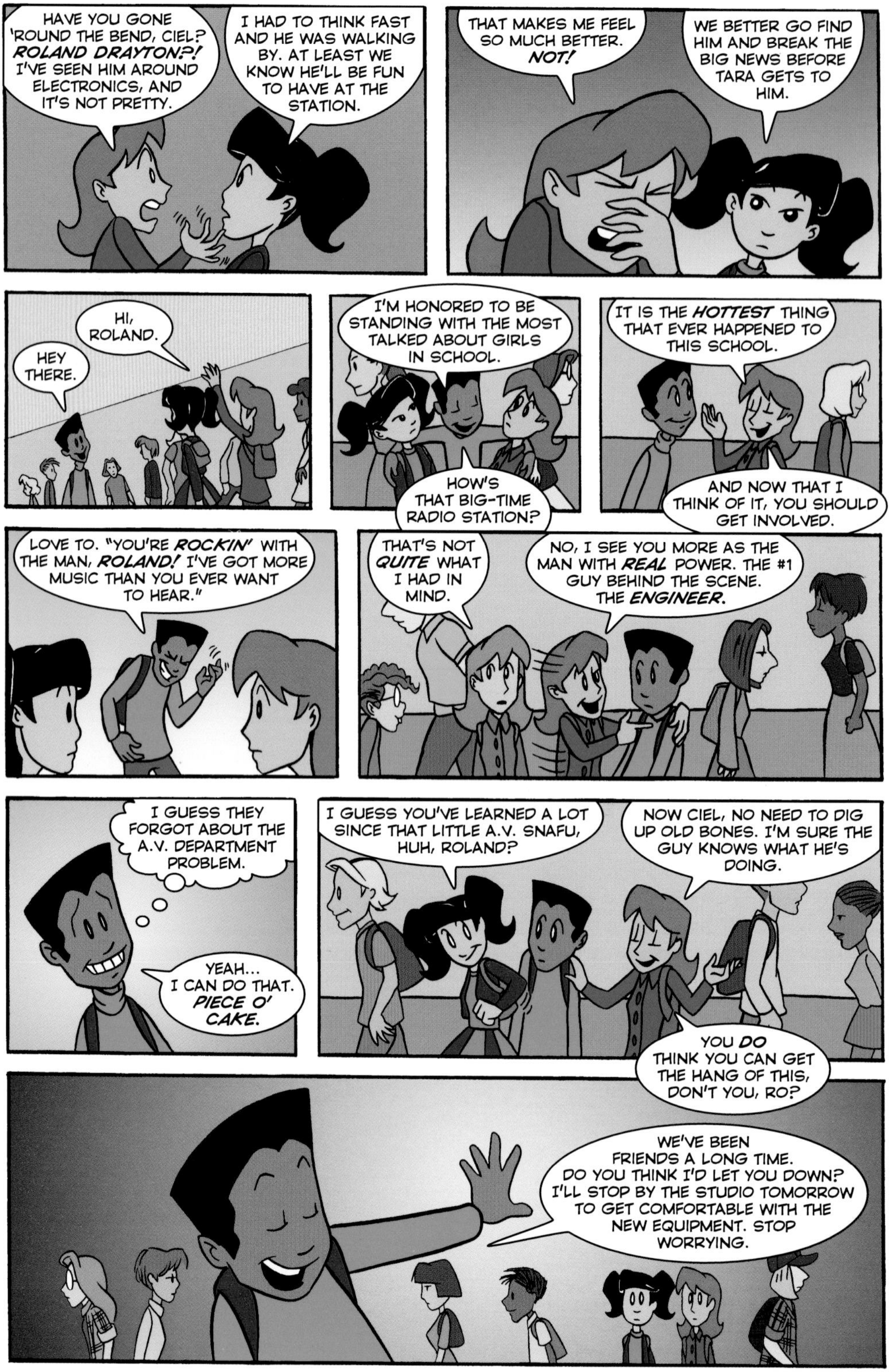
HAVE YOU GONE 'ROUND THE BEND, CIEL? ROLAND DRAYTON?! I'VE SEEN HIM AROUND ELECTRONICS, AND IT'S NOT PRETTY.
I HAD TO THINK FAST AND HE WAS WALKING BY. AT LEAST WE KNOW HE'LL BE FUN TO HAVE AT THE STATION.
THAT MAKES ME FEEL SO MUCH BETTER. NOT!
WE BETTER GO FIND HIM AND BREAK THE BIG NEWS BEFORE TARA GETS TO HIM.
HEY THERE.
HI, ROLAND.
I'M HONORED TO BE STANDING WITH THE MOST TALKED ABOUT GIRLS IN SCHOOL.
HOW'S THAT BIG-TIME RADIO STATION?
IT IS THE HOTTEST THING THAT EVER HAPPENED TO THIS SCHOOL.
AND NOW THAT I THINK OF IT, YOU SHOULD GET INVOLVED.
LOVE TO. "YOU'RE ROCKIN' WITH THE MAN, ROLAND! I'VE GOT MORE MUSIC THAN YOU EVER WANT TO HEAR."
THAT'S NOT QUITE WHAT I HAD IN MIND.
NO, I SEE YOU MORE AS THE MAN WITH REAL POWER. THE #1 GUY BEHIND THE SCENE. THE ENGINEER.
I GUESS THEY FORGOT ABOUT THE A.V. DEPARTMENT PROBLEM.
YEAH... I CAN DO THAT. PIECE O' CAKE.
I GUESS YOU'VE LEARNED A LOT SINCE THAT LITTLE A.V. SNAFU, HUH, ROLAND?
NOW CIEL, NO NEED TO DIG UP OLD BONES. I'M SURE THE GUY KNOWS WHAT HE'S DOING.
YOU DO THINK YOU CAN GET THE HANG OF THIS, DON'T YOU, RO?
WE'VE BEEN FRIENDS A LONG TIME. DO YOU THINK I'D LET YOU DOWN? I'LL STOP BY THE STUDIO TOMORROW TO GET COMFORTABLE WITH THE NEW EQUIPMENT. STOP WORRYING.

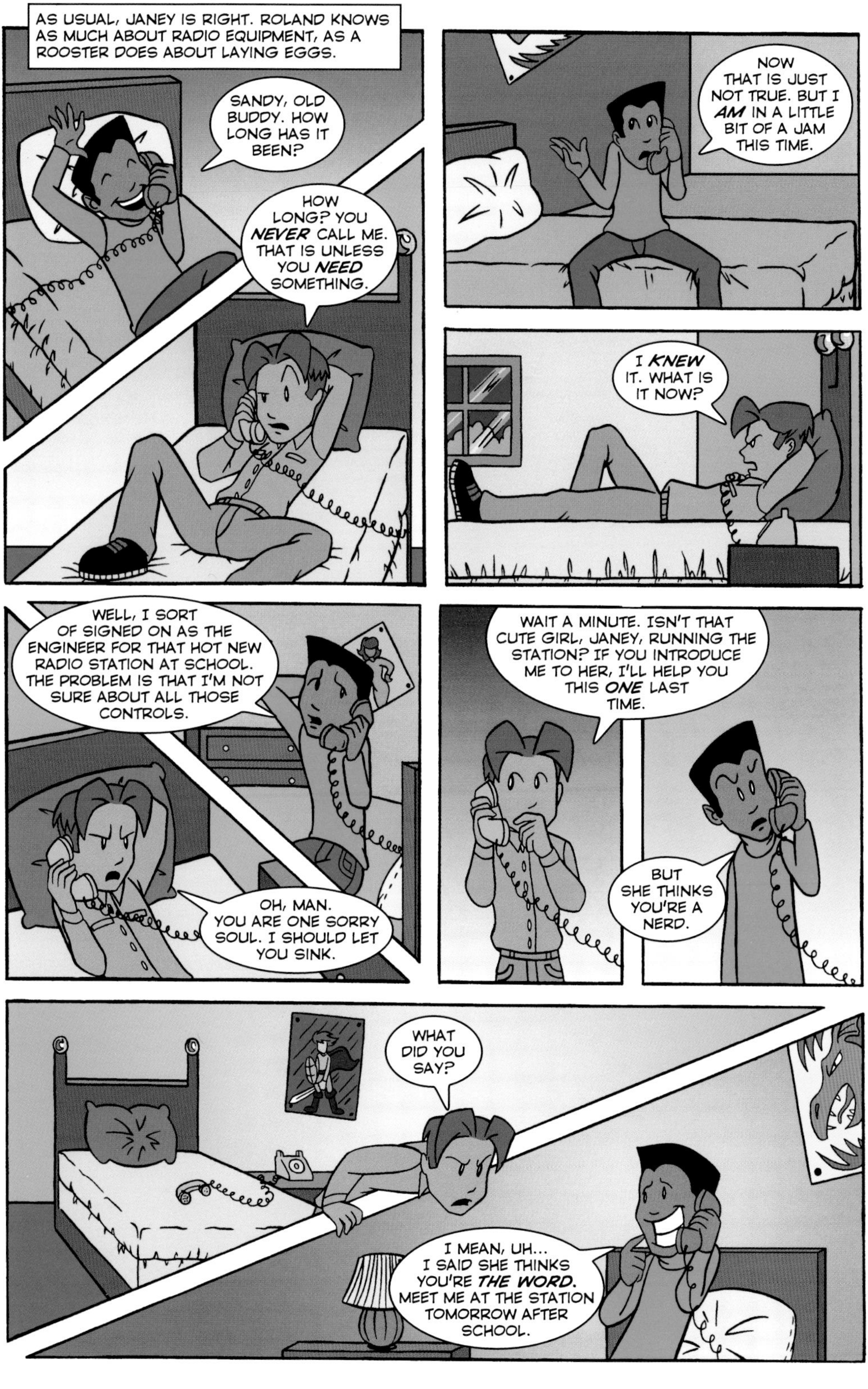
AS USUAL, JANEY IS RIGHT. ROLAND KNOWS AS MUCH ABOUT RADIO EQUIPMENT, AS A ROOSTER DOES ABOUT LAYING EGGS.
SANDY, OLD BUDDY. HOW LONG HAS IT BEEN?
HOW LONG? YOU NEVER CALL ME. THAT IS UNLESS YOU NEED SOMETHING.
NOW THAT IS JUST NOT TRUE. BUT I AM IN A LITTLE BIT OF A JAM THIS TIME.
I KNEW IT. WHAT IS IT NOW?
WELL, I SORT OF SIGNED ON AS THE ENGINEER FOR THAT HOT NEW RADIO STATION AT SCHOOL. THE PROBLEM IS THAT I'M NOT SURE ABOUT ALL THOSE CONTROLS.
OH, MAN. YOU ARE ONE SORRY SOUL. I SHOULD LET YOU SINK.
WAIT A MINUTE. ISN'T THAT CUTE GIRL, JANEY, RUNNING THE STATION? IF YOU INTRODUCE ME TO HER, I'LL HELP YOU THIS ONE LAST TIME.
BUT SHE THINKS YOU'RE A NERD.
WHAT DID YOU SAY?
I MEAN, UH... I SAID SHE THINKS YOU'RE THE WORD. MEET ME AT THE STATION TOMORROW AFTER SCHOOL.

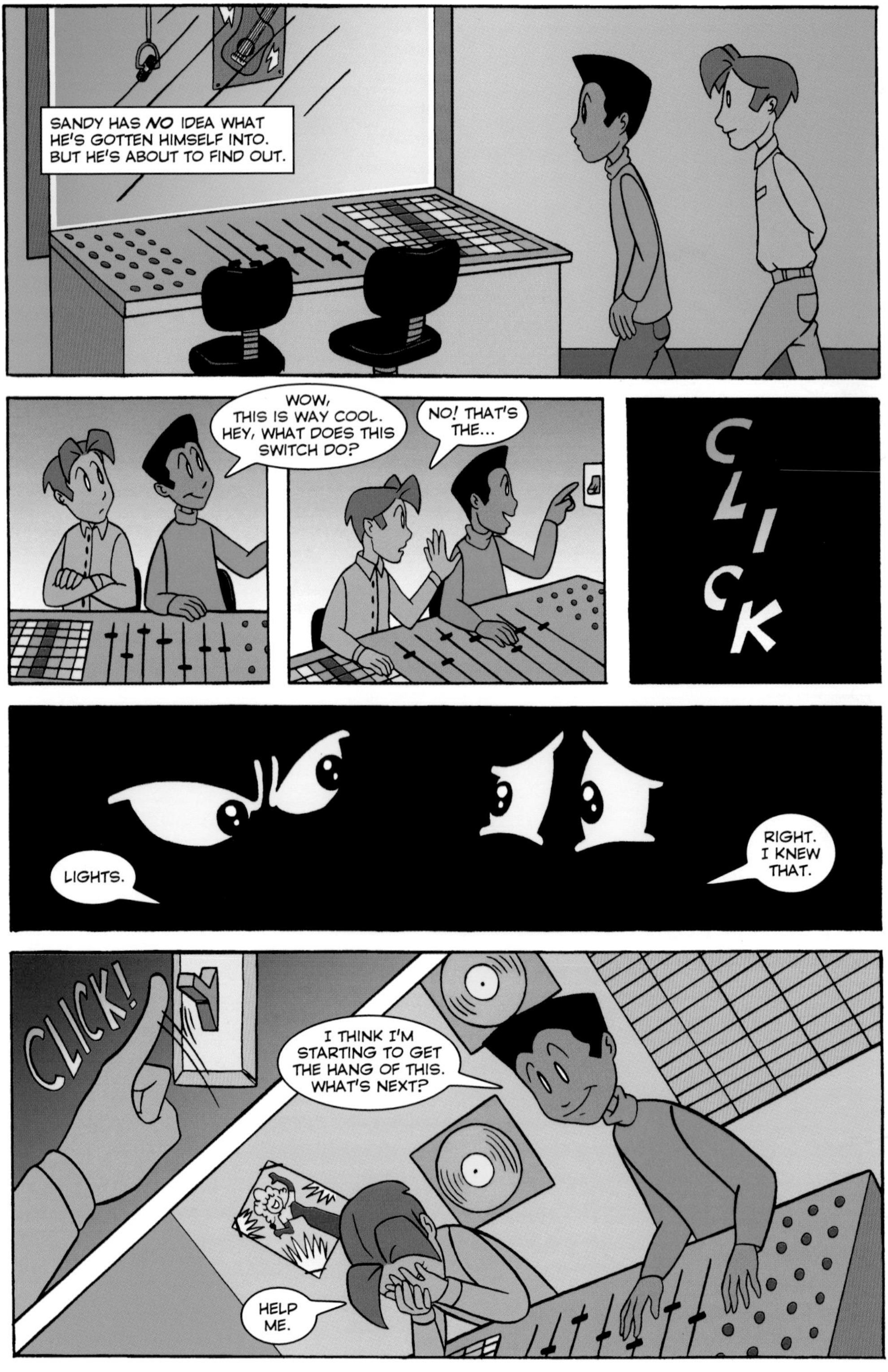
SANDY HAS NO IDEA WHAT HE'S GOTTEN HIMSELF INTO. BUT HE'S ABOUT TO FIND OUT.
WOW, THIS IS WAY COOL. HEY, WHAT DOES THIS SWITCH DO?
NO! THAT'S THE...
CLICK
LIGHTS.
RIGHT. I KNEW THAT.
CLICK!
I THINK I'M STARTING TO GET THE HANG OF THIS. WHAT'S NEXT?
HELP ME.

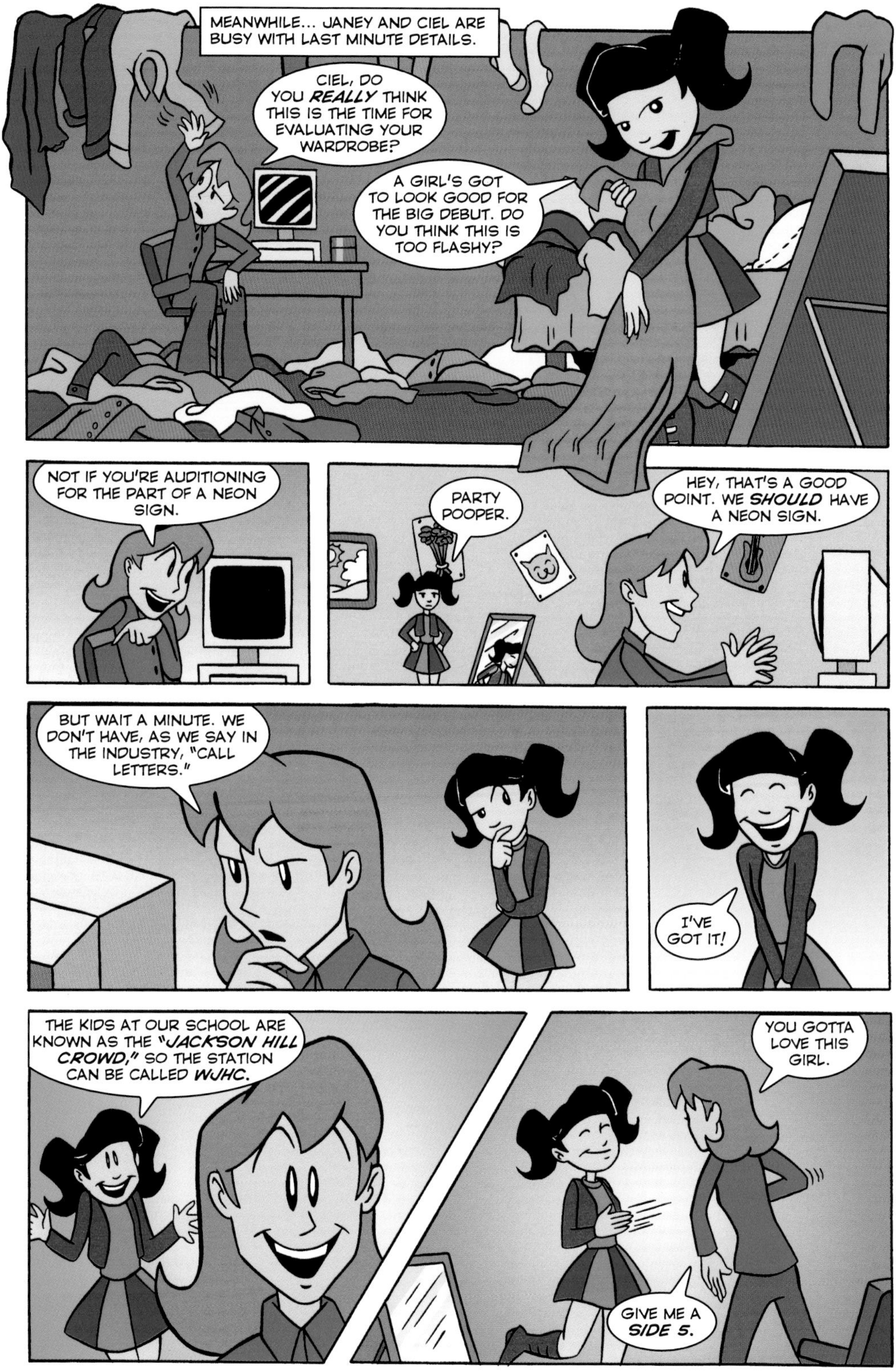
MEANWHILE... JANEY AND CIEL ARE BUSY WITH LAST MINUTE DETAILS.
CIEL, DO YOU *REALLY* THINK THIS IS THE TIME FOR EVALUATING YOUR WARDROBE?
A GIRL'S GOT TO LOOK GOOD FOR THE BIG DEBUT. DO YOU THINK THIS IS TOO FLASHY?
NOT IF YOU'RE AUDITIONING FOR THE PART OF A NEON SIGN.
PARTY POOPER.
HEY, THAT'S A GOOD POINT. WE *SHOULD* HAVE A NEON SIGN.
BUT WAIT A MINUTE. WE DON'T HAVE, AS WE SAY IN THE INDUSTRY, "CALL LETTERS."
I'VE GOT IT!
THE KIDS AT OUR SCHOOL ARE KNOWN AS THE *"JACKSON HILL CROWD,"* SO THE STATION CAN BE CALLED *WJHC*.
YOU GOTTA LOVE THIS GIRL.
GIVE ME A *SIDE 5*.

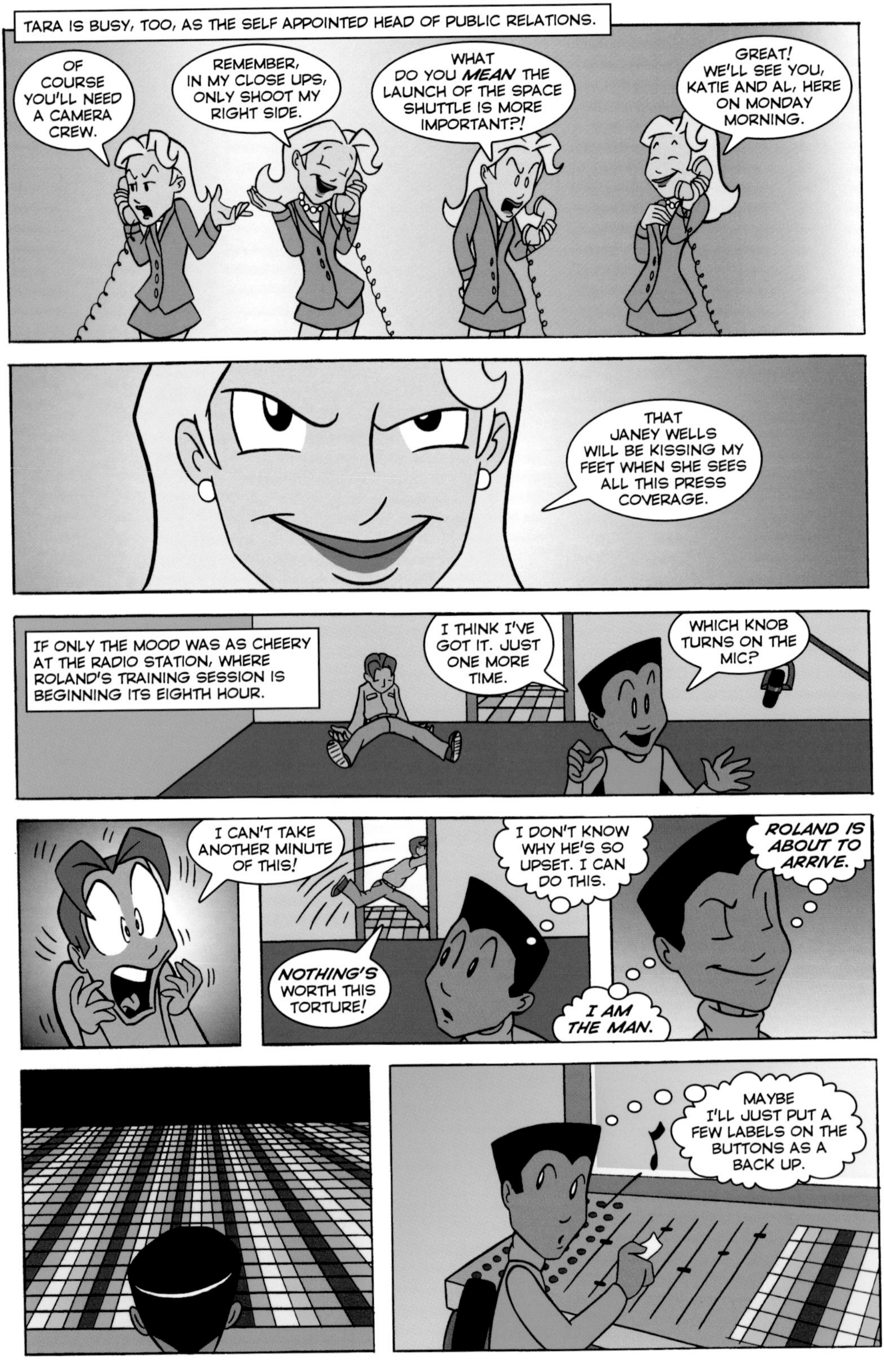
TARA IS BUSY, TOO, AS THE SELF APPOINTED HEAD OF PUBLIC RELATIONS.
OF COURSE YOU'LL NEED A CAMERA CREW.
REMEMBER, IN MY CLOSE UPS, ONLY SHOOT MY RIGHT SIDE.
WHAT DO YOU MEAN THE LAUNCH OF THE SPACE SHUTTLE IS MORE IMPORTANT?!
GREAT! WE'LL SEE YOU, KATIE AND AL, HERE ON MONDAY MORNING.
THAT JANEY WELLS WILL BE KISSING MY FEET WHEN SHE SEES ALL THIS PRESS COVERAGE.
IF ONLY THE MOOD WAS AS CHEERY AT THE RADIO STATION, WHERE ROLAND'S TRAINING SESSION IS BEGINNING ITS EIGHTH HOUR.
I THINK I'VE GOT IT. JUST ONE MORE TIME.
WHICH KNOB TURNS ON THE MIC?
I CAN'T TAKE ANOTHER MINUTE OF THIS!
NOTHING'S WORTH THIS TORTURE!
I DON'T KNOW WHY HE'S SO UPSET. I CAN DO THIS.
I AM THE MAN.
ROLAND IS ABOUT TO ARRIVE.
MAYBE I'LL JUST PUT A FEW LABELS ON THE BUTTONS AS A BACK UP.

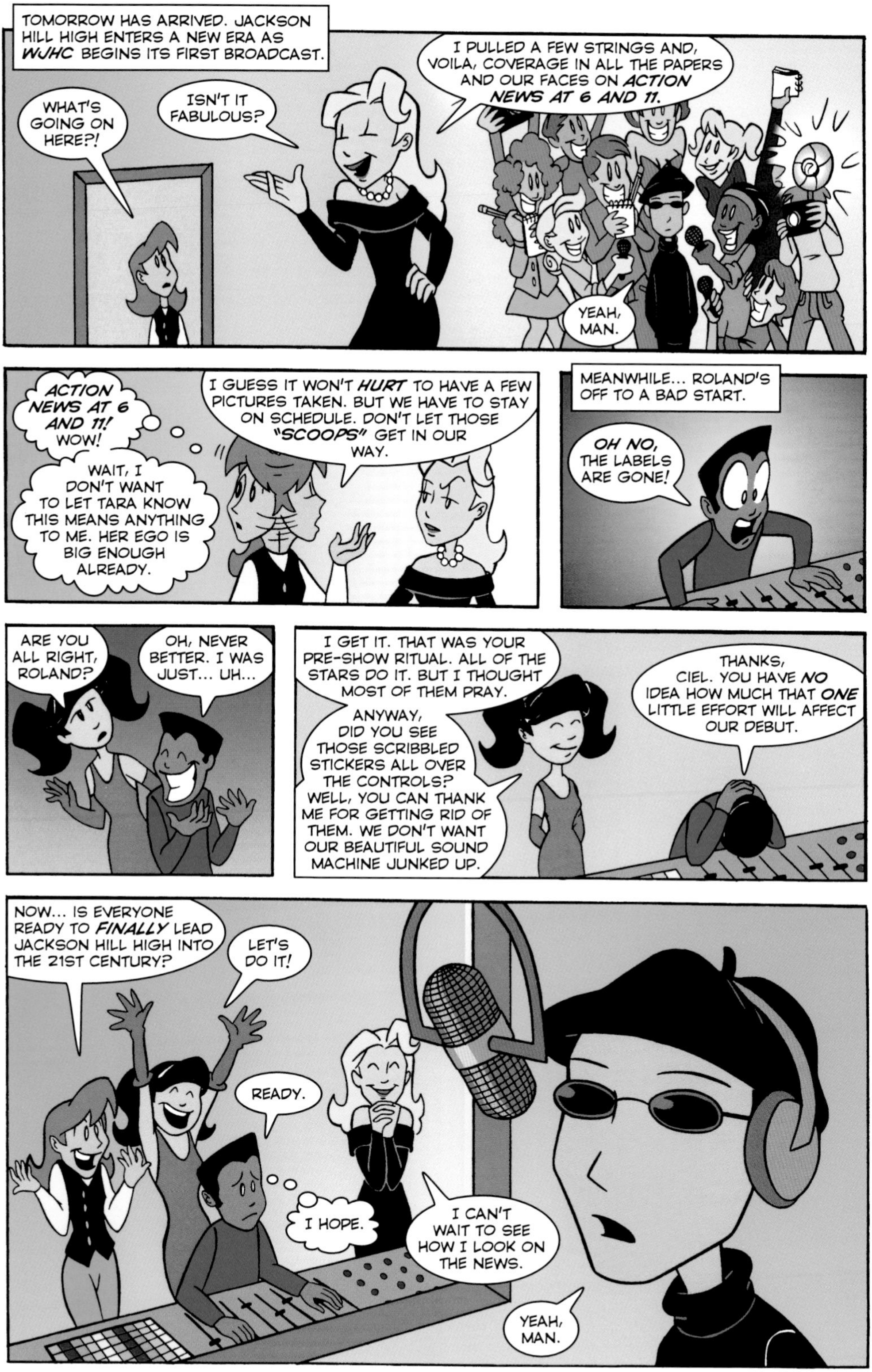
TOMORROW HAS ARRIVED. JACKSON HILL HIGH ENTERS A NEW ERA AS WJHC BEGINS ITS FIRST BROADCAST.
WHAT'S GOING ON HERE?!
ISN'T IT FABULOUS?
I PULLED A FEW STRINGS AND, VOILA, COVERAGE IN ALL THE PAPERS AND OUR FACES ON ACTION NEWS AT 6 AND 11.
YEAH, MAN.
ACTION NEWS AT 6 AND 11! WOW!
WAIT, I DON'T WANT TO LET TARA KNOW THIS MEANS ANYTHING TO ME. HER EGO IS BIG ENOUGH ALREADY.
I GUESS IT WON'T HURT TO HAVE A FEW PICTURES TAKEN. BUT WE HAVE TO STAY ON SCHEDULE. DON'T LET THOSE "SCOOPS" GET IN OUR WAY.
MEANWHILE... ROLAND'S OFF TO A BAD START.
OH NO, THE LABELS ARE GONE!
ARE YOU ALL RIGHT, ROLAND?
OH, NEVER BETTER. I WAS JUST... UH...
I GET IT. THAT WAS YOUR PRE-SHOW RITUAL. ALL OF THE STARS DO IT. BUT I THOUGHT MOST OF THEM PRAY.
ANYWAY, DID YOU SEE THOSE SCRIBBLED STICKERS ALL OVER THE CONTROLS? WELL, YOU CAN THANK ME FOR GETTING RID OF THEM. WE DON'T WANT OUR BEAUTIFUL SOUND MACHINE JUNKED UP.
THANKS, CIEL. YOU HAVE NO IDEA HOW MUCH THAT ONE LITTLE EFFORT WILL AFFECT OUR DEBUT.
NOW... IS EVERYONE READY TO FINALLY LEAD JACKSON HILL HIGH INTO THE 21ST CENTURY?
LET'S DO IT!
READY.
I HOPE.
I CAN'T WAIT TO SEE HOW I LOOK ON THE NEWS.
YEAH, MAN.

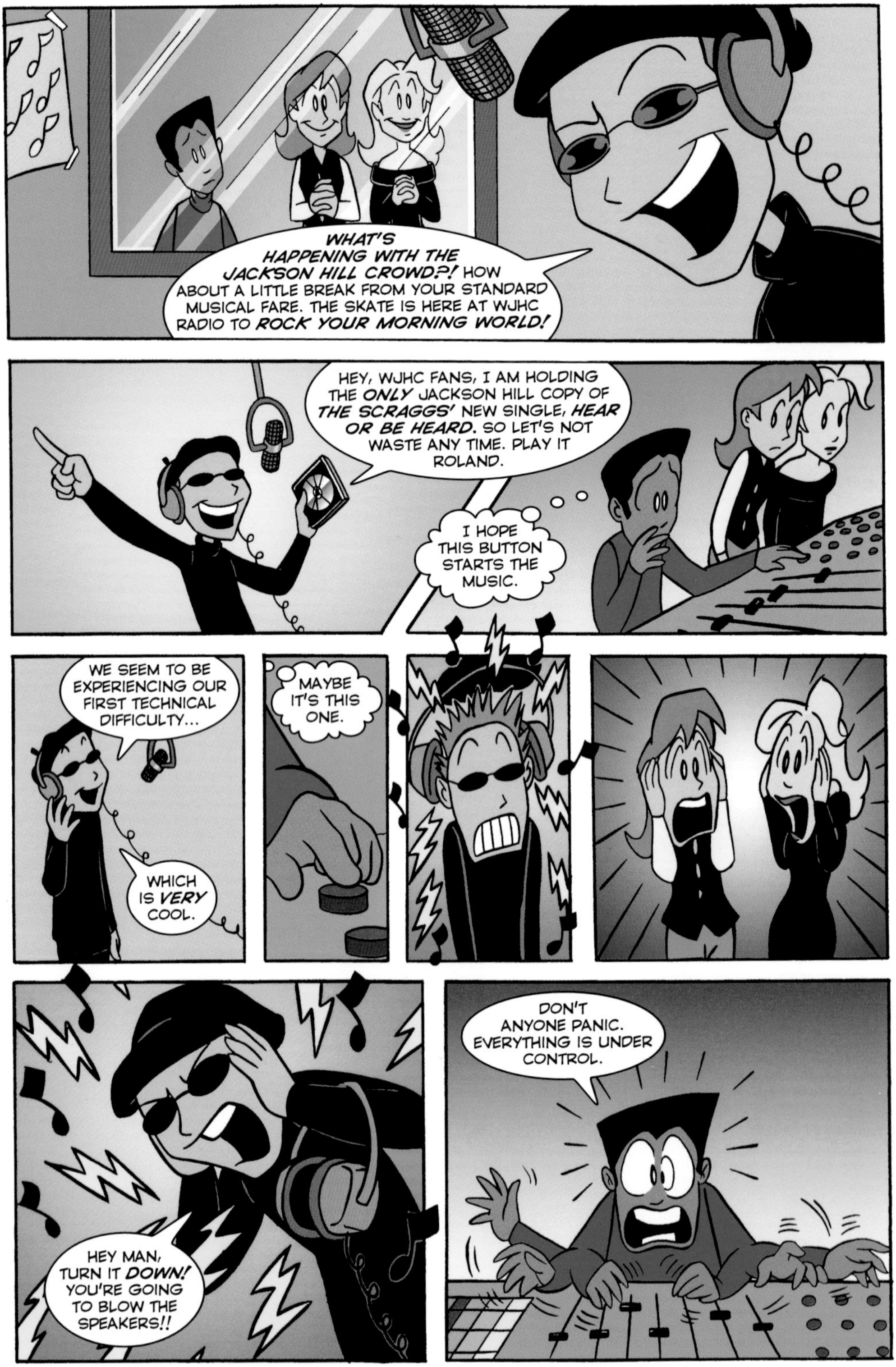
WHAT'S HAPPENING WITH THE JACKSON HILL CROWD?! HOW ABOUT A LITTLE BREAK FROM YOUR STANDARD MUSICAL FARE. THE SKATE IS HERE AT WJHC RADIO TO ROCK YOUR MORNING WORLD!
HEY, WJHC FANS, I AM HOLDING THE ONLY JACKSON HILL COPY OF THE SCRAGGS' NEW SINGLE, HEAR OR BE HEARD. SO LET'S NOT WASTE ANY TIME. PLAY IT ROLAND.
I HOPE THIS BUTTON STARTS THE MUSIC.
WE SEEM TO BE EXPERIENCING OUR FIRST TECHNICAL DIFFICULTY...
WHICH IS VERY COOL.
MAYBE IT'S THIS ONE.
HEY MAN, TURN IT DOWN! YOU'RE GOING TO BLOW THE SPEAKERS!!
DON'T ANYONE PANIC. EVERYTHING IS UNDER CONTROL.

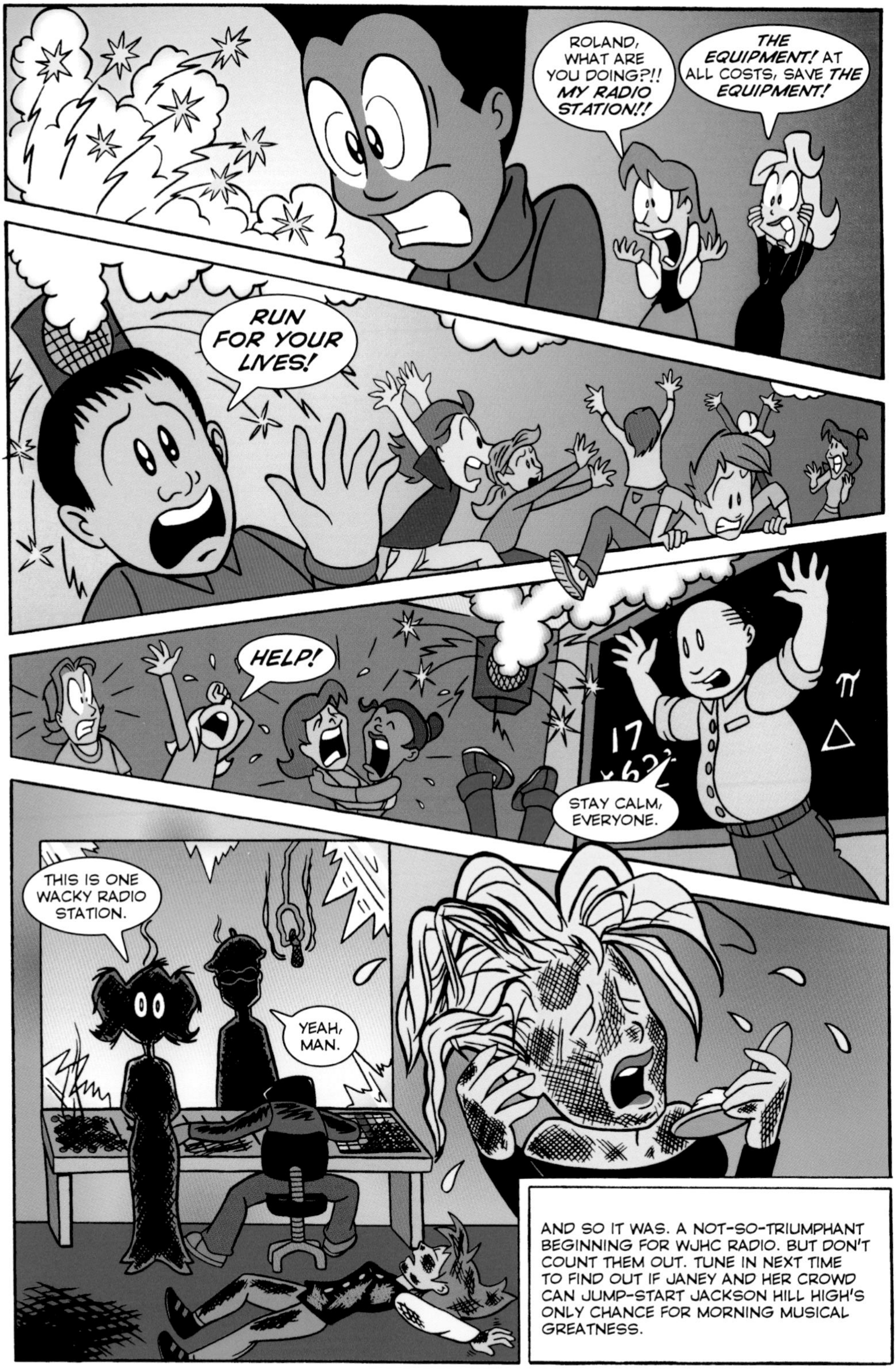
ROLAND, WHAT ARE YOU DOING?!! MY RADIO STATION!!
THE EQUIPMENT! AT ALL COSTS, SAVE THE EQUIPMENT!
RUN FOR YOUR LIVES!
HELP!
STAY CALM, EVERYONE.
THIS IS ONE WACKY RADIO STATION.
YEAH, MAN.
AND SO IT WAS. A NOT-SO-TRIUMPHANT BEGINNING FOR WJHC RADIO. BUT DON'T COUNT THEM OUT. TUNE IN NEXT TIME TO FIND OUT IF JANEY AND HER CROWD CAN JUMP-START JACKSON HILL HIGH'S ONLY CHANCE FOR MORNING MUSICAL GREATNESS.

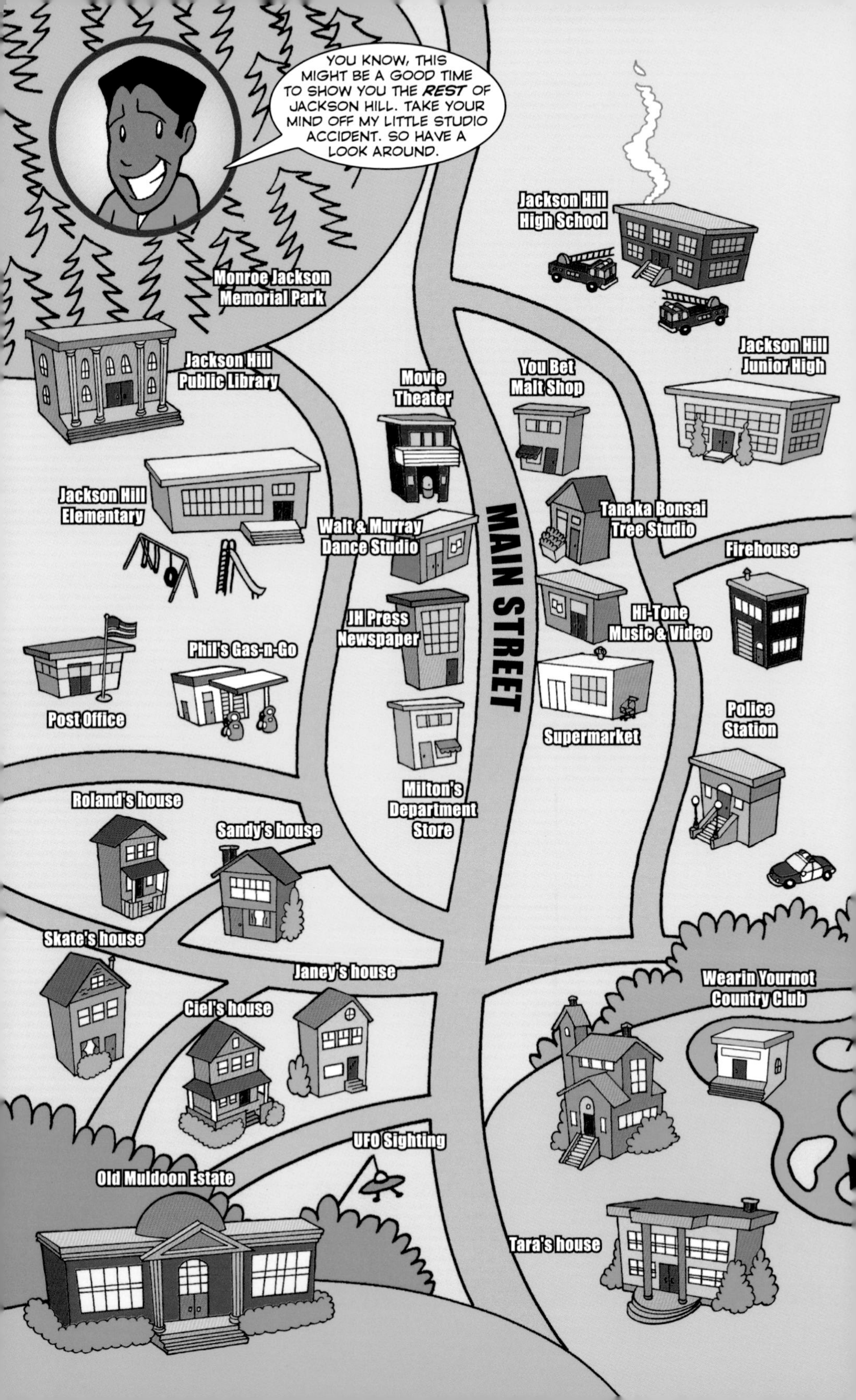
YOU KNOW, THIS MIGHT BE A GOOD TIME TO SHOW YOU THE *REST* OF JACKSON HILL. TAKE YOUR MIND OFF MY LITTLE STUDIO ACCIDENT. SO HAVE A LOOK AROUND.
Jackson Hill High School
Monroe Jackson Memorial Park
Jackson Hill Junior High
Jackson Hill Public Library
Movie Theater
You Bet Malt Shop
Jackson Hill Elementary
Tanaka Bonsai Tree Studio
Walt & Murray Dance Studio
Firehouse
MAIN STREET
JH Press Newspaper
Hi-Tone Music & Video
Phil's Gas-n-Go
Post Office
Supermarket
Police Station
Milton's Department Store
Roland's house
Sandy's house
Skate's house
Janey's house
Wearin Yournot Country Club
Ciel's house
UFO Sighting
Old Muldoon Estate
Tara's house

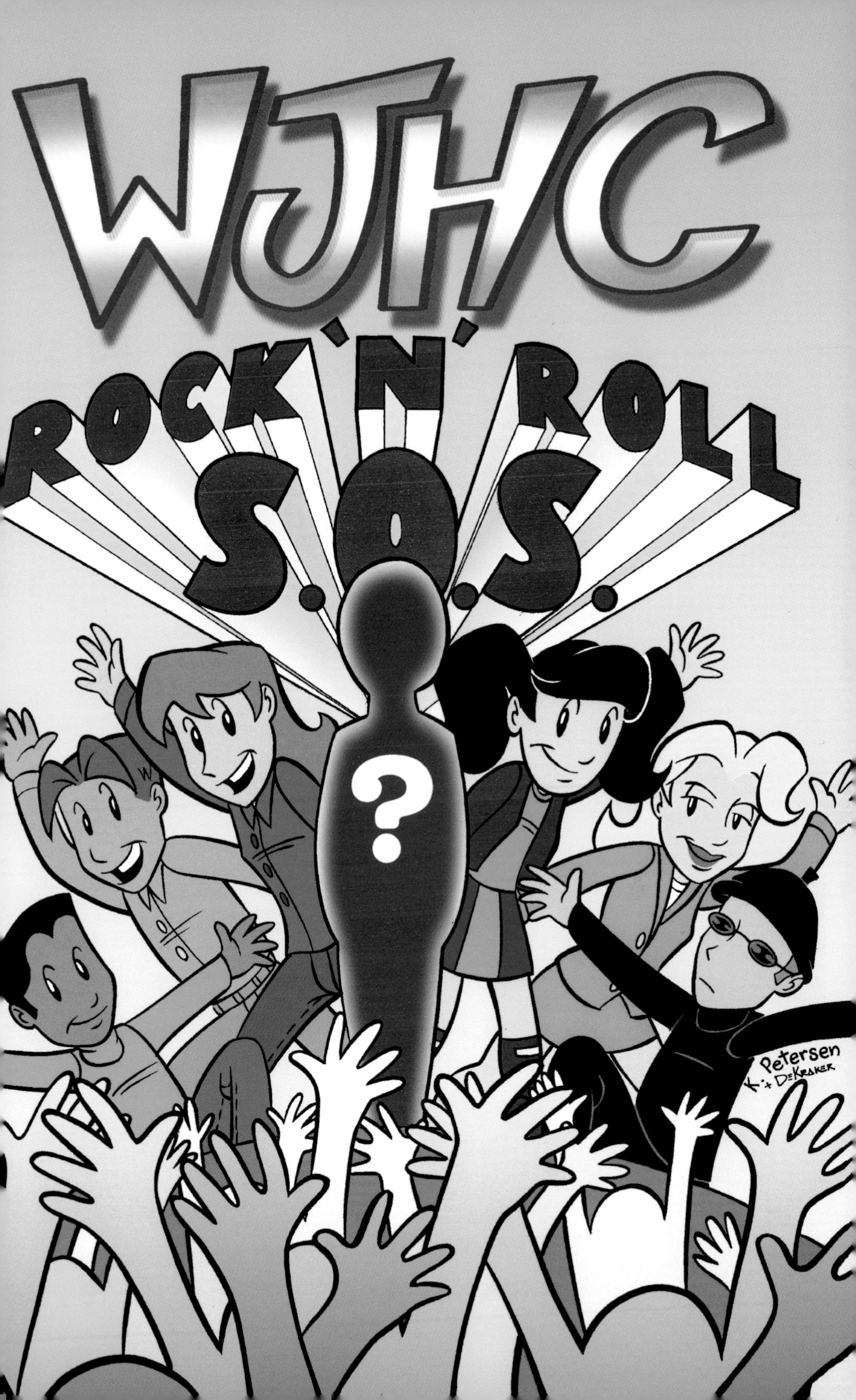
WJHC
ROCK 'N' ROLL
S.O.S.
?
Petersen
K. + DeKraker

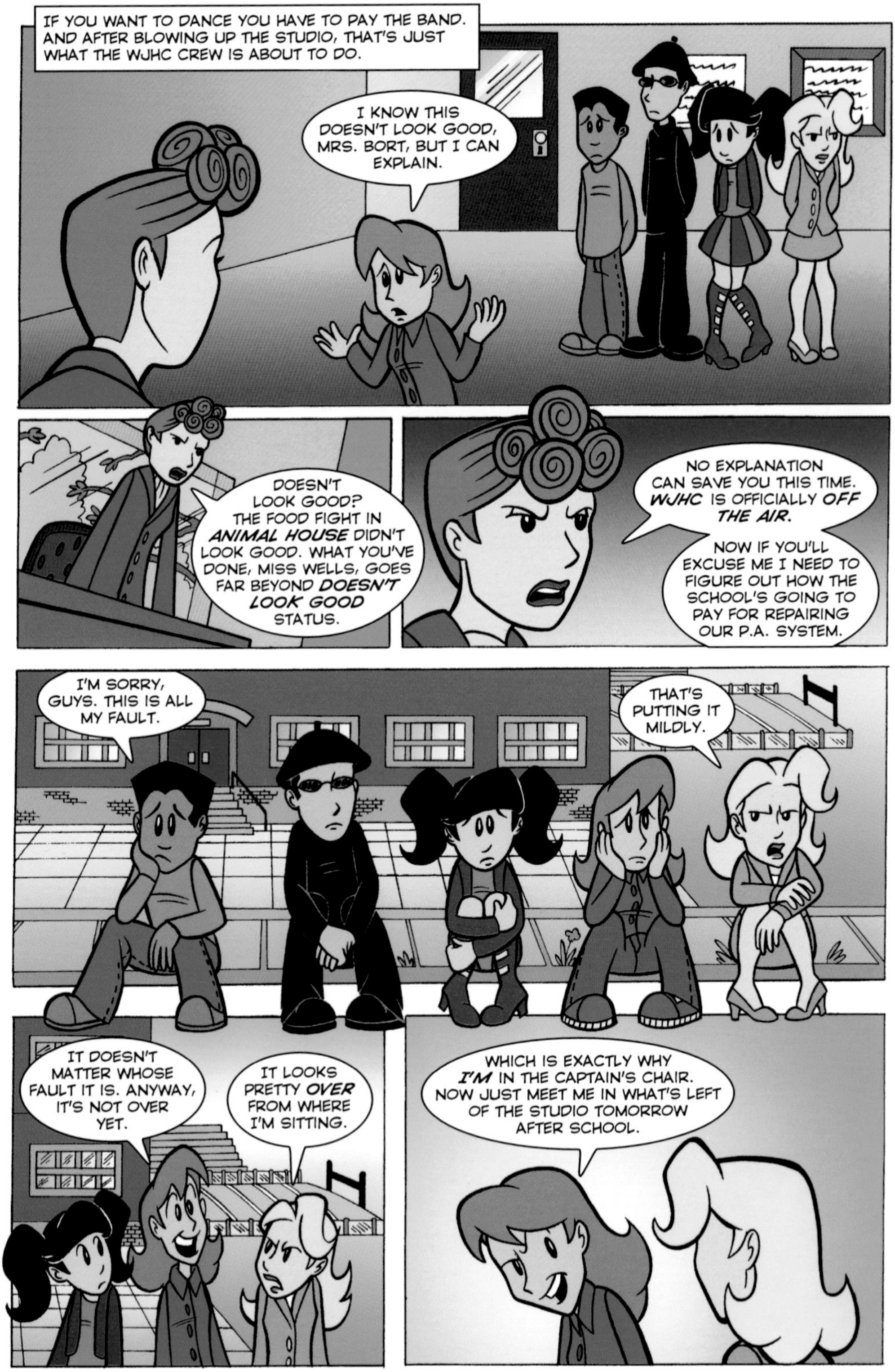
IF YOU WANT TO DANCE YOU HAVE TO PAY THE BAND. AND AFTER BLOWING UP THE STUDIO, THAT'S JUST WHAT THE WJHC CREW IS ABOUT TO DO.
I KNOW THIS DOESN'T LOOK GOOD, MRS. BORT, BUT I CAN EXPLAIN.
DOESN'T LOOK GOOD? THE FOOD FIGHT IN ***ANIMAL HOUSE*** DIDN'T LOOK GOOD. WHAT YOU'VE DONE, MISS WELLS, GOES FAR BEYOND ***DOESN'T LOOK GOOD*** STATUS.
NO EXPLANATION CAN SAVE YOU THIS TIME. ***WJHC*** IS OFFICIALLY ***OFF THE AIR.***
NOW IF YOU'LL EXCUSE ME I NEED TO FIGURE OUT HOW THE SCHOOL'S GOING TO PAY FOR REPAIRING OUR P.A. SYSTEM.
I'M SORRY, GUYS. THIS IS ALL MY FAULT.
THAT'S PUTTING IT MILDLY.
IT DOESN'T MATTER WHOSE FAULT IT IS. ANYWAY, IT'S NOT OVER YET.
IT LOOKS PRETTY ***OVER*** FROM WHERE I'M SITTING.
WHICH IS EXACTLY WHY ***I'M*** IN THE CAPTAIN'S CHAIR. NOW JUST MEET ME IN WHAT'S LEFT OF THE STUDIO TOMORROW AFTER SCHOOL.

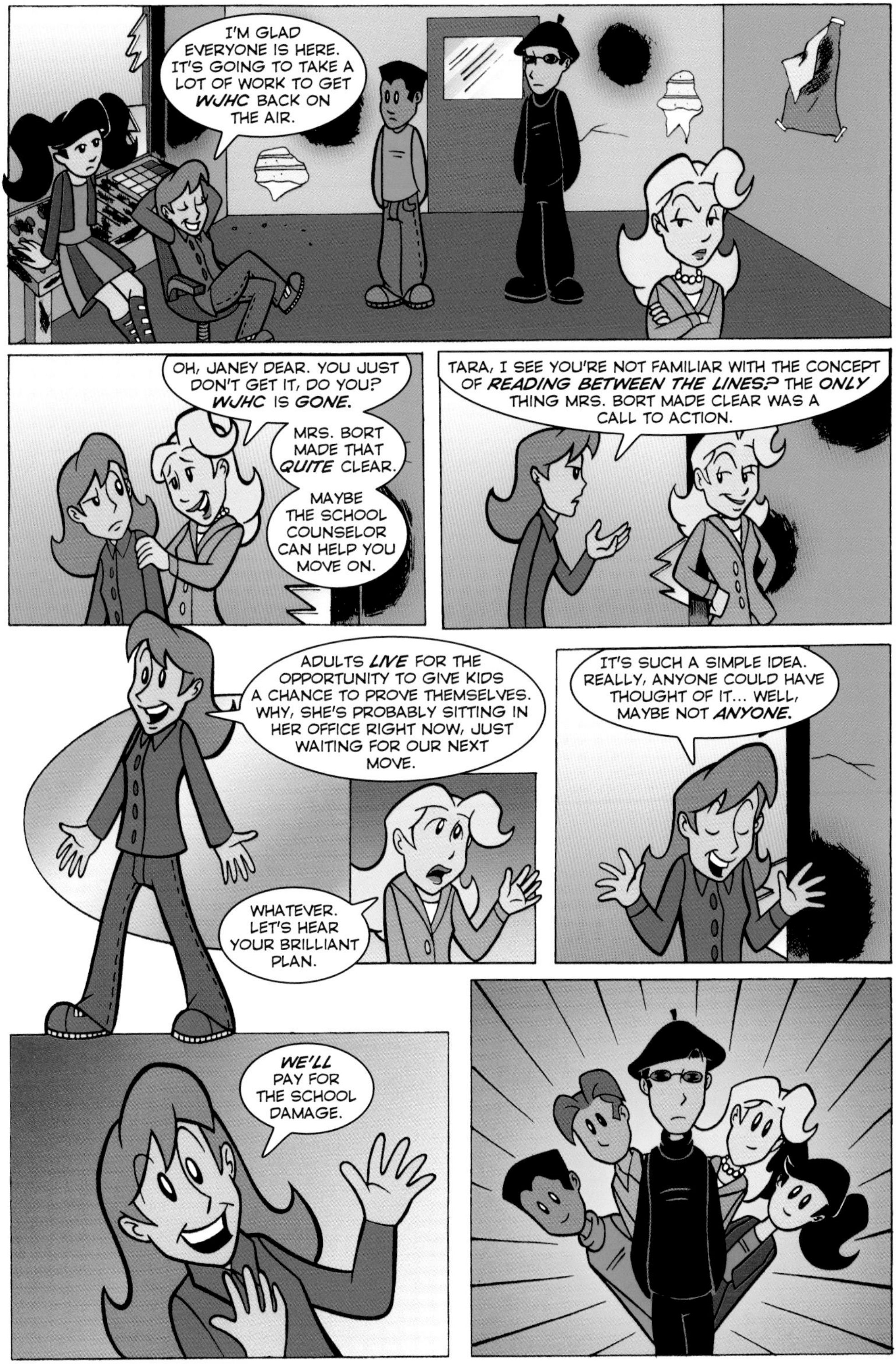
I'M GLAD EVERYONE IS HERE. IT'S GOING TO TAKE A LOT OF WORK TO GET *WJHC* BACK ON THE AIR.
OH, JANEY DEAR. YOU JUST DON'T GET IT, DO YOU? *WJHC* IS *GONE.*
MRS. BORT MADE THAT *QUITE* CLEAR.
MAYBE THE SCHOOL COUNSELOR CAN HELP YOU MOVE ON.
TARA, I SEE YOU'RE NOT FAMILIAR WITH THE CONCEPT OF *READING BETWEEN THE LINES?* THE *ONLY* THING MRS. BORT MADE CLEAR WAS A CALL TO ACTION.
ADULTS *LIVE* FOR THE OPPORTUNITY TO GIVE KIDS A CHANCE TO PROVE THEMSELVES. WHY, SHE'S PROBABLY SITTING IN HER OFFICE RIGHT NOW, JUST WAITING FOR OUR NEXT MOVE.
WHATEVER. LET'S HEAR YOUR BRILLIANT PLAN.
IT'S SUCH A SIMPLE IDEA. REALLY, ANYONE COULD HAVE THOUGHT OF IT... WELL, MAYBE NOT *ANYONE.*
WE'LL PAY FOR THE SCHOOL DAMAGE.

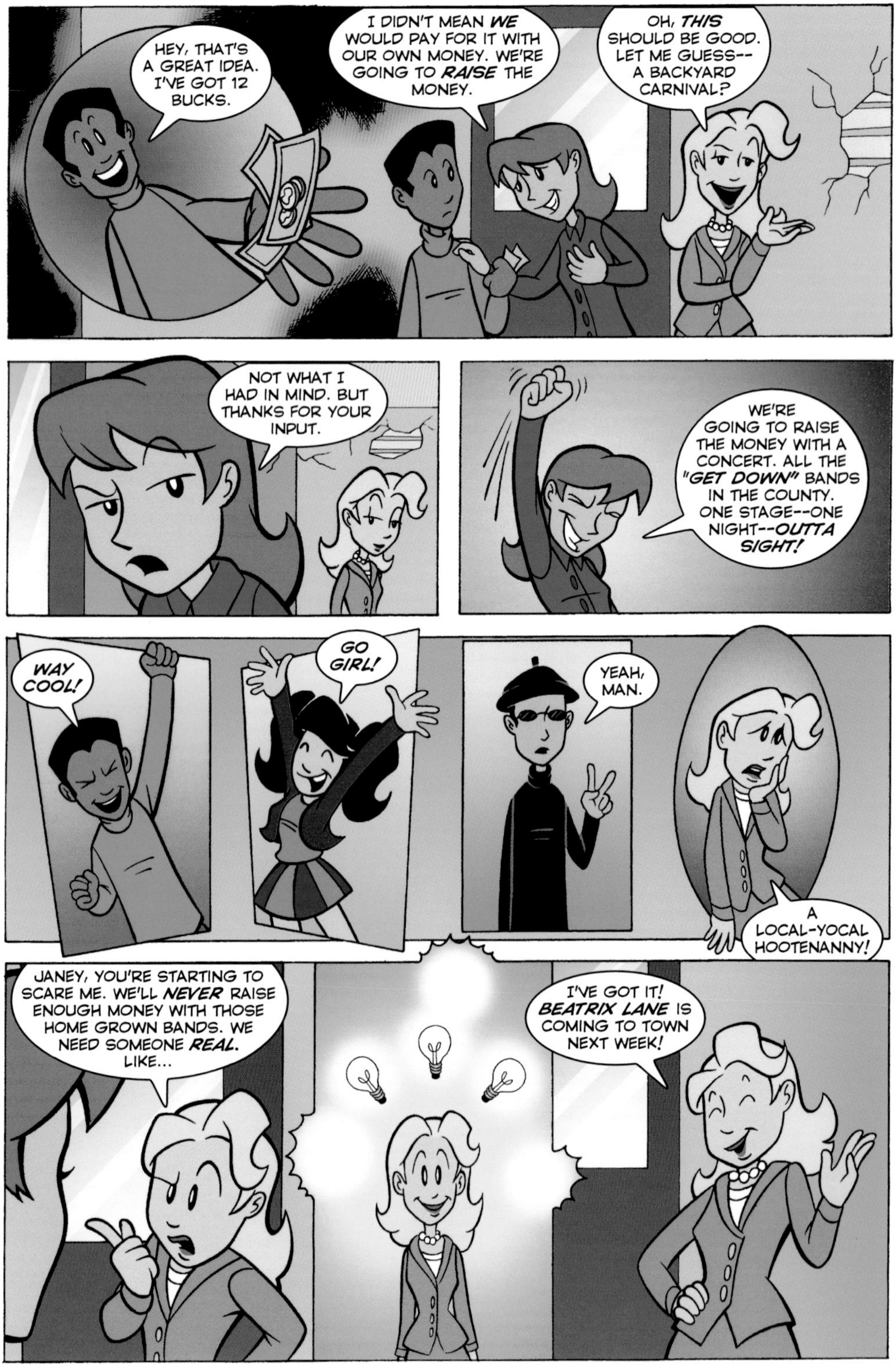
HEY, THAT'S A GREAT IDEA. I'VE GOT 12 BUCKS.
I DIDN'T MEAN *WE* WOULD PAY FOR IT WITH OUR OWN MONEY. WE'RE GOING TO *RAISE* THE MONEY.
OH, *THIS* SHOULD BE GOOD. LET ME GUESS-- A BACKYARD CARNIVAL?
NOT WHAT I HAD IN MIND. BUT THANKS FOR YOUR INPUT.
WE'RE GOING TO RAISE THE MONEY WITH A CONCERT. ALL THE *"GET DOWN"* BANDS IN THE COUNTY. ONE STAGE--ONE NIGHT--*OUTTA SIGHT!*
WAY COOL!
GO GIRL!
YEAH, MAN.
A LOCAL-YOCAL HOOTENANNY!
JANEY, YOU'RE STARTING TO SCARE ME. WE'LL *NEVER* RAISE ENOUGH MONEY WITH THOSE HOME GROWN BANDS. WE NEED SOMEONE *REAL.* LIKE...
I'VE GOT IT! *BEATRIX LANE* IS COMING TO TOWN NEXT WEEK!

BEATRIX LANE IS ONLY THE HOTTEST SINGER ALIVE. TARA SURE CAN PICK 'EM.

LIKE WE COULD EVER GET A HEADLINER LIKE THAT.

JANEY, I LOVE BEATRIX LANE. MAYBE WE *CAN* GET HER?

WELL, *WE* CAN'T. BUT *I* CAN. DADDY'S KNOWN BEATRIX FOR A LONG TIME. I'M SURE SHE'D LOVE TO HELP. UNLESS YOU THINK YOUR HOOTENANNY IS THE WAY TO GO.

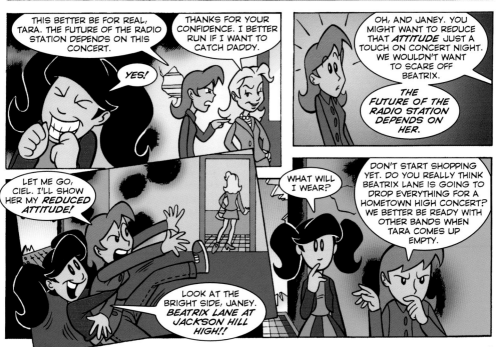

THIS BETTER BE FOR REAL, TARA. THE FUTURE OF THE RADIO STATION DEPENDS ON THIS CONCERT.

YES!

THANKS FOR YOUR CONFIDENCE. I BETTER RUN IF I WANT TO CATCH DADDY.

OH, AND JANEY. YOU MIGHT WANT TO REDUCE THAT *ATTITUDE* JUST A TOUCH ON CONCERT NIGHT. WE WOULDN'T WANT TO SCARE OFF BEATRIX.

THE FUTURE OF THE RADIO STATION DEPENDS ON HER.

LET ME GO, CIEL. I'LL SHOW HER MY *REDUCED ATTITUDE!*

WHAT WILL I WEAR?

DON'T START SHOPPING YET. DO YOU REALLY THINK BEATRIX LANE IS GOING TO DROP EVERYTHING FOR A HOMETOWN HIGH CONCERT? WE BETTER BE READY WITH OTHER BANDS WHEN TARA COMES UP EMPTY.

LOOK AT THE BRIGHT SIDE, JANEY. *BEATRIX LANE AT JACKSON HILL HIGH!!*

ROLAND, I'M COUNTING ON YOU TO FIND THE BOSS BANDS. I'M TALKIN' THE *REAL JAM!*

YOU GOT IT, JANEY!

TALK ABOUT NOT HOLDING A GRUDGE AFTER I BLEW UP THE STUDIO.

I HOPE I DON'T REGRET THIS MOVE.

WE BETTER START SPREADING THE WORD AROUND SCHOOL. WE'LL CALL IT THE *MYSTERY CONCERT.* THAT WAY WE'RE COVERED IF TARA DOESN'T COME THROUGH.

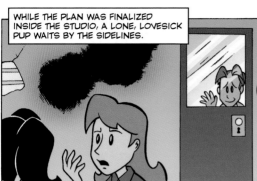

WHILE THE PLAN WAS FINALIZED INSIDE THE STUDIO, A LONE, LOVESICK PUP WAITS BY THE SIDELINES.

OH, JANEY. IF ONLY YOU KNEW. YOUR PRINCE AWAITS YOU.

MAN, HE'S GOT IT BAD. I DIDN'T EVEN SHOOT THE ARROW.

CAN YOU BELIEVE IT, CIEL?! OUR POPULARITY WILL *SOAR* AFTER THIS CONCERT.

NOT SO FAST, PAL. IT'S *PAYBACK* TIME.

YOU *DO* REMEMBER OUR DEAL. *I* POINTLESSLY TRY TO TEACH YOU SOMETHING ABOUT RADIO ENGINEERING AND *YOU* HOOK ME UP WITH JANEY WELLS.

YEAH... YEAH, I *DO* REMEMBER SOMETHING ABOUT THAT. HMMMM... THIS COULD BE TOUGH. SHE'S PRETTY BUSY PUTTING THE RADIO STATION BACK TOGETHER.

WAIT, I'VE GOT THE TICKET! YOU CAN FIX THE STUDIO EQUIPMENT. THEN, AS JANEY IS THANKING YOU FOR YOUR ENORMOUS CONTRIBUTION, YOU MAKE YOUR MOVE. *PERFECT.*

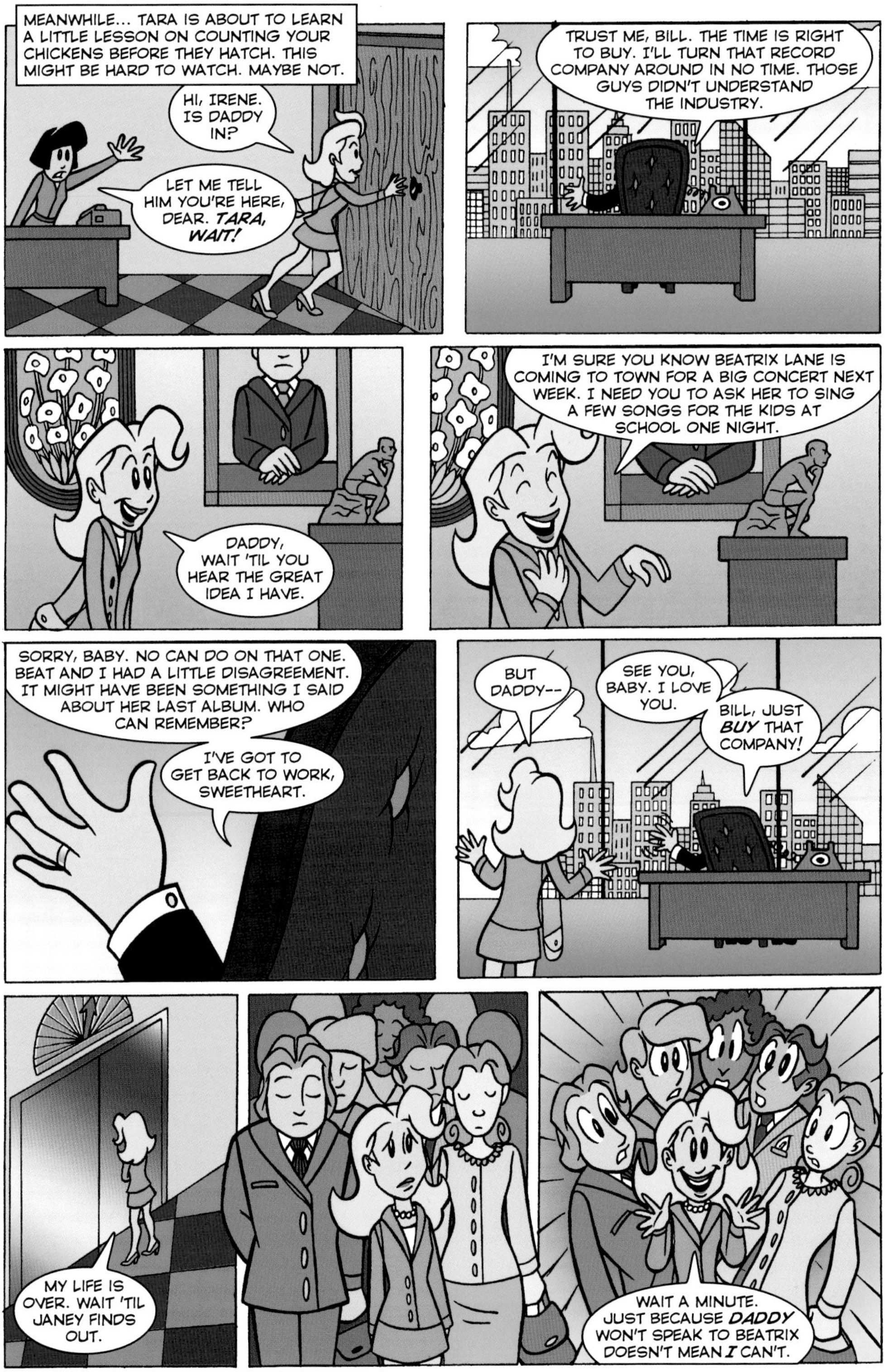
MEANWHILE... TARA IS ABOUT TO LEARN A LITTLE LESSON ON COUNTING YOUR CHICKENS BEFORE THEY HATCH. THIS MIGHT BE HARD TO WATCH. MAYBE NOT.
HI, IRENE. IS DADDY IN?
LET ME TELL HIM YOU'RE HERE, DEAR. TARA, WAIT!
TRUST ME, BILL. THE TIME IS RIGHT TO BUY. I'LL TURN THAT RECORD COMPANY AROUND IN NO TIME. THOSE GUYS DIDN'T UNDERSTAND THE INDUSTRY.
DADDY, WAIT 'TIL YOU HEAR THE GREAT IDEA I HAVE.
I'M SURE YOU KNOW BEATRIX LANE IS COMING TO TOWN FOR A BIG CONCERT NEXT WEEK. I NEED YOU TO ASK HER TO SING A FEW SONGS FOR THE KIDS AT SCHOOL ONE NIGHT.
SORRY, BABY. NO CAN DO ON THAT ONE. BEAT AND I HAD A LITTLE DISAGREEMENT. IT MIGHT HAVE BEEN SOMETHING I SAID ABOUT HER LAST ALBUM. WHO CAN REMEMBER?
I'VE GOT TO GET BACK TO WORK, SWEETHEART.
BUT DADDY--
SEE YOU, BABY. I LOVE YOU.
BILL, JUST BUY THAT COMPANY!
MY LIFE IS OVER. WAIT 'TIL JANEY FINDS OUT.
WAIT A MINUTE. JUST BECAUSE DADDY WON'T SPEAK TO BEATRIX DOESN'T MEAN I CAN'T.

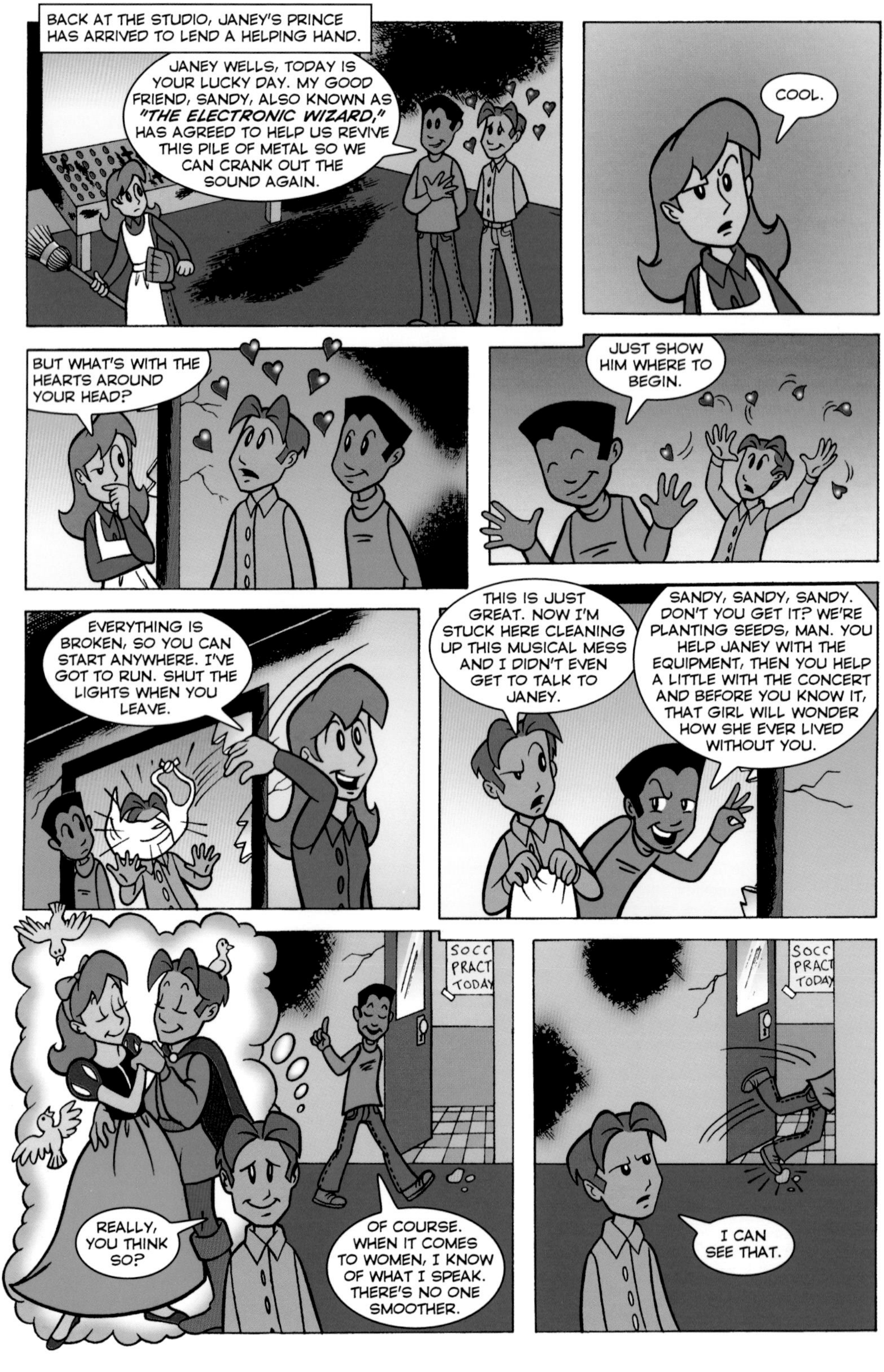
BACK AT THE STUDIO, JANEY'S PRINCE HAS ARRIVED TO LEND A HELPING HAND.
JANEY WELLS, TODAY IS YOUR LUCKY DAY. MY GOOD FRIEND, SANDY, ALSO KNOWN AS "THE ELECTRONIC WIZARD," HAS AGREED TO HELP US REVIVE THIS PILE OF METAL SO WE CAN CRANK OUT THE SOUND AGAIN.
COOL.
BUT WHAT'S WITH THE HEARTS AROUND YOUR HEAD?
JUST SHOW HIM WHERE TO BEGIN.
EVERYTHING IS BROKEN, SO YOU CAN START ANYWHERE. I'VE GOT TO RUN. SHUT THE LIGHTS WHEN YOU LEAVE.
THIS IS JUST GREAT. NOW I'M STUCK HERE CLEANING UP THIS MUSICAL MESS AND I DIDN'T EVEN GET TO TALK TO JANEY.
SANDY, SANDY, SANDY. DON'T YOU GET IT? WE'RE PLANTING SEEDS, MAN. YOU HELP JANEY WITH THE EQUIPMENT, THEN YOU HELP A LITTLE WITH THE CONCERT AND BEFORE YOU KNOW IT, THAT GIRL WILL WONDER HOW SHE EVER LIVED WITHOUT YOU.
SOCC PRACT TODAY
REALLY, YOU THINK SO?
OF COURSE. WHEN IT COMES TO WOMEN, I KNOW OF WHAT I SPEAK. THERE'S NO ONE SMOOTHER.
SOCC PRACT TODAY
I CAN SEE THAT.

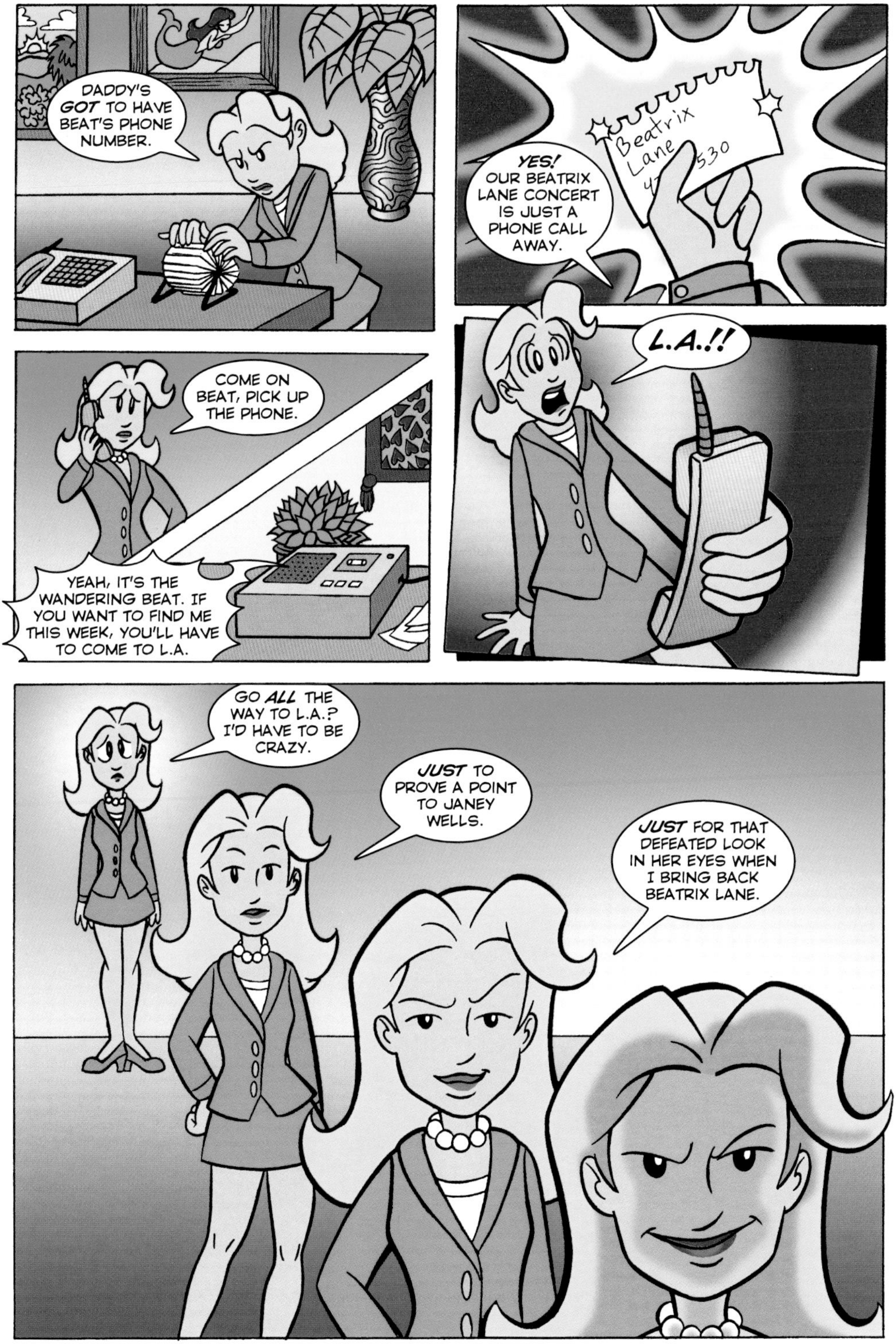
DADDY'S GOT TO HAVE BEAT'S PHONE NUMBER.
Beatrix Lane 4?? 530
YES! OUR BEATRIX LANE CONCERT IS JUST A PHONE CALL AWAY.
COME ON BEAT, PICK UP THE PHONE.
YEAH, IT'S THE WANDERING BEAT. IF YOU WANT TO FIND ME THIS WEEK, YOU'LL HAVE TO COME TO L.A.
L.A.!!
GO ALL THE WAY TO L.A.? I'D HAVE TO BE CRAZY.
JUST TO PROVE A POINT TO JANEY WELLS.
JUST FOR THAT DEFEATED LOOK IN HER EYES WHEN I BRING BACK BEATRIX LANE.

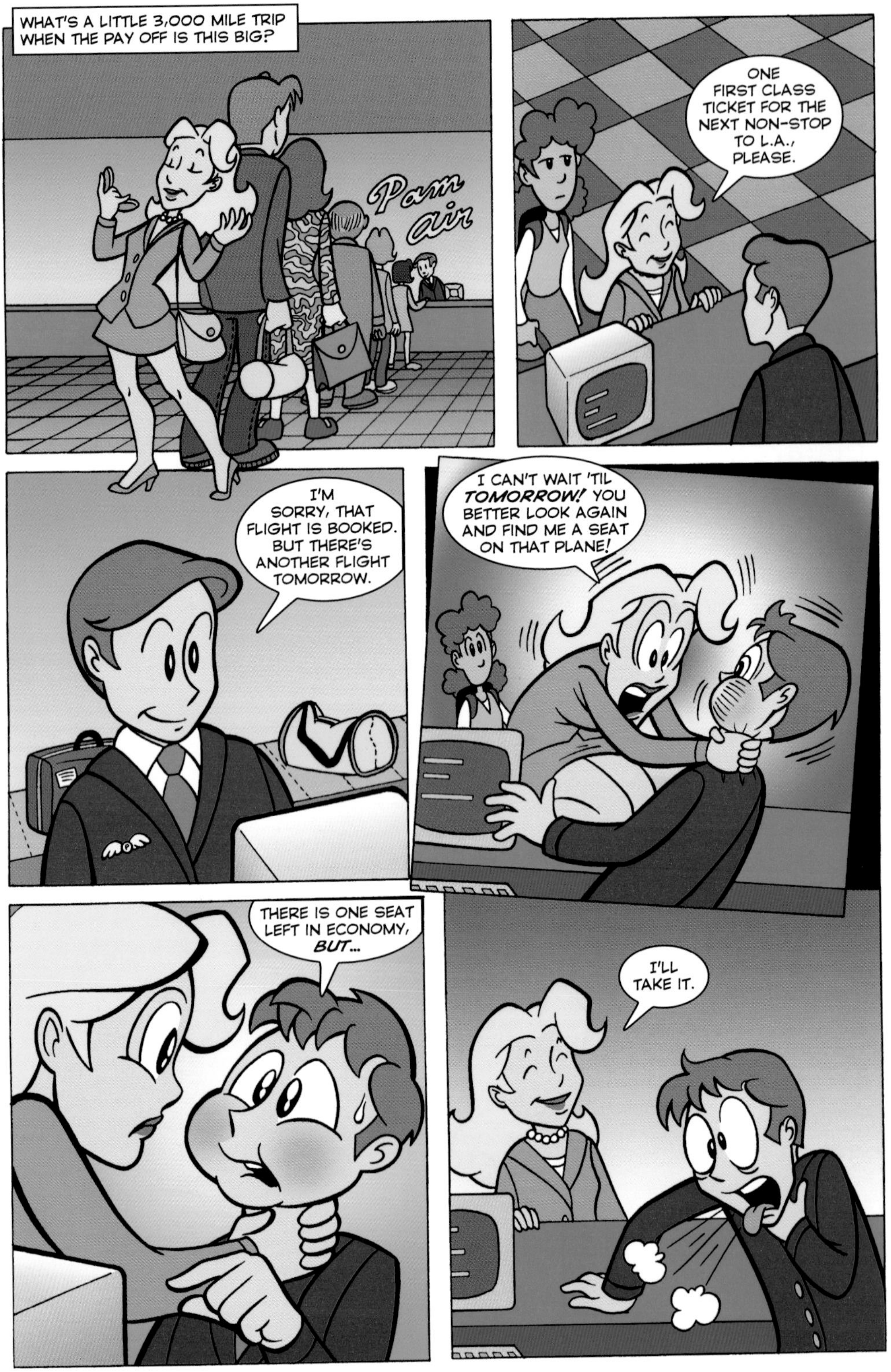
WHAT'S A LITTLE 3,000 MILE TRIP WHEN THE PAY OFF IS THIS BIG?
Pam air
ONE FIRST CLASS TICKET FOR THE NEXT NON-STOP TO L.A., PLEASE.
I'M SORRY, THAT FLIGHT IS BOOKED. BUT THERE'S ANOTHER FLIGHT TOMORROW.
I CAN'T WAIT 'TIL ***TOMORROW!*** YOU BETTER LOOK AGAIN AND FIND ME A SEAT ON THAT PLANE!
THERE IS ONE SEAT LEFT IN ECONOMY, ***BUT...***
I'LL TAKE IT.

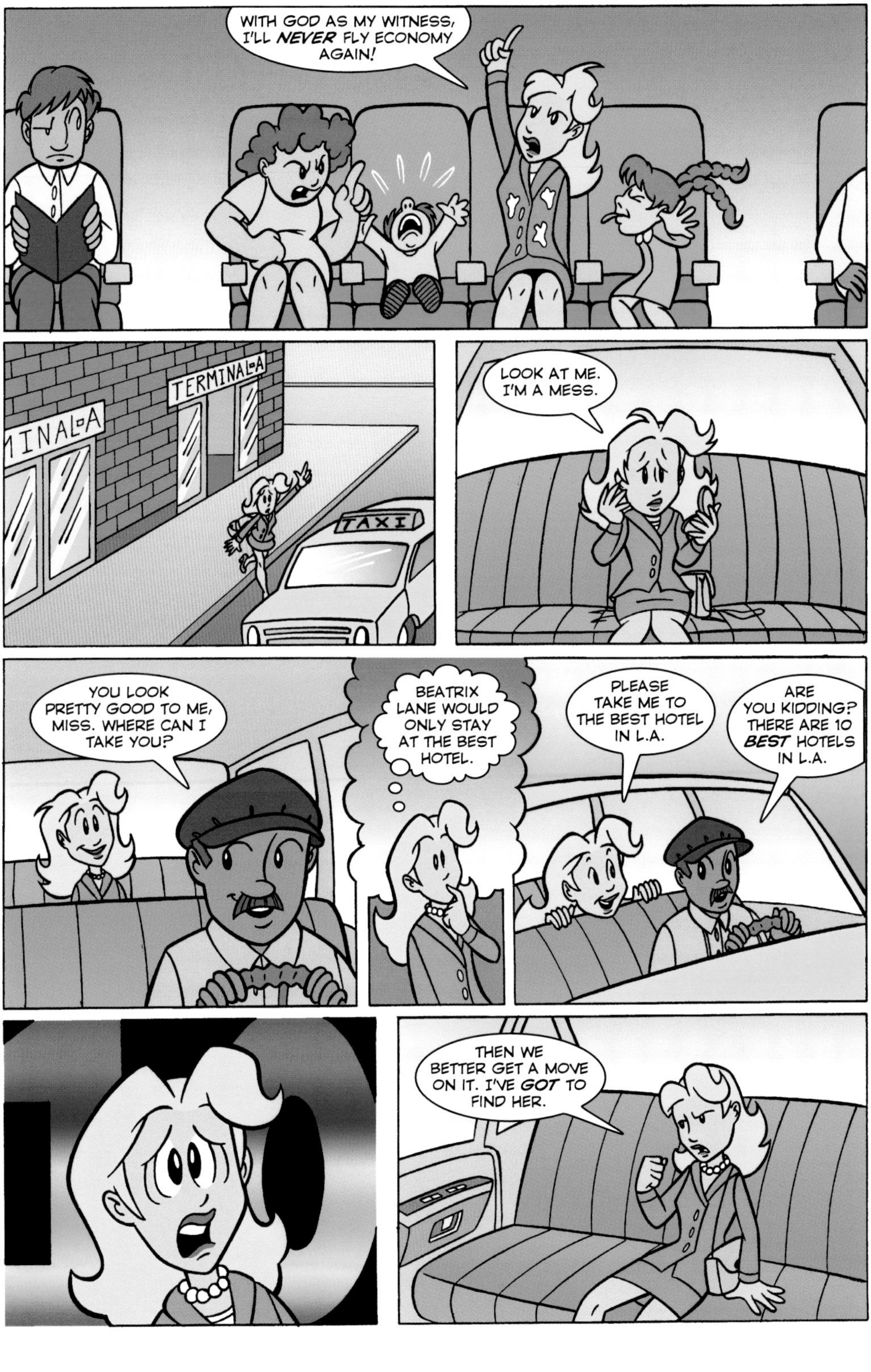
WITH GOD AS MY WITNESS, I'LL **NEVER** FLY ECONOMY AGAIN!
TERMINAL A
INAL A
TAXI
LOOK AT ME. I'M A MESS.
YOU LOOK PRETTY GOOD TO ME, MISS. WHERE CAN I TAKE YOU?
BEATRIX LANE WOULD ONLY STAY AT THE BEST HOTEL.
PLEASE TAKE ME TO THE BEST HOTEL IN L.A.
ARE YOU KIDDING? THERE ARE 10 **BEST** HOTELS IN L.A.
THEN WE BETTER GET A MOVE ON IT. I'VE **GOT** TO FIND HER.

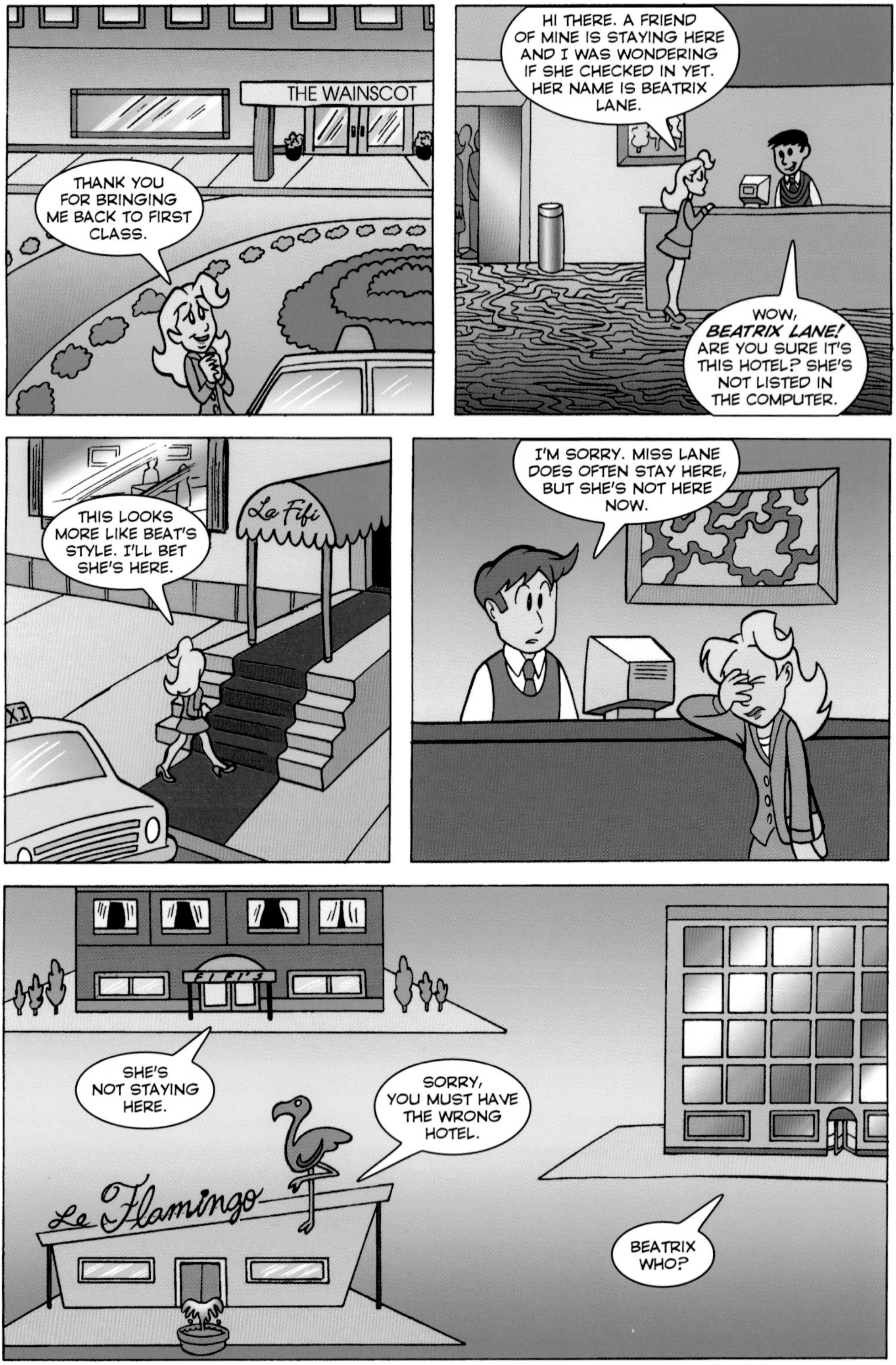
THE WAINSCOT
THANK YOU FOR BRINGING ME BACK TO FIRST CLASS.
HI THERE. A FRIEND OF MINE IS STAYING HERE AND I WAS WONDERING IF SHE CHECKED IN YET. HER NAME IS BEATRIX LANE.
WOW, ***BEATRIX LANE!*** ARE YOU SURE IT'S THIS HOTEL? SHE'S NOT LISTED IN THE COMPUTER.
La Fifi
THIS LOOKS MORE LIKE BEAT'S STYLE. I'LL BET SHE'S HERE.
I'M SORRY. MISS LANE DOES OFTEN STAY HERE, BUT SHE'S NOT HERE NOW.
SHE'S NOT STAYING HERE.
SORRY, YOU MUST HAVE THE WRONG HOTEL.
Le Flamingo
BEATRIX WHO?

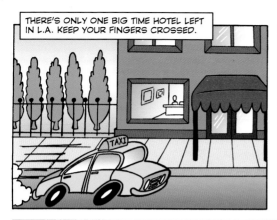

THERE'S ONLY ONE BIG TIME HOTEL LEFT IN L.A. KEEP YOUR FINGERS CROSSED.

PLEASE TELL ME THAT BEATRIX LANE IS STAYING HERE.

WELL, SHE *WAS*. SHE CHECKED OUT THIS MORNING.

CHECKED OUT!!

OK. I'VE GOT TO STAY CALM.

I KNOW. I'LL CALL HER HOME AGAIN TO FIND OUT WHERE SHE IS.

TELEPHONE

SUN AND SURF BEAT HERE. I'M FINALLY RESTING AND RELAXING AT MY SECRET HIDEAWAY. I'LL BE BACK TO REALITY AT THE END OF THE WEEK, WHEN I LAND AT THE JACKSON HILL STADIUM.

AGHHH!!

TELEPHONE

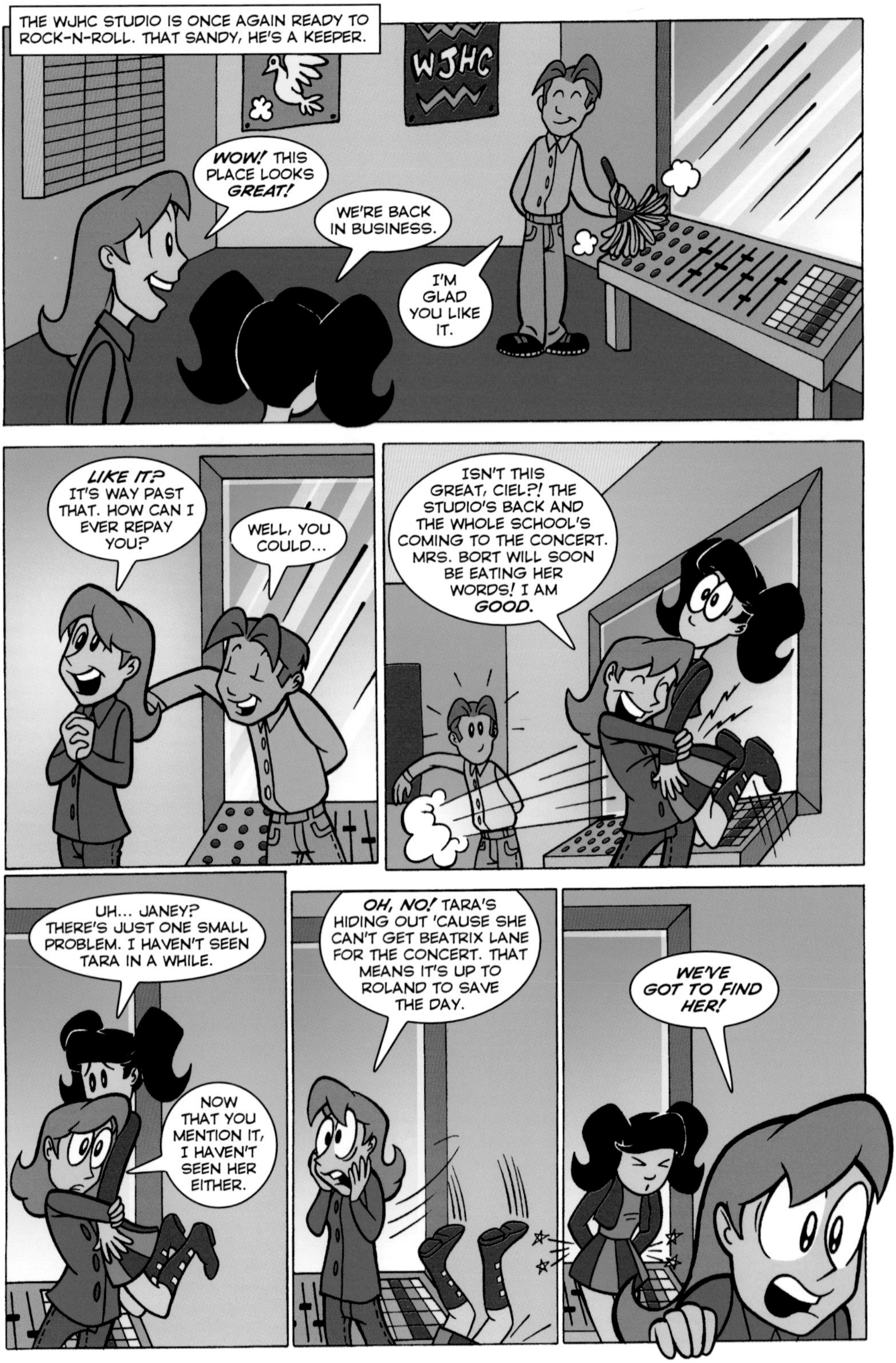
THE WJHC STUDIO IS ONCE AGAIN READY TO ROCK-N-ROLL. THAT SANDY, HE'S A KEEPER.
WJHC
WOW! THIS PLACE LOOKS GREAT!
WE'RE BACK IN BUSINESS.
I'M GLAD YOU LIKE IT.
LIKE IT? IT'S WAY PAST THAT. HOW CAN I EVER REPAY YOU?
WELL, YOU COULD...
ISN'T THIS GREAT, CIEL?! THE STUDIO'S BACK AND THE WHOLE SCHOOL'S COMING TO THE CONCERT. MRS. BORT WILL SOON BE EATING HER WORDS! I AM GOOD.
UH... JANEY? THERE'S JUST ONE SMALL PROBLEM. I HAVEN'T SEEN TARA IN A WHILE.
NOW THAT YOU MENTION IT, I HAVEN'T SEEN HER EITHER.
OH, NO! TARA'S HIDING OUT 'CAUSE SHE CAN'T GET BEATRIX LANE FOR THE CONCERT. THAT MEANS IT'S UP TO ROLAND TO SAVE THE DAY.
WE'VE GOT TO FIND HER!

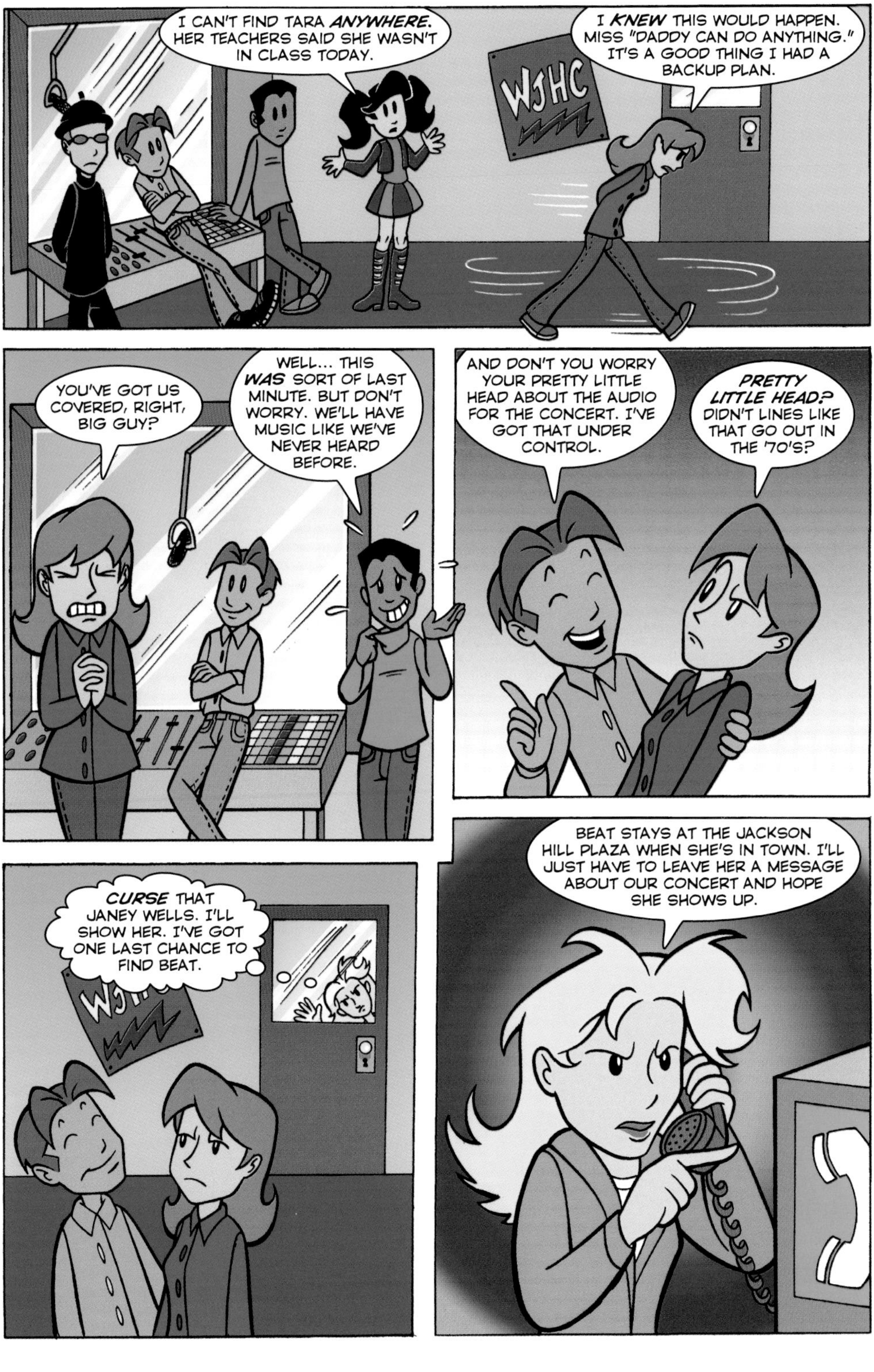
I CAN'T FIND TARA *ANYWHERE.* HER TEACHERS SAID SHE WASN'T IN CLASS TODAY.
I *KNEW* THIS WOULD HAPPEN. MISS "DADDY CAN DO ANYTHING." IT'S A GOOD THING I HAD A BACKUP PLAN.
WJHC
YOU'VE GOT US COVERED, RIGHT, BIG GUY?
WELL... THIS *WAS* SORT OF LAST MINUTE. BUT DON'T WORRY. WE'LL HAVE MUSIC LIKE WE'VE NEVER HEARD BEFORE.
AND DON'T YOU WORRY YOUR PRETTY LITTLE HEAD ABOUT THE AUDIO FOR THE CONCERT. I'VE GOT THAT UNDER CONTROL.
PRETTY LITTLE HEAD? DIDN'T LINES LIKE THAT GO OUT IN THE '70'S?
CURSE THAT JANEY WELLS. I'LL SHOW HER. I'VE GOT ONE LAST CHANCE TO FIND BEAT.
BEAT STAYS AT THE JACKSON HILL PLAZA WHEN SHE'S IN TOWN. I'LL JUST HAVE TO LEAVE HER A MESSAGE ABOUT OUR CONCERT AND HOPE SHE SHOWS UP.

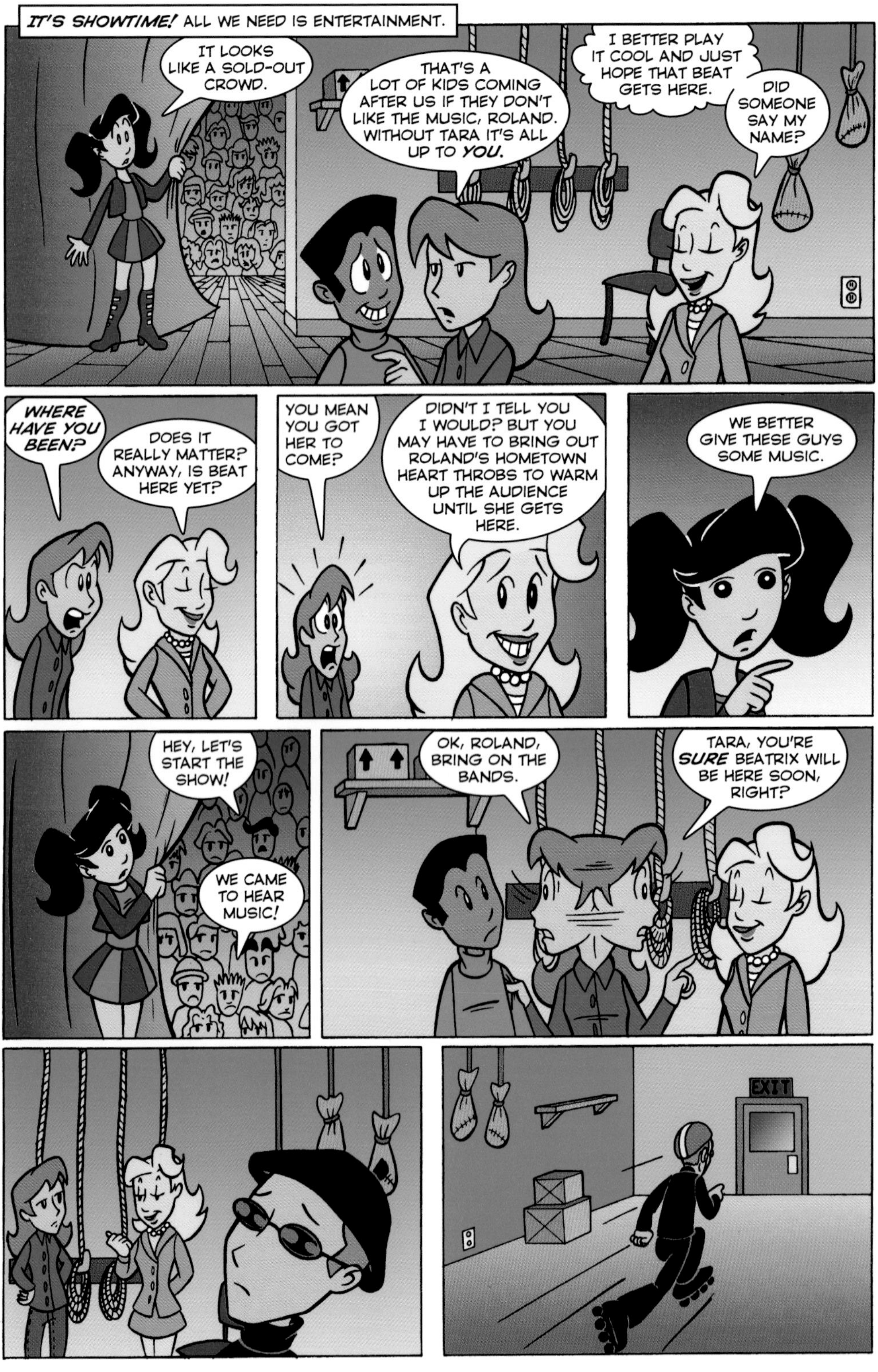
IT'S SHOWTIME! ALL WE NEED IS ENTERTAINMENT.
IT LOOKS LIKE A SOLD-OUT CROWD.
THAT'S A LOT OF KIDS COMING AFTER US IF THEY DON'T LIKE THE MUSIC, ROLAND. WITHOUT TARA IT'S ALL UP TO YOU.
I BETTER PLAY IT COOL AND JUST HOPE THAT BEAT GETS HERE.
DID SOMEONE SAY MY NAME?
WHERE HAVE YOU BEEN?
DOES IT REALLY MATTER? ANYWAY, IS BEAT HERE YET?
YOU MEAN YOU GOT HER TO COME?
DIDN'T I TELL YOU I WOULD? BUT YOU MAY HAVE TO BRING OUT ROLAND'S HOMETOWN HEART THROBS TO WARM UP THE AUDIENCE UNTIL SHE GETS HERE.
WE BETTER GIVE THESE GUYS SOME MUSIC.
HEY, LET'S START THE SHOW!
WE CAME TO HEAR MUSIC!
OK, ROLAND, BRING ON THE BANDS.
TARA, YOU'RE SURE BEATRIX WILL BE HERE SOON, RIGHT?
EXIT

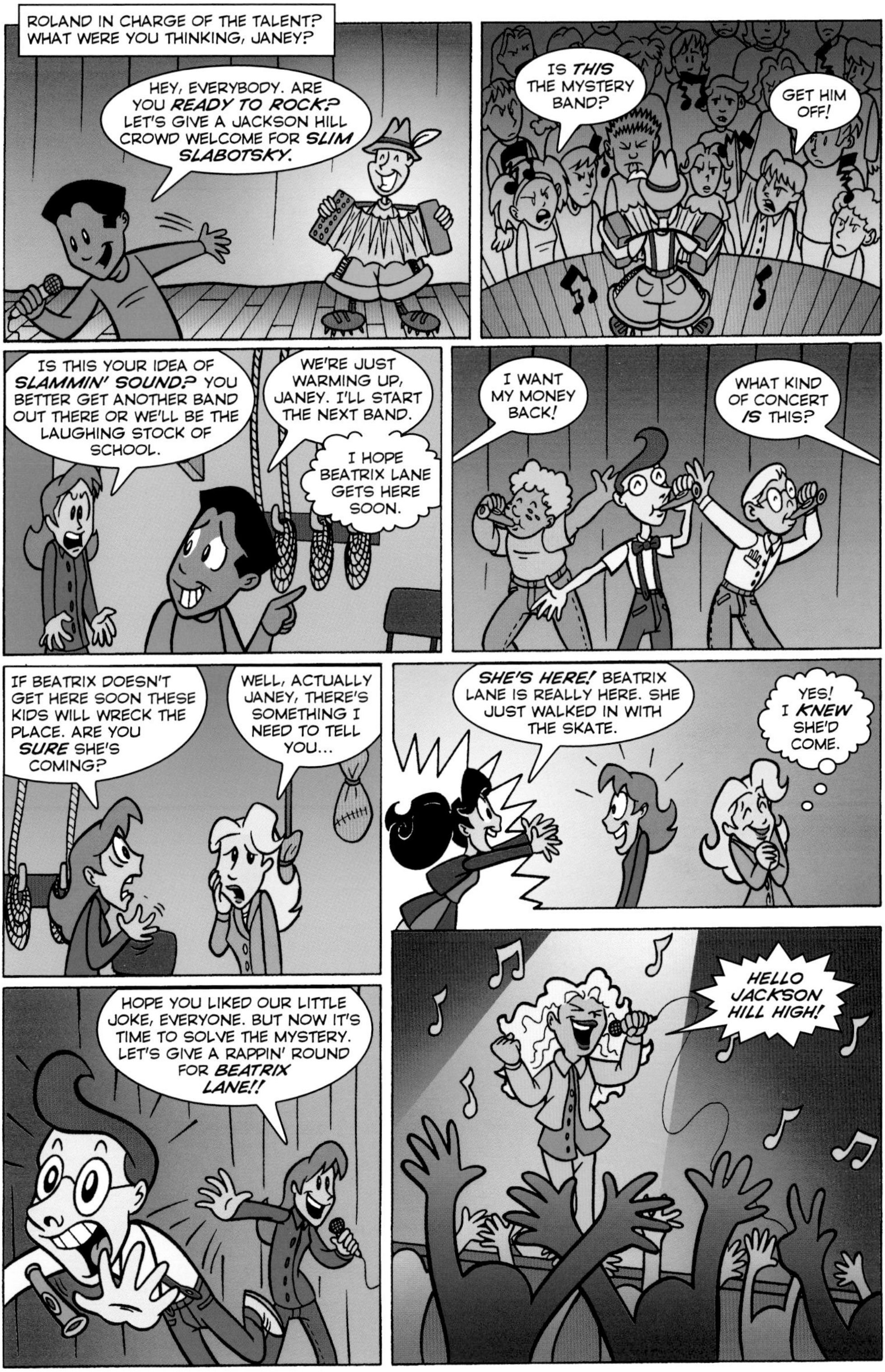
ROLAND IN CHARGE OF THE TALENT? WHAT WERE YOU THINKING, JANEY?
HEY, EVERYBODY. ARE YOU READY TO ROCK? LET'S GIVE A JACKSON HILL CROWD WELCOME FOR SLIM SLABOTSKY.
IS THIS THE MYSTERY BAND?
GET HIM OFF!
IS THIS YOUR IDEA OF SLAMMIN' SOUND? YOU BETTER GET ANOTHER BAND OUT THERE OR WE'LL BE THE LAUGHING STOCK OF SCHOOL.
WE'RE JUST WARMING UP, JANEY. I'LL START THE NEXT BAND.
I HOPE BEATRIX LANE GETS HERE SOON.
I WANT MY MONEY BACK!
WHAT KIND OF CONCERT IS THIS?
IF BEATRIX DOESN'T GET HERE SOON THESE KIDS WILL WRECK THE PLACE. ARE YOU SURE SHE'S COMING?
WELL, ACTUALLY JANEY, THERE'S SOMETHING I NEED TO TELL YOU...
SHE'S HERE! BEATRIX LANE IS REALLY HERE. SHE JUST WALKED IN WITH THE SKATE.
YES! I KNEW SHE'D COME.
HOPE YOU LIKED OUR LITTLE JOKE, EVERYONE. BUT NOW IT'S TIME TO SOLVE THE MYSTERY. LET'S GIVE A RAPPIN' ROUND FOR BEATRIX LANE!!
HELLO JACKSON HILL HIGH!

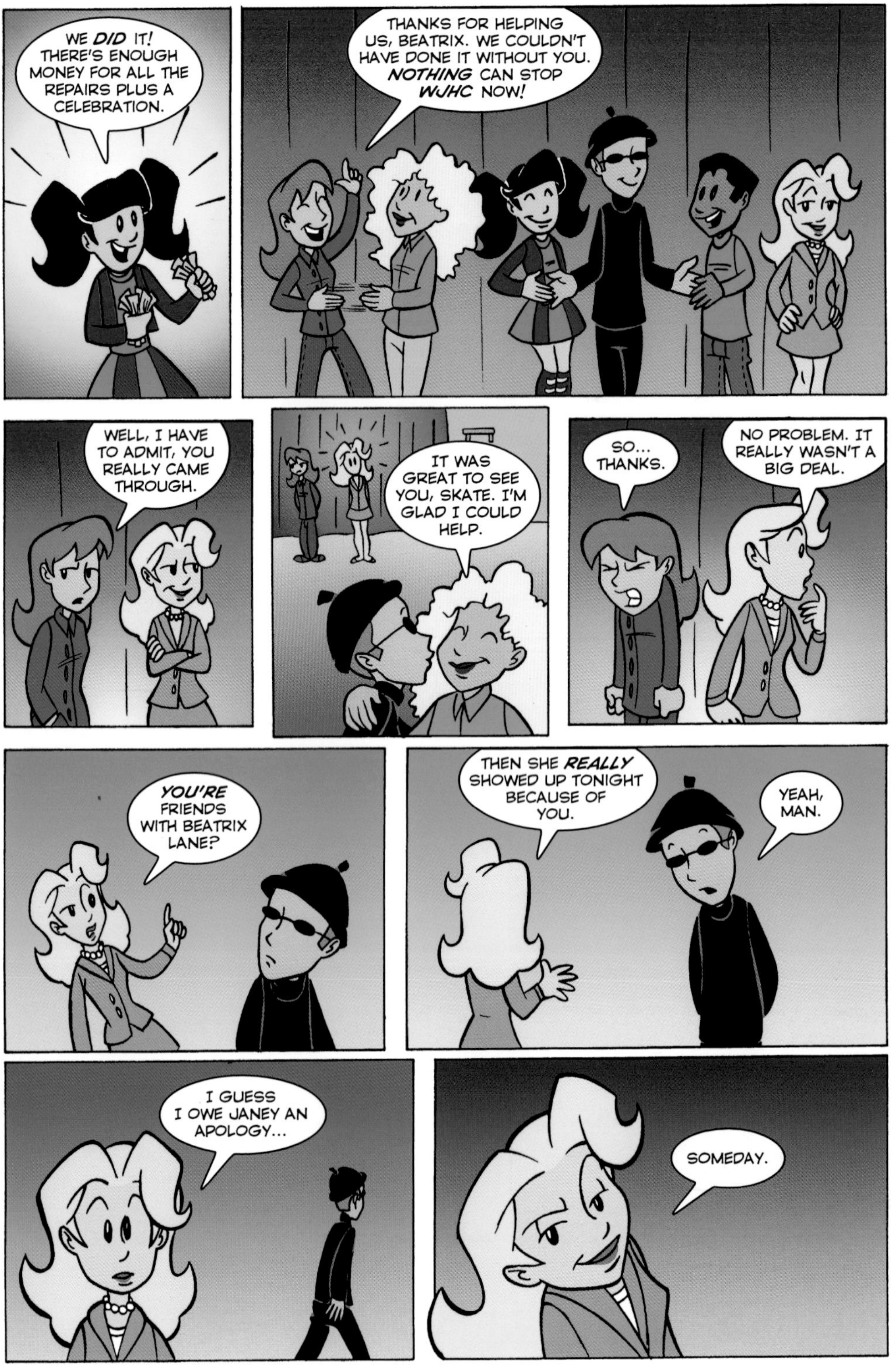
WE DID IT! THERE'S ENOUGH MONEY FOR ALL THE REPAIRS PLUS A CELEBRATION.
THANKS FOR HELPING US, BEATRIX. WE COULDN'T HAVE DONE IT WITHOUT YOU. NOTHING CAN STOP WJHC NOW!
WELL, I HAVE TO ADMIT, YOU REALLY CAME THROUGH.
IT WAS GREAT TO SEE YOU, SKATE. I'M GLAD I COULD HELP.
SO... THANKS.
NO PROBLEM. IT REALLY WASN'T A BIG DEAL.
YOU'RE FRIENDS WITH BEATRIX LANE?
THEN SHE REALLY SHOWED UP TONIGHT BECAUSE OF YOU.
YEAH, MAN.
I GUESS I OWE JANEY AN APOLOGY...
SOMEDAY.

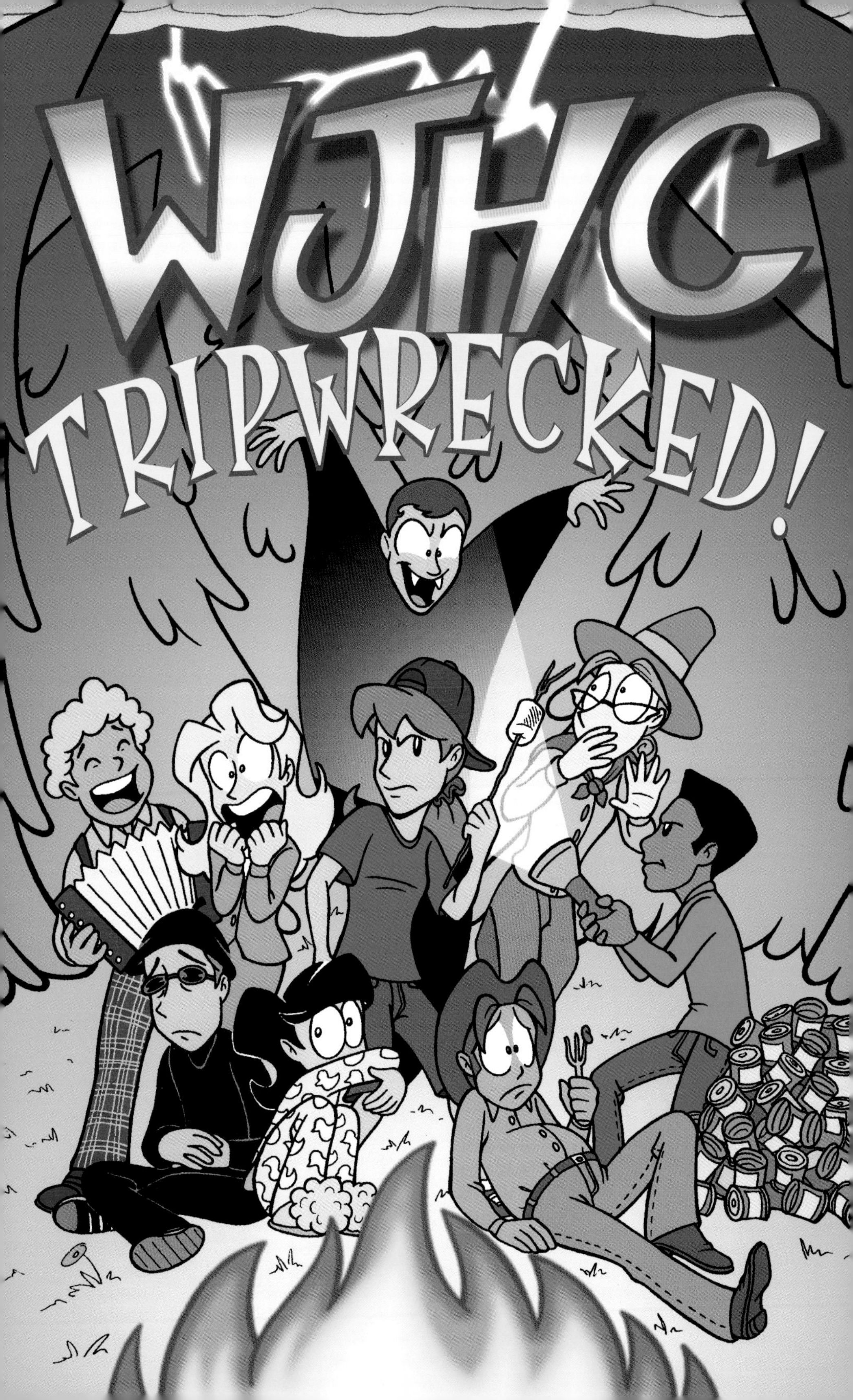
WJHC
TRIPWRECKED!

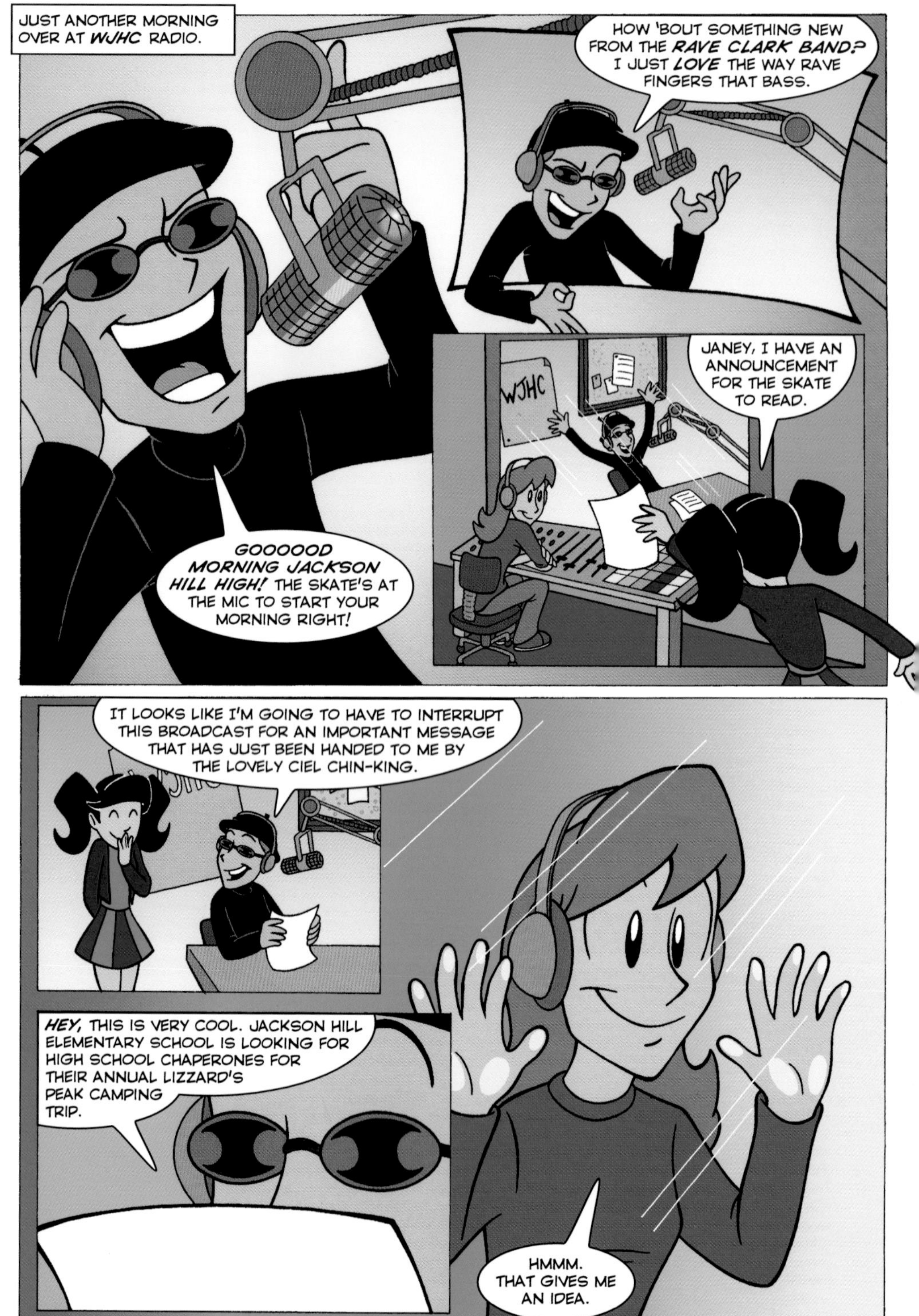

JUST ANOTHER MORNING OVER AT *WJHC* RADIO.
GOOOOOD MORNING JACKSON HILL HIGH! THE SKATE'S AT THE MIC TO START YOUR MORNING RIGHT!
HOW 'BOUT SOMETHING NEW FROM THE *RAVE CLARK BAND?* I JUST *LOVE* THE WAY RAVE FINGERS THAT BASS.
WJHC
JANEY, I HAVE AN ANNOUNCEMENT FOR THE SKATE TO READ.
IT LOOKS LIKE I'M GOING TO HAVE TO INTERRUPT THIS BROADCAST FOR AN IMPORTANT MESSAGE THAT HAS JUST BEEN HANDED TO ME BY THE LOVELY CIEL CHIN-KING.
HEY, THIS IS VERY COOL. JACKSON HILL ELEMENTARY SCHOOL IS LOOKING FOR HIGH SCHOOL CHAPERONES FOR THEIR ANNUAL LIZZARD'S PEAK CAMPING TRIP.
HMMM. THAT GIVES ME AN IDEA.

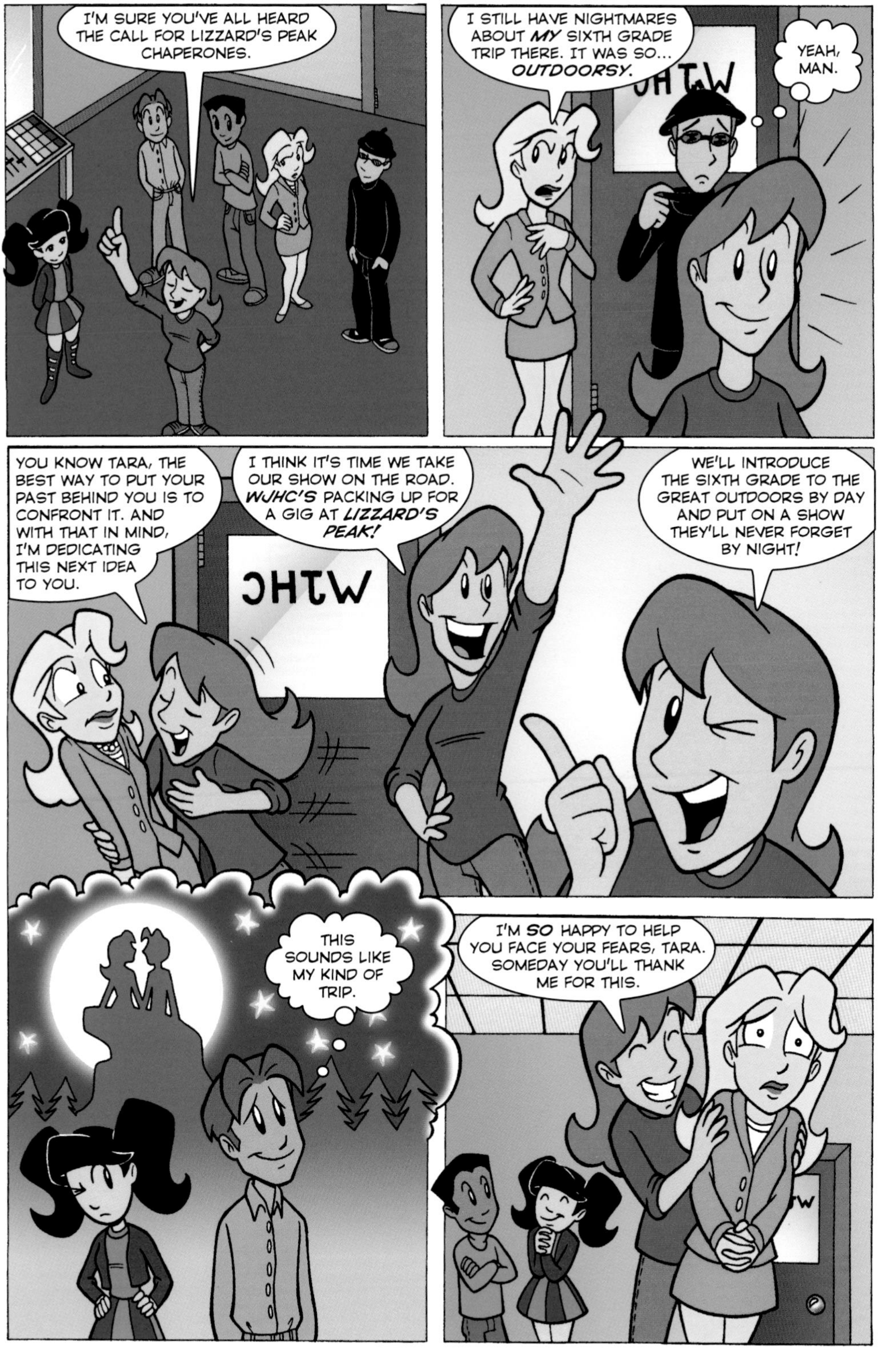
I'M SURE YOU'VE ALL HEARD THE CALL FOR LIZZARD'S PEAK CHAPERONES.
I STILL HAVE NIGHTMARES ABOUT *MY* SIXTH GRADE TRIP THERE. IT WAS SO... *OUTDOORSY.*
YEAH, MAN.
YOU KNOW TARA, THE BEST WAY TO PUT YOUR PAST BEHIND YOU IS TO CONFRONT IT. AND WITH THAT IN MIND, I'M DEDICATING THIS NEXT IDEA TO YOU.
I THINK IT'S TIME WE TAKE OUR SHOW ON THE ROAD. *WJHC'S* PACKING UP FOR A GIG AT *LIZZARD'S PEAK!*
WE'LL INTRODUCE THE SIXTH GRADE TO THE GREAT OUTDOORS BY DAY AND PUT ON A SHOW THEY'LL NEVER FORGET BY NIGHT!
THIS SOUNDS LIKE MY KIND OF TRIP.
I'M *SO* HAPPY TO HELP YOU FACE YOUR FEARS, TARA. SOMEDAY YOU'LL THANK ME FOR THIS.

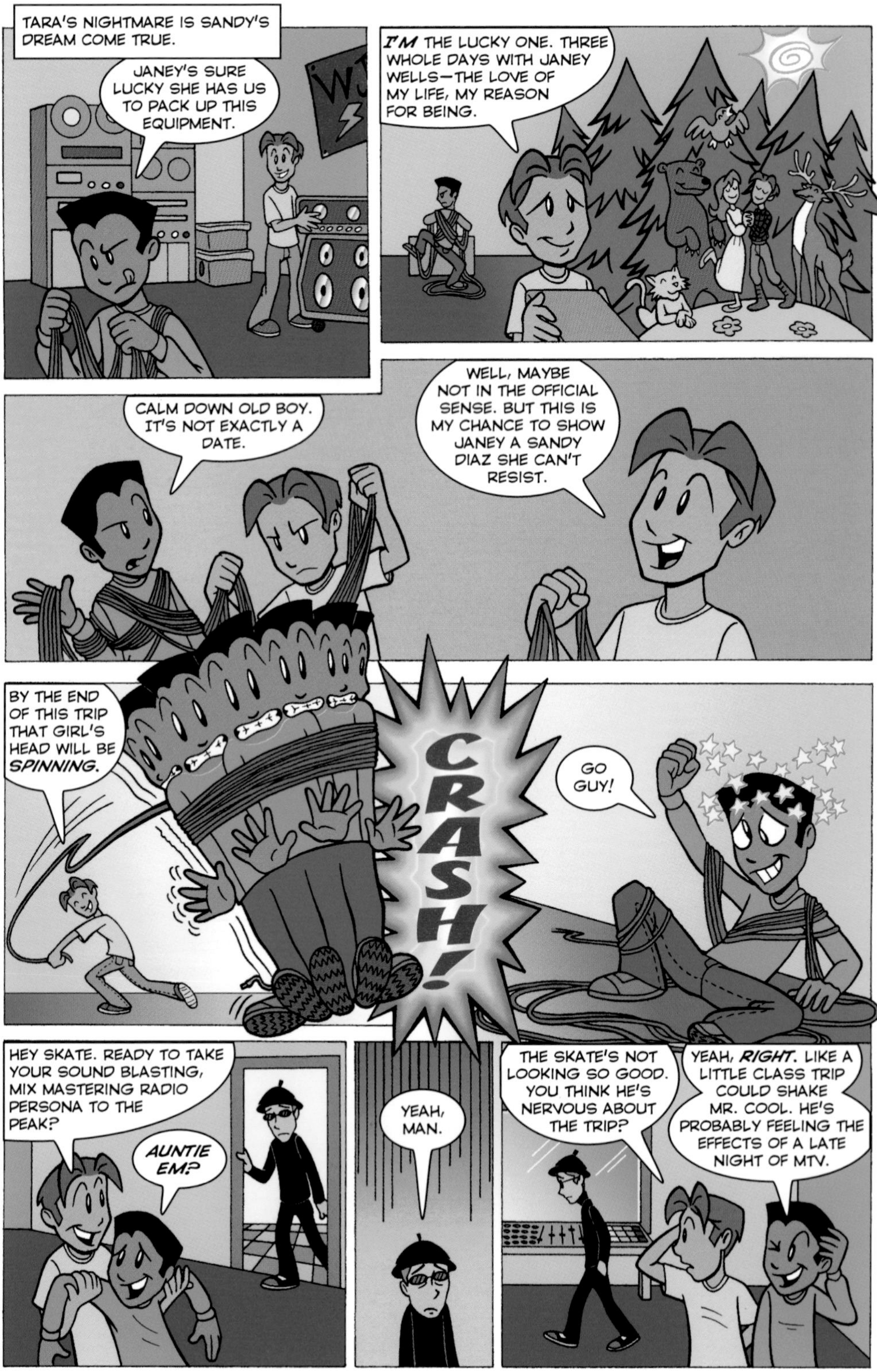
TARA'S NIGHTMARE IS SANDY'S DREAM COME TRUE.
JANEY'S SURE LUCKY SHE HAS US TO PACK UP THIS EQUIPMENT.
I'M THE LUCKY ONE. THREE WHOLE DAYS WITH JANEY WELLS—THE LOVE OF MY LIFE, MY REASON FOR BEING.
CALM DOWN OLD BOY. IT'S NOT EXACTLY A DATE.
WELL, MAYBE NOT IN THE OFFICIAL SENSE. BUT THIS IS MY CHANCE TO SHOW JANEY A SANDY DIAZ SHE CAN'T RESIST.
BY THE END OF THIS TRIP THAT GIRL'S HEAD WILL BE SPINNING.
CRASH!
GO GUY!
HEY SKATE. READY TO TAKE YOUR SOUND BLASTING, MIX MASTERING RADIO PERSONA TO THE PEAK?
AUNTIE EM?
YEAH, MAN.
THE SKATE'S NOT LOOKING SO GOOD. YOU THINK HE'S NERVOUS ABOUT THE TRIP?
YEAH, RIGHT. LIKE A LITTLE CLASS TRIP COULD SHAKE MR. COOL. HE'S PROBABLY FEELING THE EFFECTS OF A LATE NIGHT OF MTV.

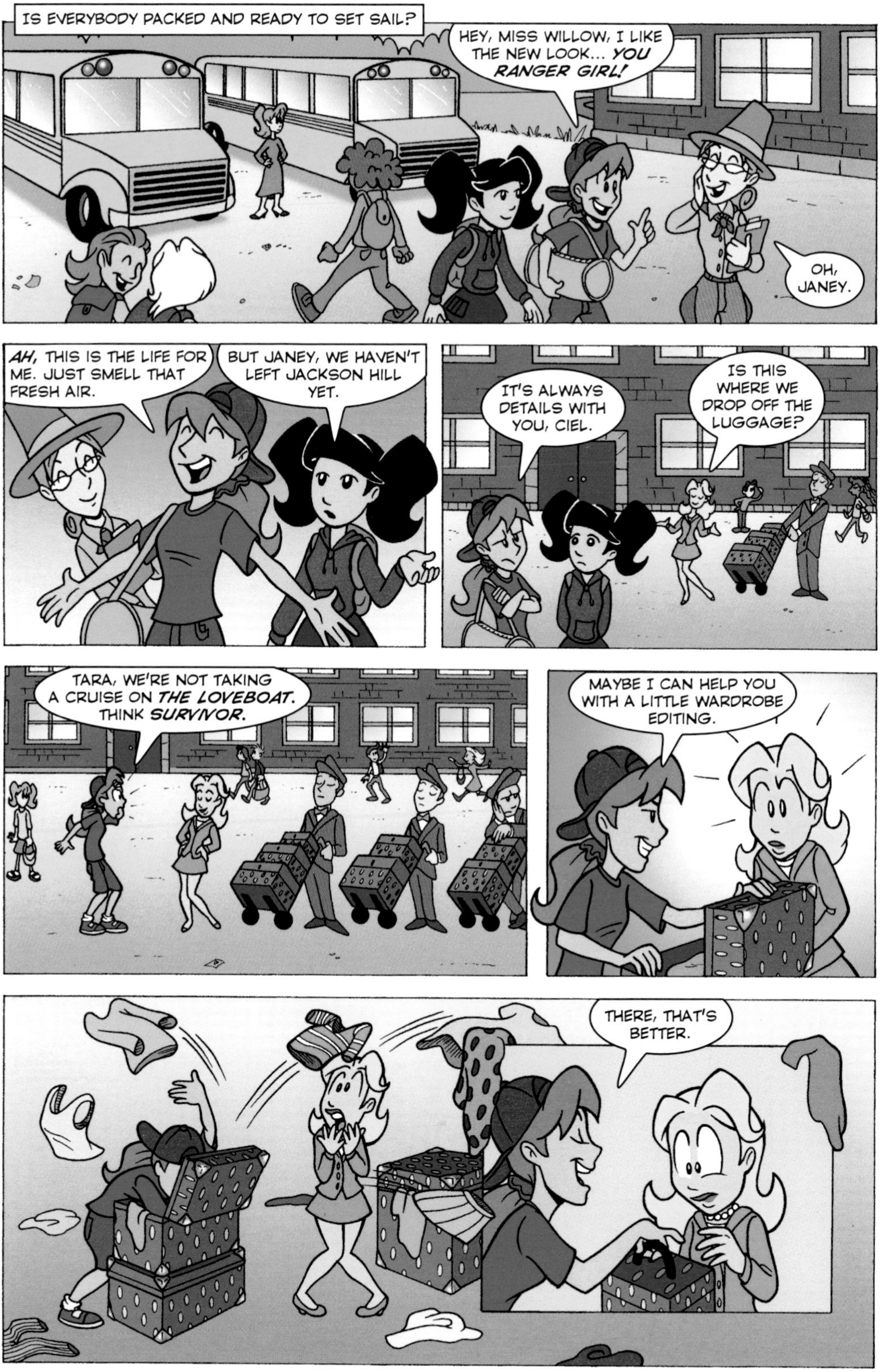
IS EVERYBODY PACKED AND READY TO SET SAIL?
HEY, MISS WILLOW, I LIKE THE NEW LOOK... YOU RANGER GIRL!
OH, JANEY.
AH, THIS IS THE LIFE FOR ME. JUST SMELL THAT FRESH AIR.
BUT JANEY, WE HAVEN'T LEFT JACKSON HILL YET.
IT'S ALWAYS DETAILS WITH YOU, CIEL.
IS THIS WHERE WE DROP OFF THE LUGGAGE?
TARA, WE'RE NOT TAKING A CRUISE ON THE LOVEBOAT. THINK SURVIVOR.
MAYBE I CAN HELP YOU WITH A LITTLE WARDROBE EDITING.
THERE, THAT'S BETTER.

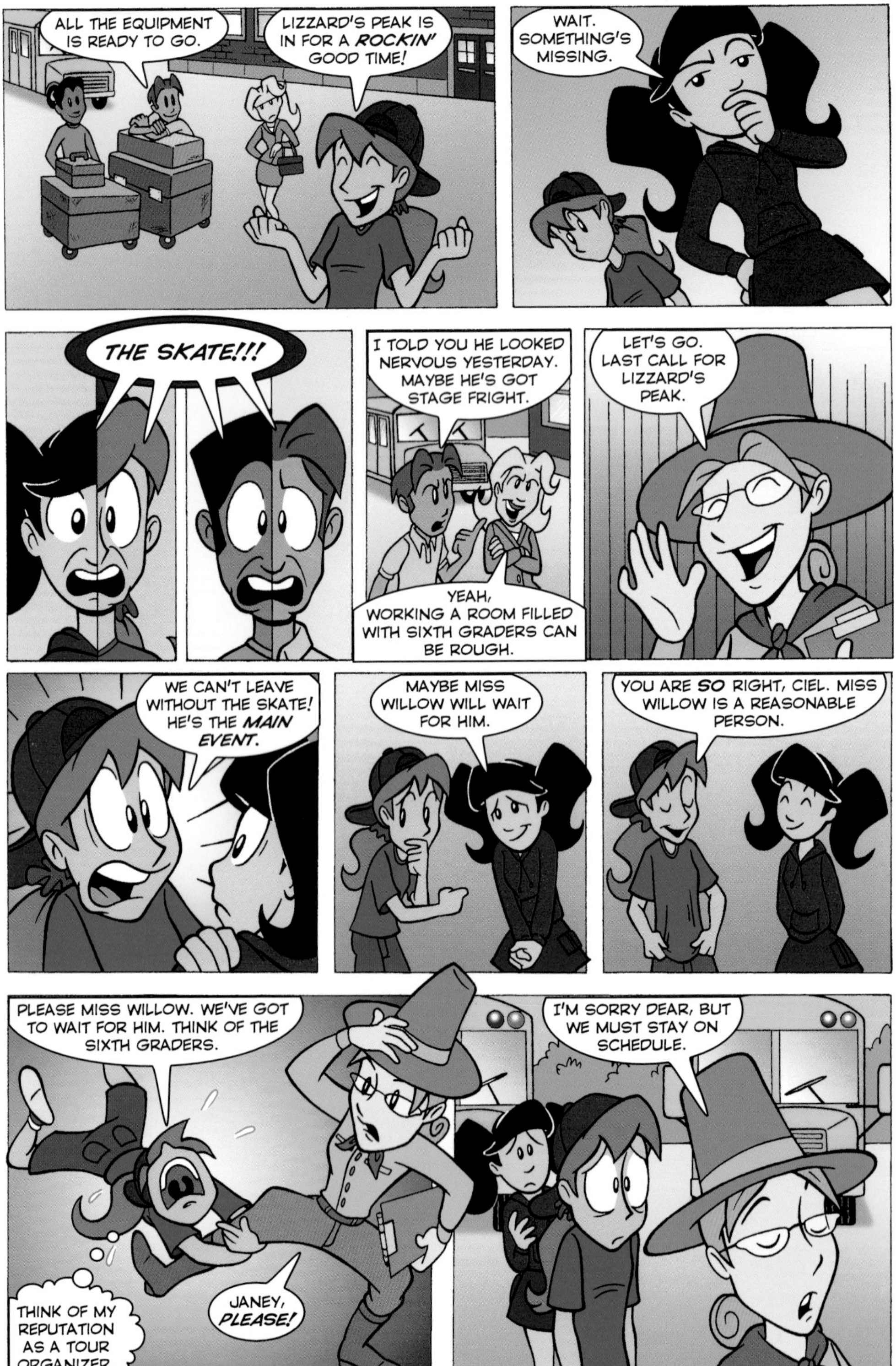
ALL THE EQUIPMENT IS READY TO GO.
LIZZARD'S PEAK IS IN FOR A ROCKIN' GOOD TIME!
WAIT. SOMETHING'S MISSING.
THE SKATE!!!
I TOLD YOU HE LOOKED NERVOUS YESTERDAY. MAYBE HE'S GOT STAGE FRIGHT.
YEAH, WORKING A ROOM FILLED WITH SIXTH GRADERS CAN BE ROUGH.
LET'S GO. LAST CALL FOR LIZZARD'S PEAK.
WE CAN'T LEAVE WITHOUT THE SKATE! HE'S THE MAIN EVENT.
MAYBE MISS WILLOW WILL WAIT FOR HIM.
YOU ARE SO RIGHT, CIEL. MISS WILLOW IS A REASONABLE PERSON.
PLEASE MISS WILLOW. WE'VE GOT TO WAIT FOR HIM. THINK OF THE SIXTH GRADERS.
THINK OF MY REPUTATION AS A TOUR ORGANIZER.
JANEY, PLEASE!
I'M SORRY DEAR, BUT WE MUST STAY ON SCHEDULE.

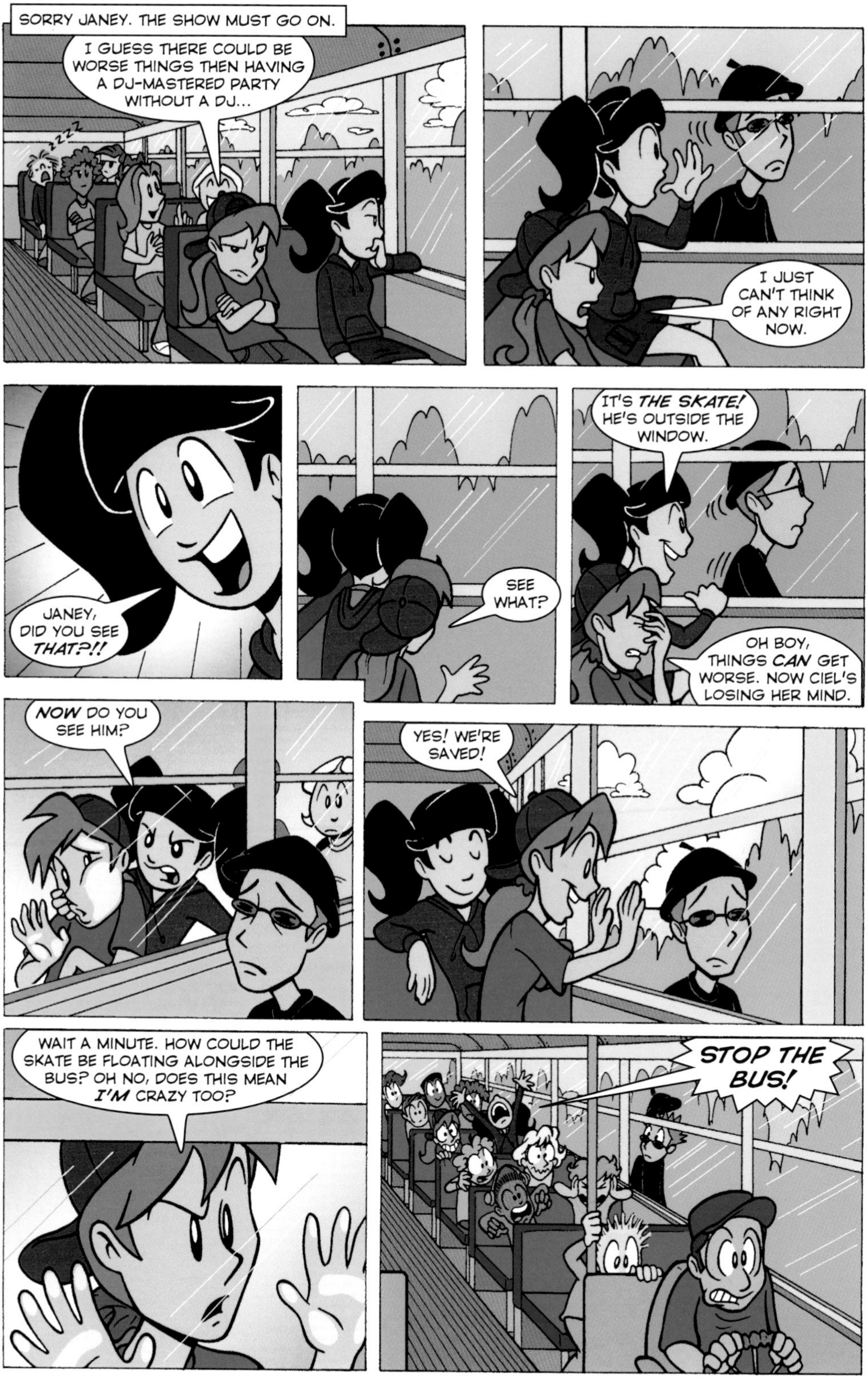
SORRY JANEY. THE SHOW MUST GO ON.
I GUESS THERE COULD BE WORSE THINGS THEN HAVING A DJ-MASTERED PARTY WITHOUT A DJ...
I JUST CAN'T THINK OF ANY RIGHT NOW.
JANEY, DID YOU SEE THAT?!!
SEE WHAT?
IT'S THE SKATE! HE'S OUTSIDE THE WINDOW.
OH BOY, THINGS CAN GET WORSE. NOW CIEL'S LOSING HER MIND.
NOW DO YOU SEE HIM?
YES! WE'RE SAVED!
WAIT A MINUTE. HOW COULD THE SKATE BE FLOATING ALONGSIDE THE BUS? OH NO, DOES THIS MEAN I'M CRAZY TOO?
STOP THE BUS!

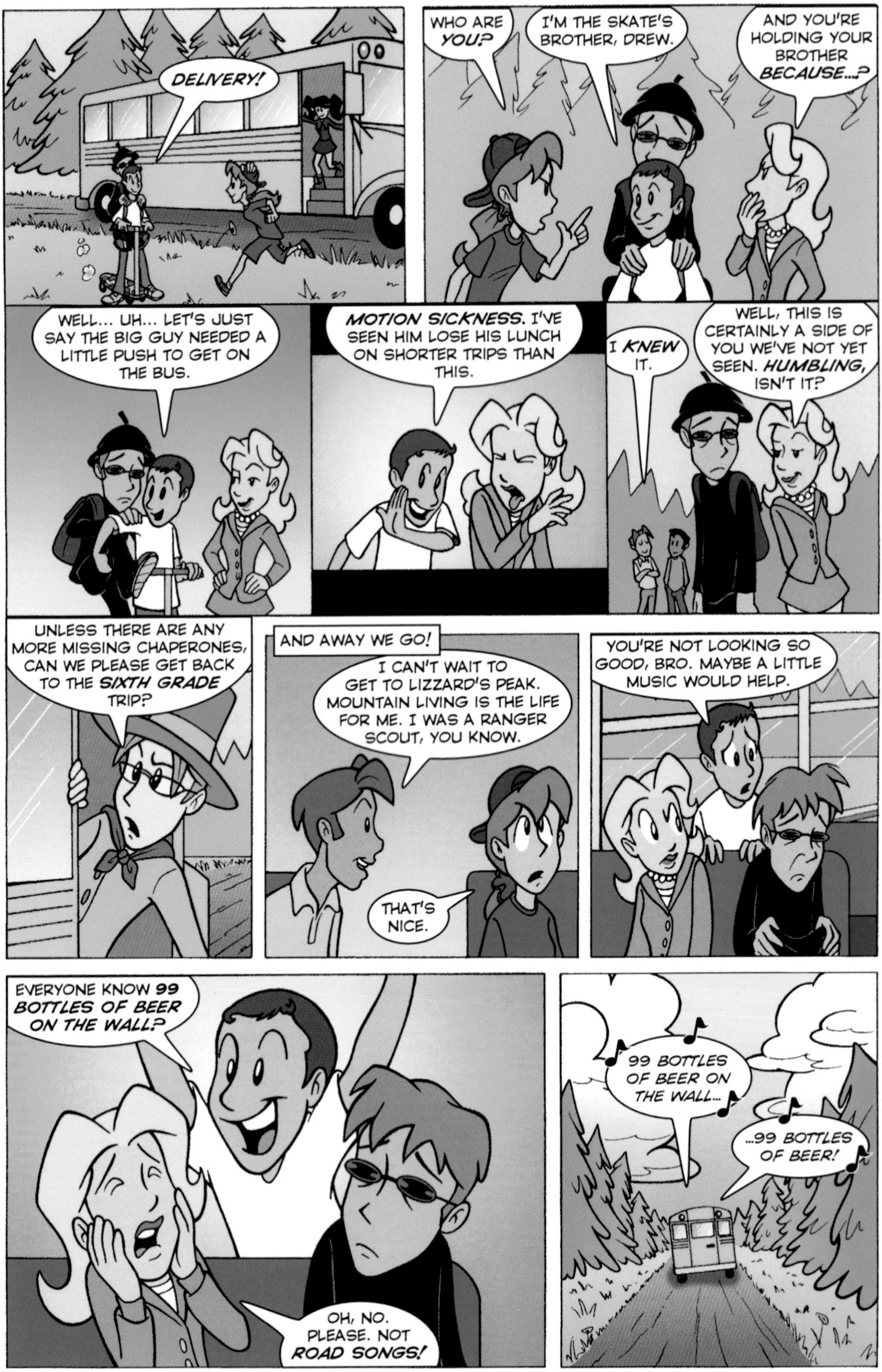
DELIVERY!
WHO ARE YOU?
I'M THE SKATE'S BROTHER, DREW.
AND YOU'RE HOLDING YOUR BROTHER BECAUSE...?
WELL... UH... LET'S JUST SAY THE BIG GUY NEEDED A LITTLE PUSH TO GET ON THE BUS.
MOTION SICKNESS. I'VE SEEN HIM LOSE HIS LUNCH ON SHORTER TRIPS THAN THIS.
I KNEW IT.
WELL, THIS IS CERTAINLY A SIDE OF YOU WE'VE NOT YET SEEN. HUMBLING, ISN'T IT?
UNLESS THERE ARE ANY MORE MISSING CHAPERONES, CAN WE PLEASE GET BACK TO THE SIXTH GRADE TRIP?
AND AWAY WE GO!
I CAN'T WAIT TO GET TO LIZZARD'S PEAK. MOUNTAIN LIVING IS THE LIFE FOR ME. I WAS A RANGER SCOUT, YOU KNOW.
THAT'S NICE.
YOU'RE NOT LOOKING SO GOOD, BRO. MAYBE A LITTLE MUSIC WOULD HELP.
EVERYONE KNOW 99 BOTTLES OF BEER ON THE WALL?
OH, NO. PLEASE. NOT ROAD SONGS!
99 BOTTLES OF BEER ON THE WALL...
...99 BOTTLES OF BEER!

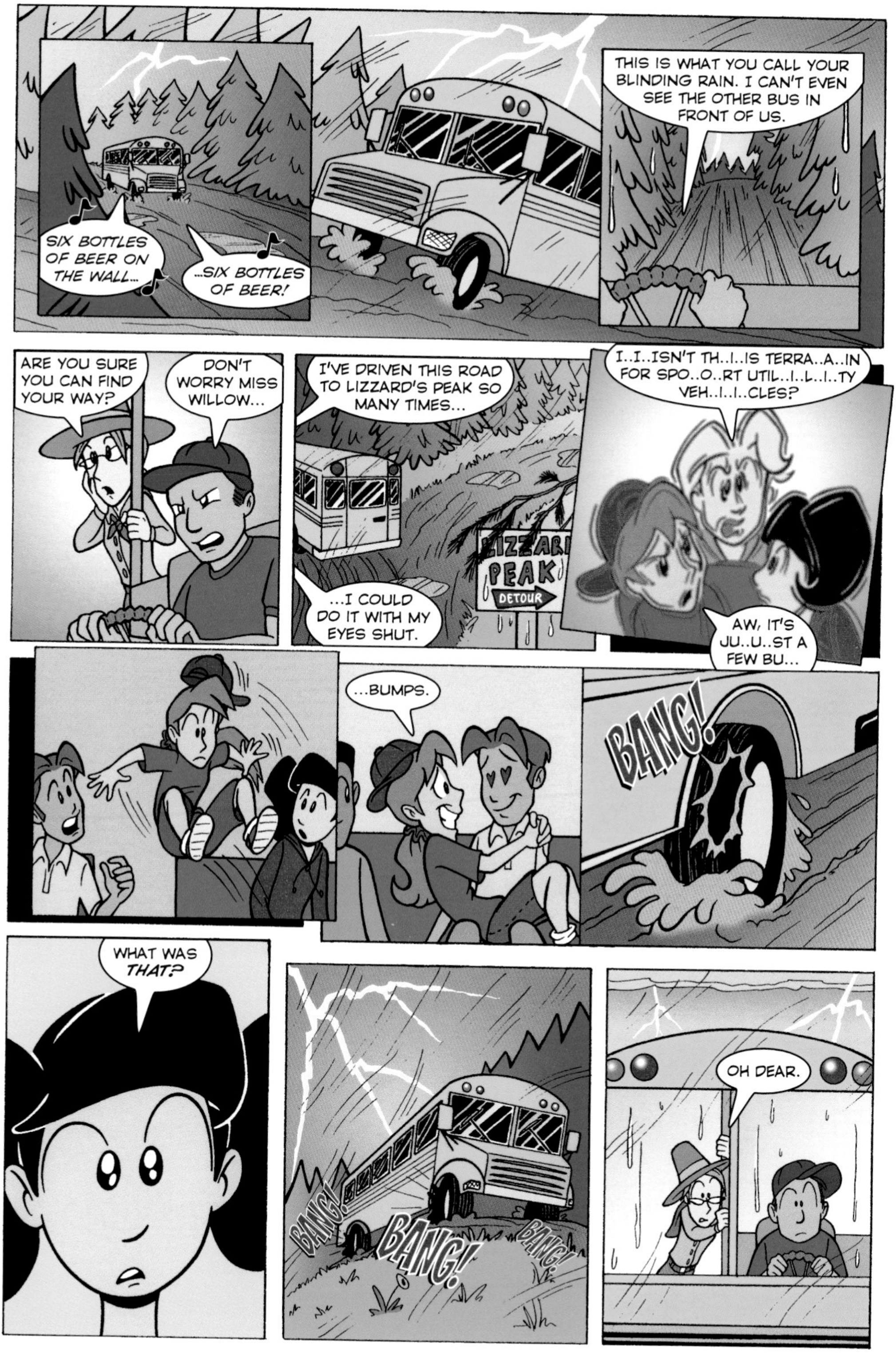
SIX BOTTLES OF BEER ON THE WALL...
...SIX BOTTLES OF BEER!
THIS IS WHAT YOU CALL YOUR BLINDING RAIN. I CAN'T EVEN SEE THE OTHER BUS IN FRONT OF US.
ARE YOU SURE YOU CAN FIND YOUR WAY?
DON'T WORRY MISS WILLOW...
I'VE DRIVEN THIS ROAD TO LIZZARD'S PEAK SO MANY TIMES...
...I COULD DO IT WITH MY EYES SHUT.
PEAK
DETOUR
I..I..ISN'T TH..I..IS TERRA..A..IN FOR SPO..O..RT UTIL..I..L..I..TY VEH..I..I..CLES?
AW, IT'S JU..U..ST A FEW BU...
...BUMPS.
BANG!
WHAT WAS THAT?
BANG!
BANG!
BANG!
OH DEAR.

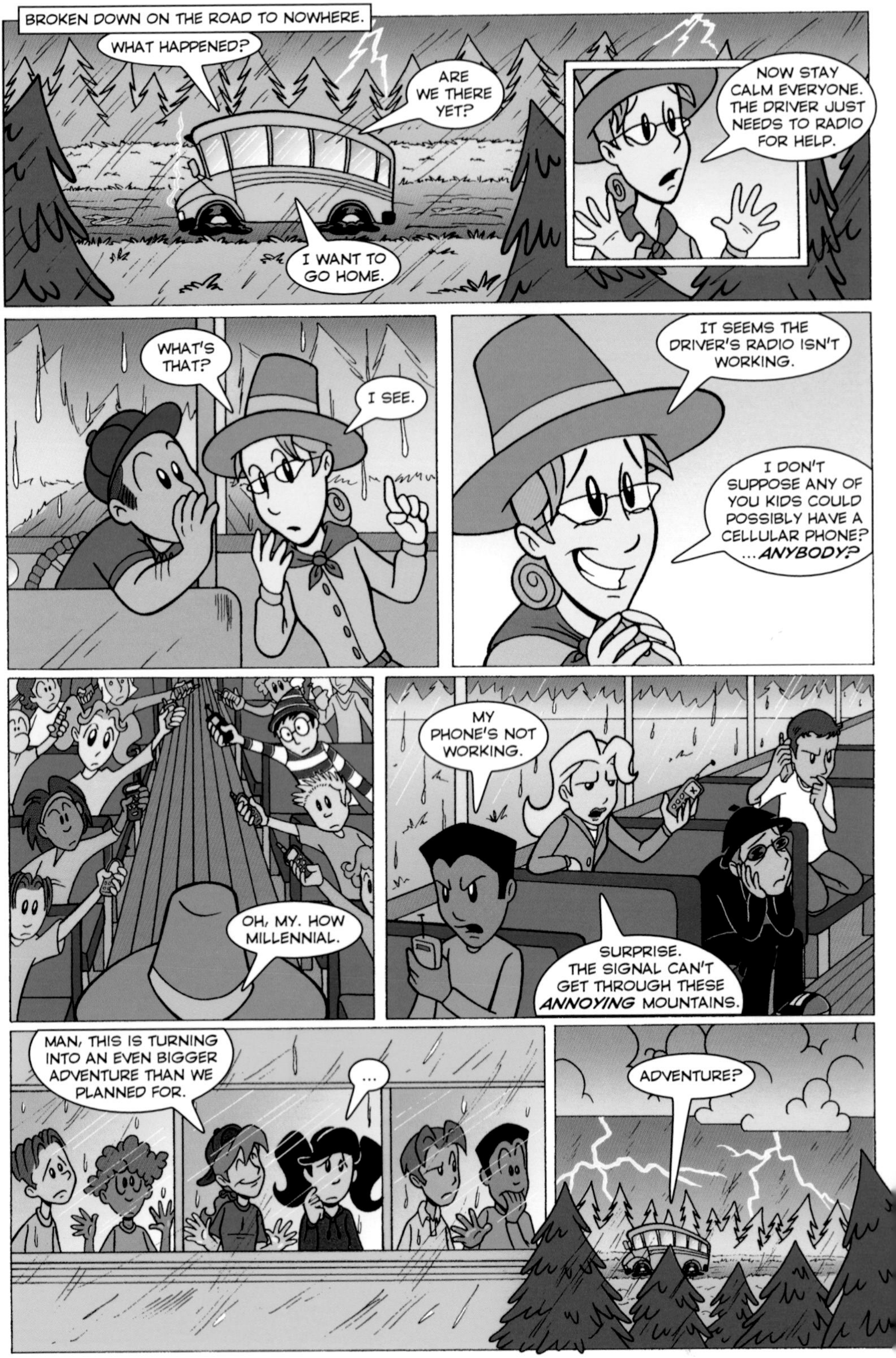
BROKEN DOWN ON THE ROAD TO NOWHERE.
WHAT HAPPENED?
ARE WE THERE YET?
I WANT TO GO HOME.
NOW STAY CALM EVERYONE. THE DRIVER JUST NEEDS TO RADIO FOR HELP.
WHAT'S THAT?
I SEE.
IT SEEMS THE DRIVER'S RADIO ISN'T WORKING.
I DON'T SUPPOSE ANY OF YOU KIDS COULD POSSIBLY HAVE A CELLULAR PHONE? ...ANYBODY?
OH, MY. HOW MILLENNIAL.
MY PHONE'S NOT WORKING.
SURPRISE. THE SIGNAL CAN'T GET THROUGH THESE ANNOYING MOUNTAINS.
MAN, THIS IS TURNING INTO AN EVEN BIGGER ADVENTURE THAN WE PLANNED FOR.
...
ADVENTURE?

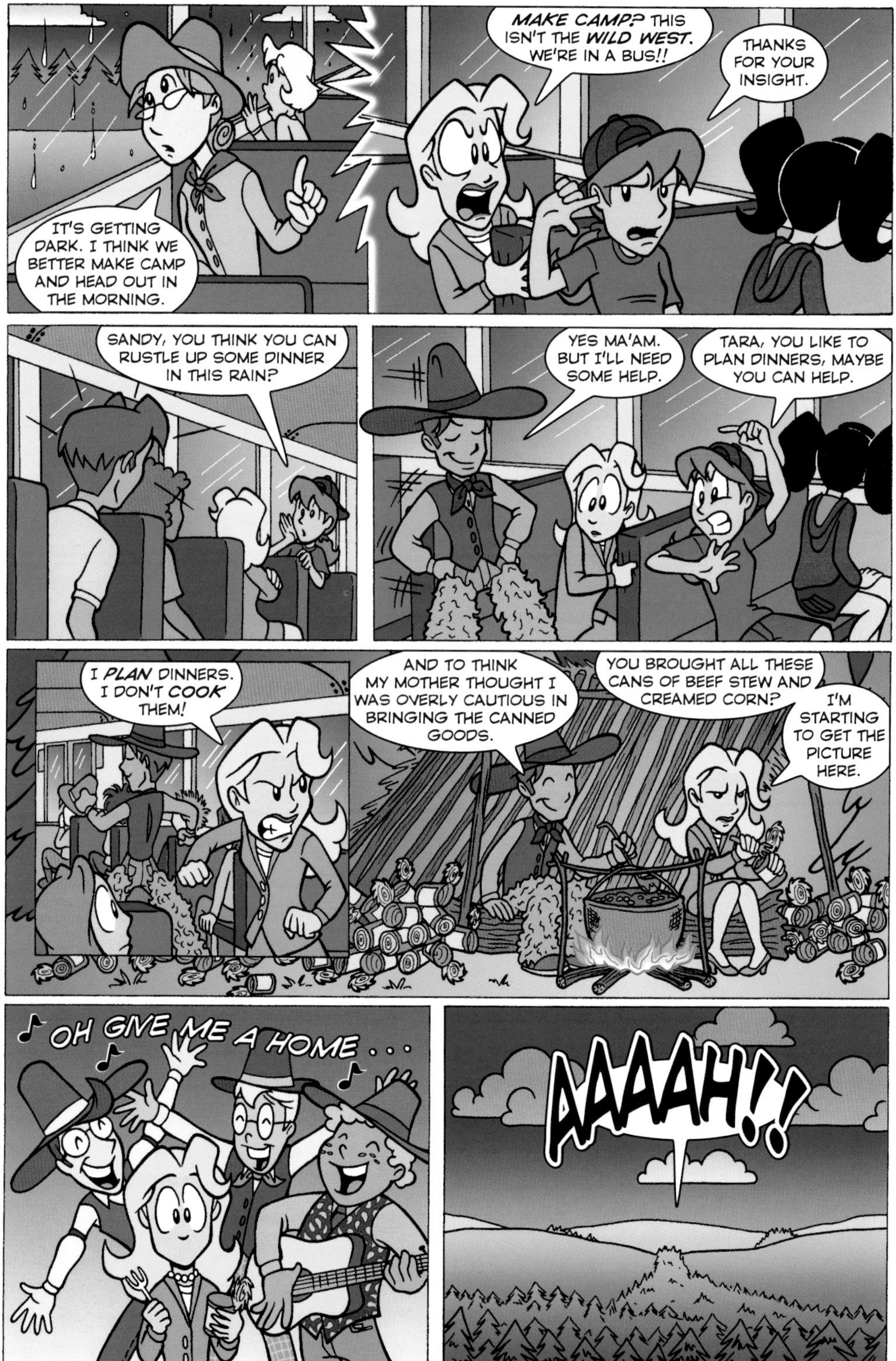
IT'S GETTING DARK. I THINK WE BETTER MAKE CAMP AND HEAD OUT IN THE MORNING.
MAKE CAMP? THIS ISN'T THE WILD WEST. WE'RE IN A BUS!!
THANKS FOR YOUR INSIGHT.
SANDY, YOU THINK YOU CAN RUSTLE UP SOME DINNER IN THIS RAIN?
YES MA'AM. BUT I'LL NEED SOME HELP.
TARA, YOU LIKE TO PLAN DINNERS, MAYBE YOU CAN HELP.
I PLAN DINNERS. I DON'T COOK THEM!
AND TO THINK MY MOTHER THOUGHT I WAS OVERLY CAUTIOUS IN BRINGING THE CANNED GOODS.
YOU BROUGHT ALL THESE CANS OF BEEF STEW AND CREAMED CORN?
I'M STARTING TO GET THE PICTURE HERE.
OH GIVE ME A HOME . . .
AAAAH!!

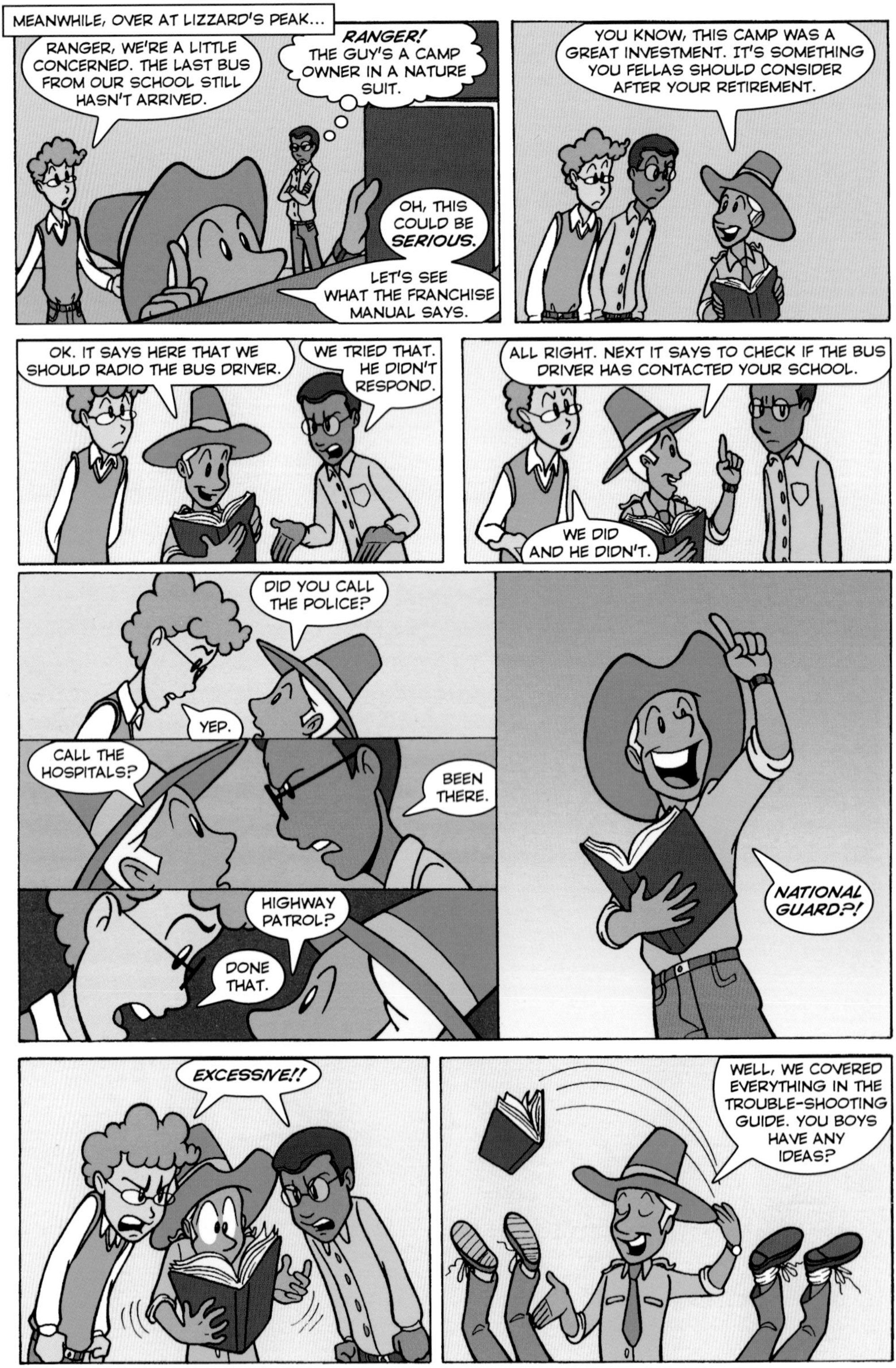
MEANWHILE, OVER AT LIZZARD'S PEAK...
RANGER, WE'RE A LITTLE CONCERNED. THE LAST BUS FROM OUR SCHOOL STILL HASN'T ARRIVED.
RANGER! THE GUY'S A CAMP OWNER IN A NATURE SUIT.
OH, THIS COULD BE SERIOUS.
LET'S SEE WHAT THE FRANCHISE MANUAL SAYS.
YOU KNOW, THIS CAMP WAS A GREAT INVESTMENT. IT'S SOMETHING YOU FELLAS SHOULD CONSIDER AFTER YOUR RETIREMENT.
OK. IT SAYS HERE THAT WE SHOULD RADIO THE BUS DRIVER.
WE TRIED THAT. HE DIDN'T RESPOND.
ALL RIGHT. NEXT IT SAYS TO CHECK IF THE BUS DRIVER HAS CONTACTED YOUR SCHOOL.
WE DID AND HE DIDN'T.
DID YOU CALL THE POLICE?
YEP.
CALL THE HOSPITALS?
BEEN THERE.
HIGHWAY PATROL?
DONE THAT.
NATIONAL GUARD?!
EXCESSIVE!!
WELL, WE COVERED EVERYTHING IN THE TROUBLE-SHOOTING GUIDE. YOU BOYS HAVE ANY IDEAS?

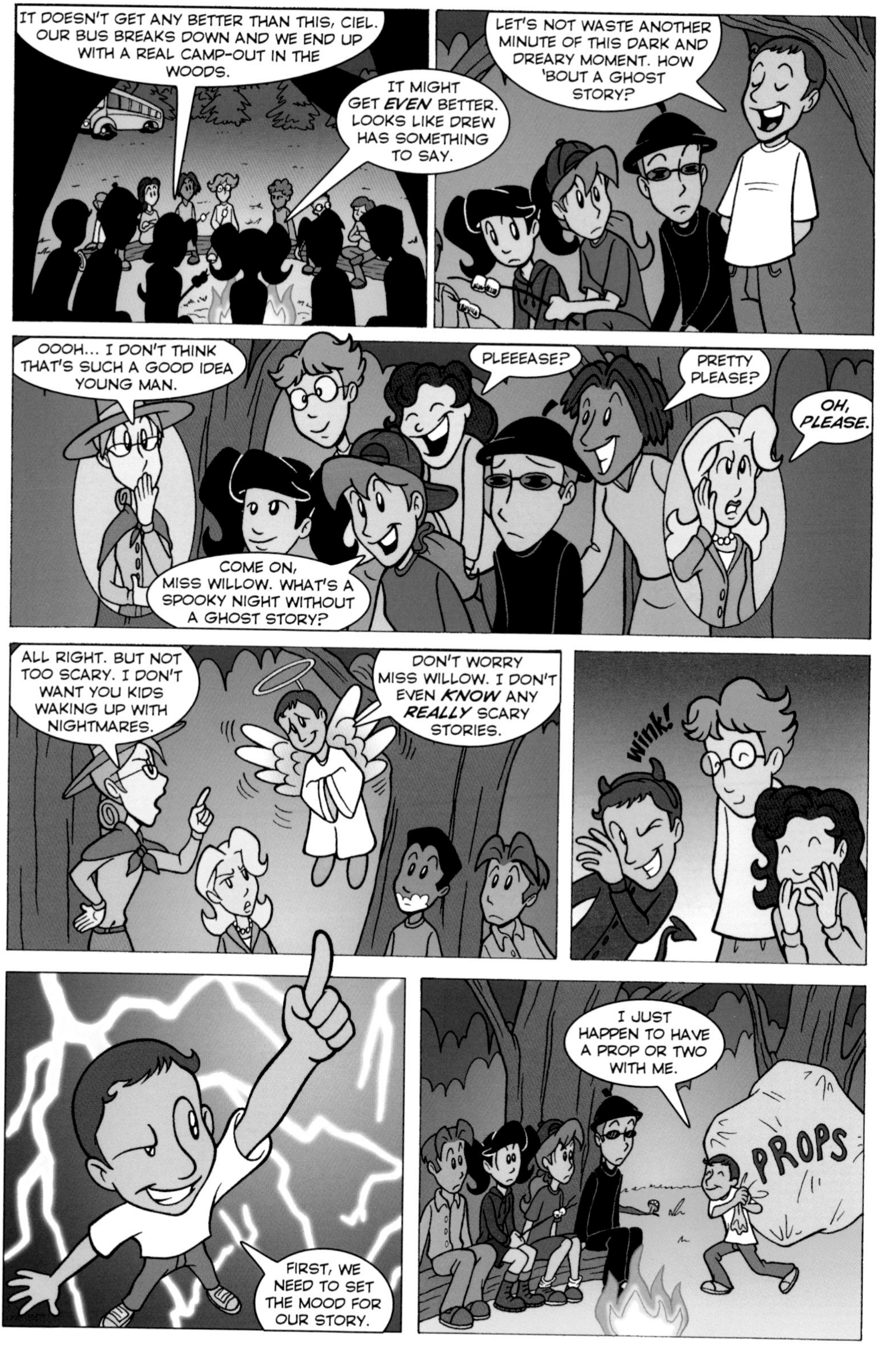
IT DOESN'T GET ANY BETTER THAN THIS, CIEL. OUR BUS BREAKS DOWN AND WE END UP WITH A REAL CAMP-OUT IN THE WOODS.
IT MIGHT GET EVEN BETTER. LOOKS LIKE DREW HAS SOMETHING TO SAY.
LET'S NOT WASTE ANOTHER MINUTE OF THIS DARK AND DREARY MOMENT. HOW 'BOUT A GHOST STORY?
OOOH... I DON'T THINK THAT'S SUCH A GOOD IDEA YOUNG MAN.
PLEEEASE?
PRETTY PLEASE?
OH, PLEASE.
COME ON, MISS WILLOW. WHAT'S A SPOOKY NIGHT WITHOUT A GHOST STORY?
ALL RIGHT. BUT NOT TOO SCARY. I DON'T WANT YOU KIDS WAKING UP WITH NIGHTMARES.
DON'T WORRY MISS WILLOW. I DON'T EVEN KNOW ANY REALLY SCARY STORIES.
wink!
FIRST, WE NEED TO SET THE MOOD FOR OUR STORY.
I JUST HAPPEN TO HAVE A PROP OR TWO WITH ME.
PROPS

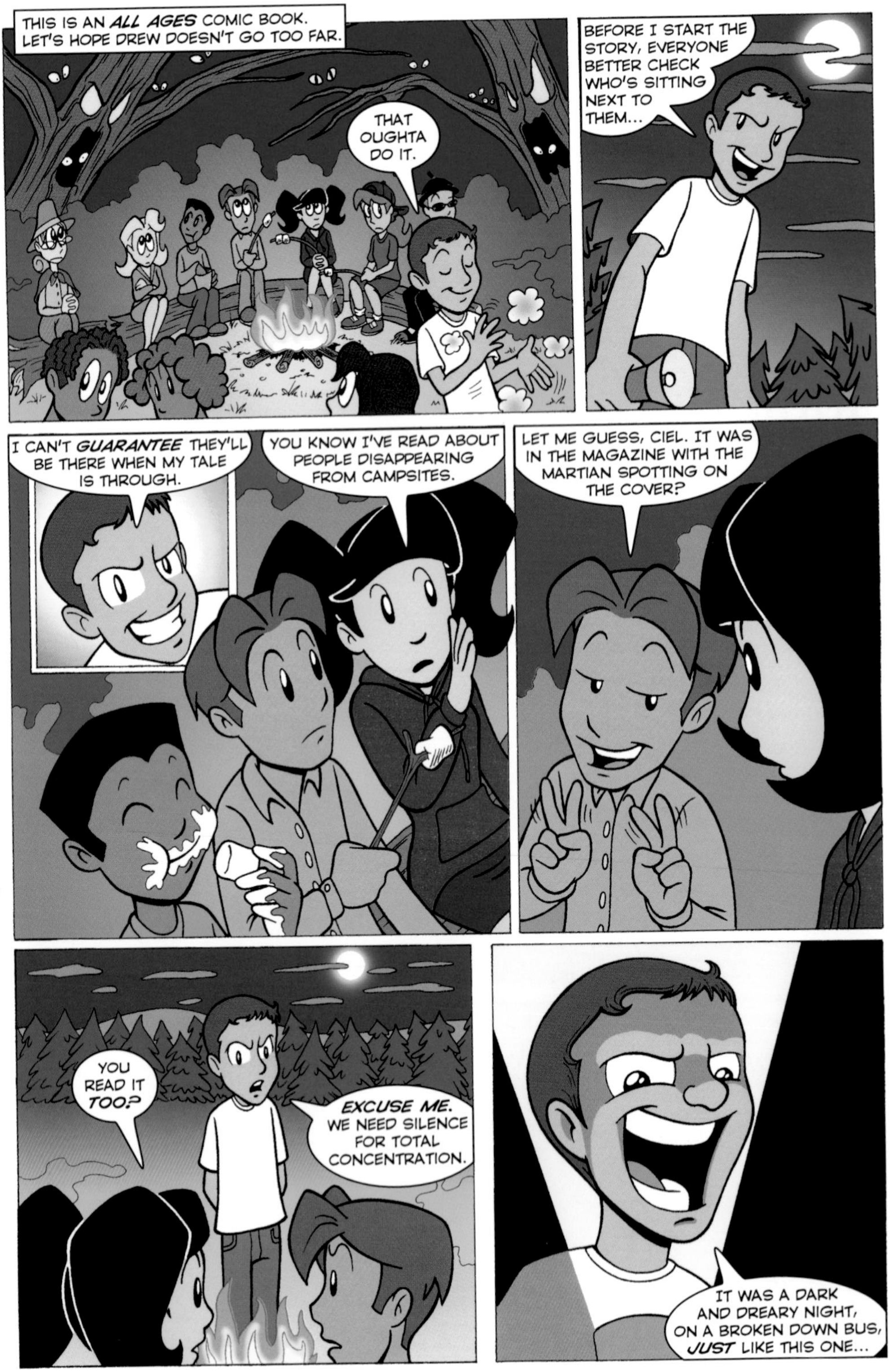
THIS IS AN *ALL AGES* COMIC BOOK. LET'S HOPE DREW DOESN'T GO TOO FAR.
THAT OUGHTA DO IT.
BEFORE I START THE STORY, EVERYONE BETTER CHECK WHO'S SITTING NEXT TO THEM...
I CAN'T *GUARANTEE* THEY'LL BE THERE WHEN MY TALE IS THROUGH.
YOU KNOW I'VE READ ABOUT PEOPLE DISAPPEARING FROM CAMPSITES.
LET ME GUESS, CIEL. IT WAS IN THE MAGAZINE WITH THE MARTIAN SPOTTING ON THE COVER?
YOU READ IT *TOO?*
EXCUSE ME. WE NEED SILENCE FOR TOTAL CONCENTRATION.
IT WAS A DARK AND DREARY NIGHT, ON A BROKEN DOWN BUS, *JUST* LIKE THIS ONE...

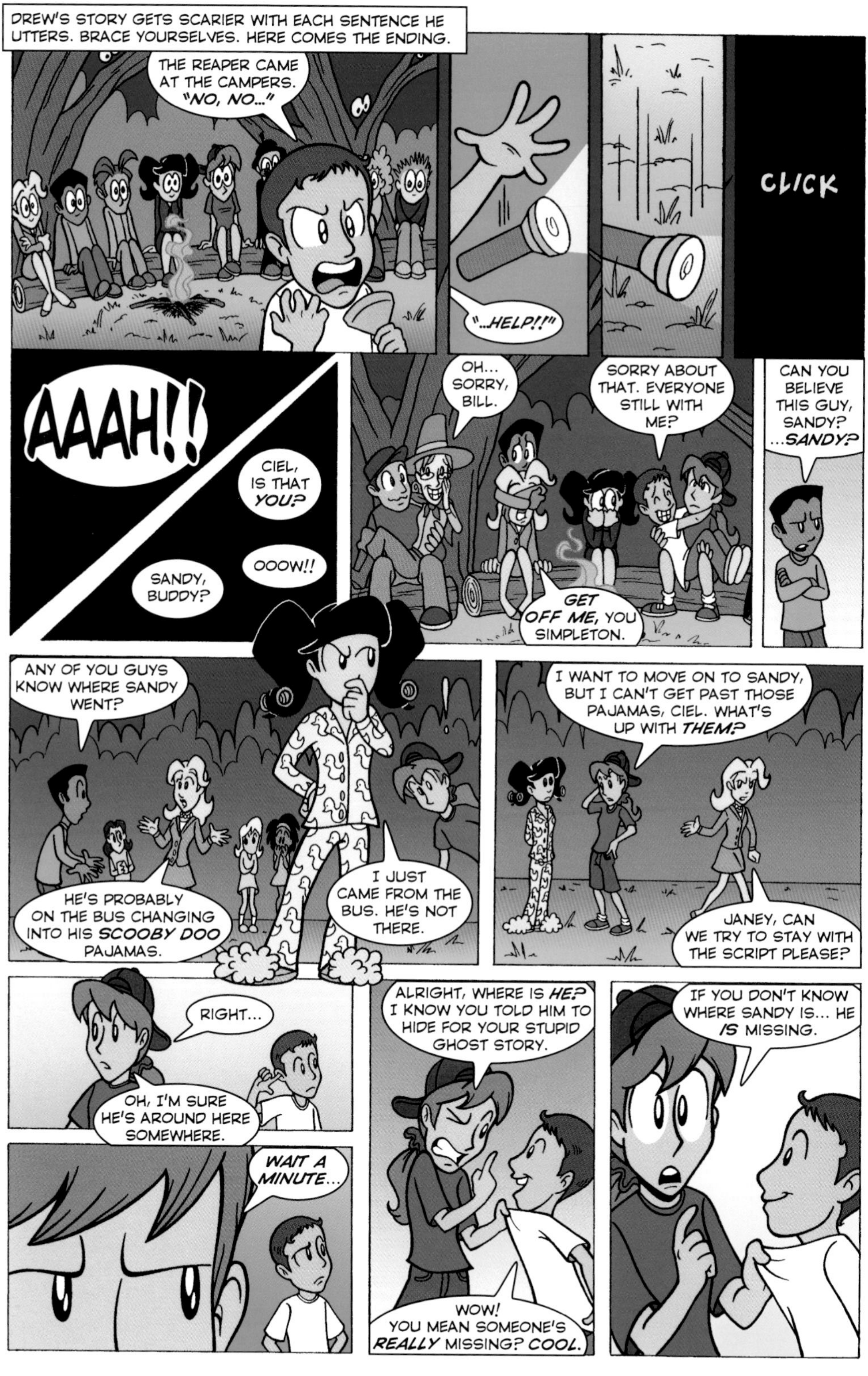
DREW'S STORY GETS SCARIER WITH EACH SENTENCE HE UTTERS. BRACE YOURSELVES. HERE COMES THE ENDING.
THE REAPER CAME AT THE CAMPERS. *"NO, NO..."*
"...HELP!!"
CLICK
AAAH!!
CIEL, IS THAT *YOU?*
SANDY, BUDDY?
OOOW!!
OH... SORRY, BILL.
SORRY ABOUT THAT. EVERYONE STILL WITH ME?
GET OFF ME, YOU SIMPLETON.
CAN YOU BELIEVE THIS GUY, SANDY? ...*SANDY?*
ANY OF YOU GUYS KNOW WHERE SANDY WENT?
HE'S PROBABLY ON THE BUS CHANGING INTO HIS *SCOOBY DOO* PAJAMAS.
I JUST CAME FROM THE BUS. HE'S NOT THERE.
I WANT TO MOVE ON TO SANDY, BUT I CAN'T GET PAST THOSE PAJAMAS, CIEL. WHAT'S UP WITH *THEM?*
JANEY, CAN WE TRY TO STAY WITH THE SCRIPT PLEASE?
RIGHT...
OH, I'M SURE HE'S AROUND HERE SOMEWHERE.
WAIT A MINUTE...
ALRIGHT, WHERE IS *HE?* I KNOW YOU TOLD HIM TO HIDE FOR YOUR STUPID GHOST STORY.
WOW! YOU MEAN SOMEONE'S *REALLY* MISSING? *COOL.*
IF YOU DON'T KNOW WHERE SANDY IS... HE *IS* MISSING.

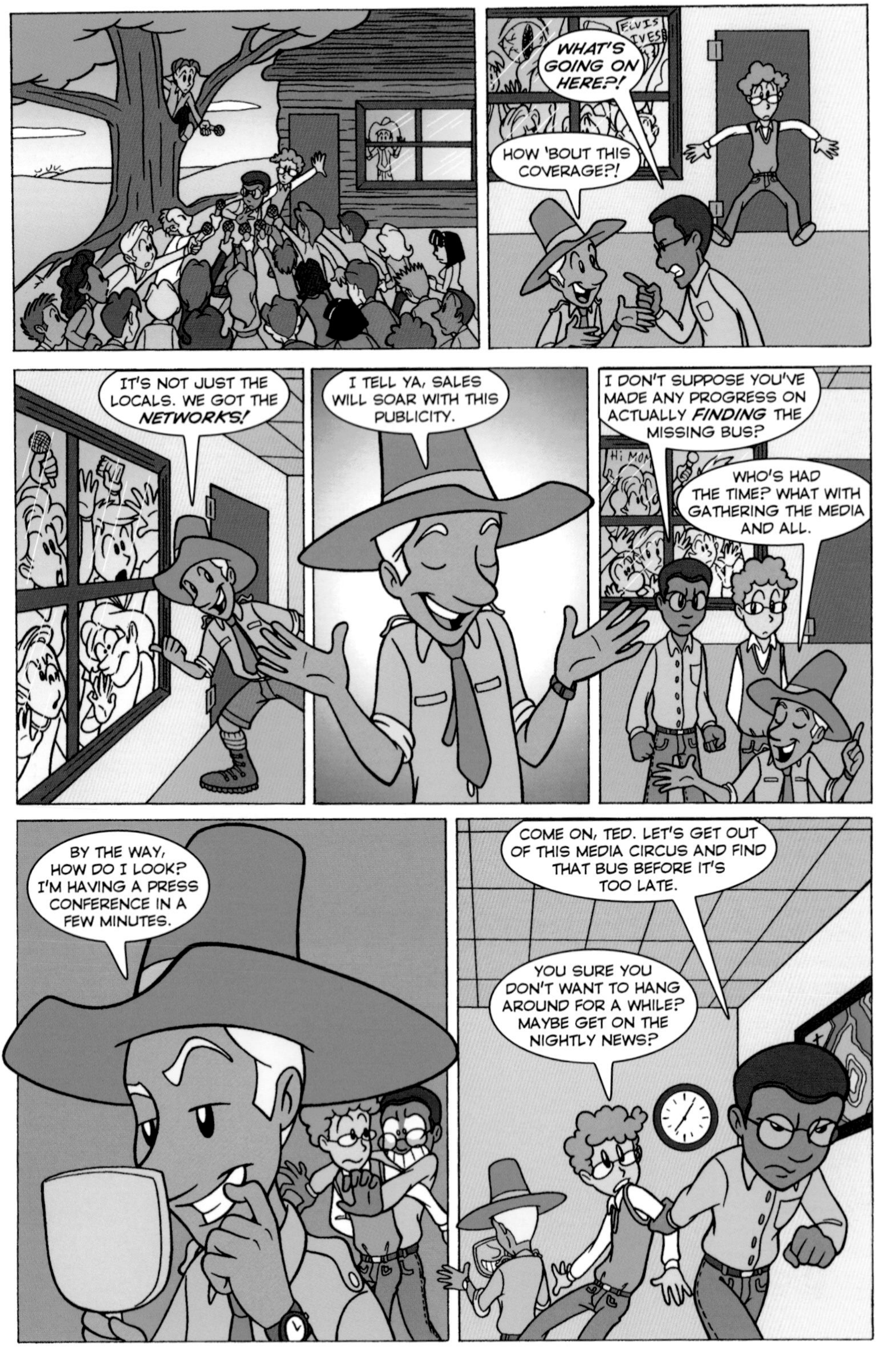
WHAT'S GOING ON HERE?!
HOW 'BOUT THIS COVERAGE?!
IT'S NOT JUST THE LOCALS. WE GOT THE NETWORKS!
I TELL YA, SALES WILL SOAR WITH THIS PUBLICITY.
I DON'T SUPPOSE YOU'VE MADE ANY PROGRESS ON ACTUALLY FINDING THE MISSING BUS?
Hi MOM
WHO'S HAD THE TIME? WHAT WITH GATHERING THE MEDIA AND ALL.
BY THE WAY, HOW DO I LOOK? I'M HAVING A PRESS CONFERENCE IN A FEW MINUTES.
COME ON, TED. LET'S GET OUT OF THIS MEDIA CIRCUS AND FIND THAT BUS BEFORE IT'S TOO LATE.
YOU SURE YOU DON'T WANT TO HANG AROUND FOR A WHILE? MAYBE GET ON THE NIGHTLY NEWS?

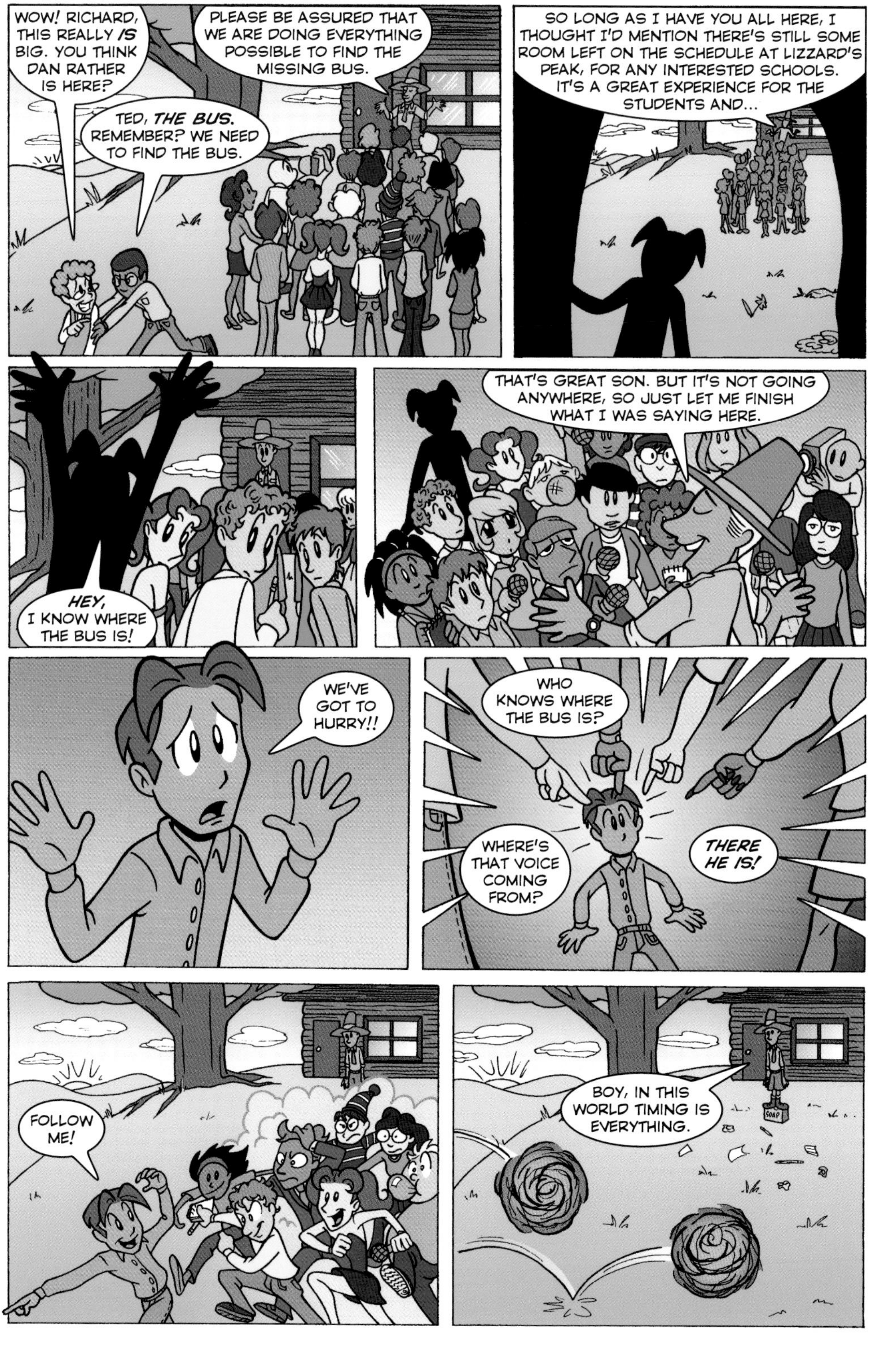
WOW! RICHARD, THIS REALLY IS BIG. YOU THINK DAN RATHER IS HERE?
PLEASE BE ASSURED THAT WE ARE DOING EVERYTHING POSSIBLE TO FIND THE MISSING BUS.
TED, THE BUS. REMEMBER? WE NEED TO FIND THE BUS.
SO LONG AS I HAVE YOU ALL HERE, I THOUGHT I'D MENTION THERE'S STILL SOME ROOM LEFT ON THE SCHEDULE AT LIZZARD'S PEAK, FOR ANY INTERESTED SCHOOLS. IT'S A GREAT EXPERIENCE FOR THE STUDENTS AND...
HEY, I KNOW WHERE THE BUS IS!
THAT'S GREAT SON. BUT IT'S NOT GOING ANYWHERE, SO JUST LET ME FINISH WHAT I WAS SAYING HERE.
WE'VE GOT TO HURRY!!
WHO KNOWS WHERE THE BUS IS?
WHERE'S THAT VOICE COMING FROM?
THERE HE IS!
FOLLOW ME!
BOY, IN THIS WORLD TIMING IS EVERYTHING.
SOAP

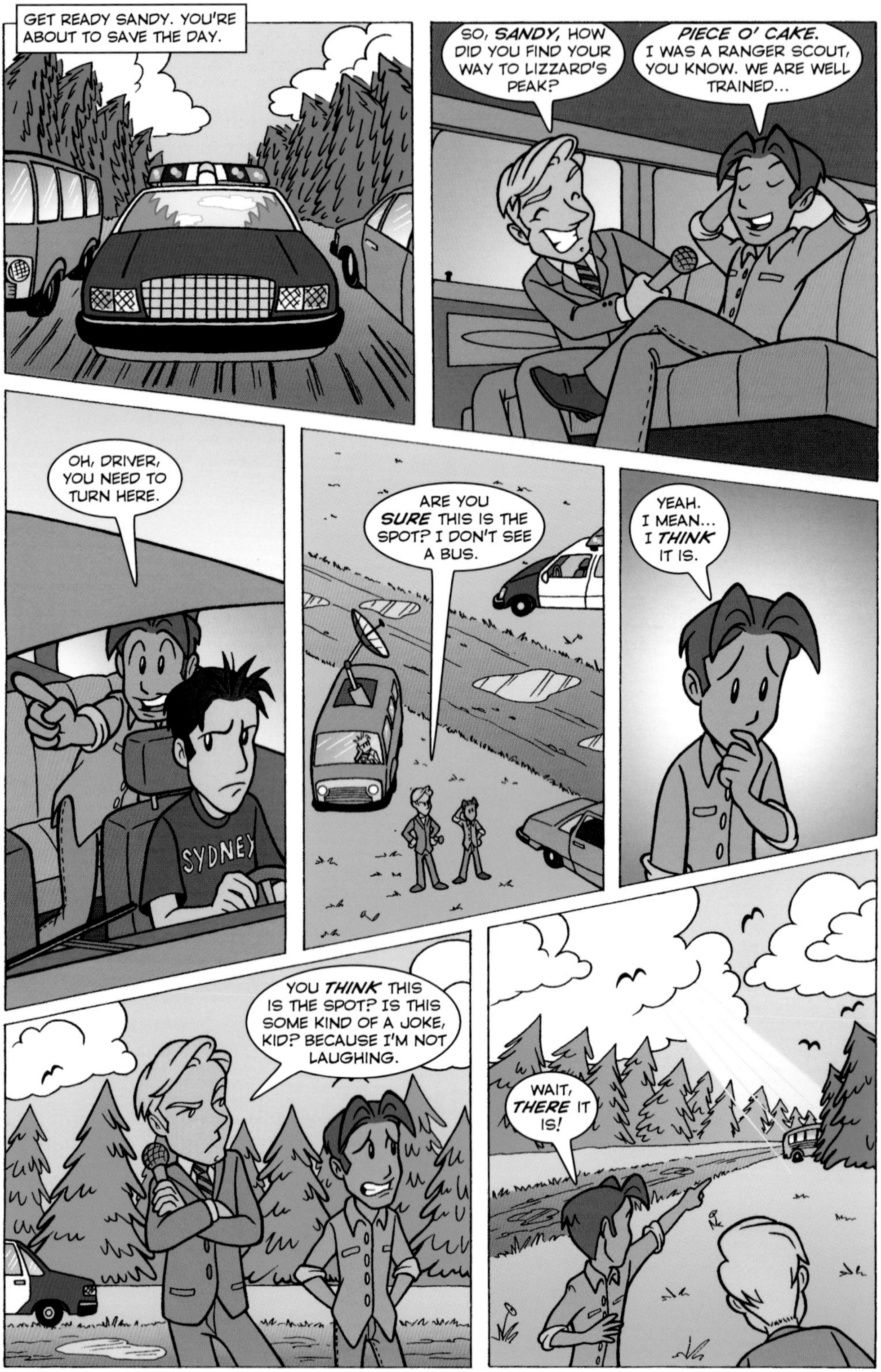
GET READY SANDY. YOU'RE ABOUT TO SAVE THE DAY.
SO, SANDY, HOW DID YOU FIND YOUR WAY TO LIZZARD'S PEAK?
PIECE O' CAKE. I WAS A RANGER SCOUT, YOU KNOW. WE ARE WELL TRAINED...
OH, DRIVER, YOU NEED TO TURN HERE.
SYDNEY
ARE YOU SURE THIS IS THE SPOT? I DON'T SEE A BUS.
YEAH. I MEAN... I THINK IT IS.
YOU THINK THIS IS THE SPOT? IS THIS SOME KIND OF A JOKE, KID? BECAUSE I'M NOT LAUGHING.
WAIT, THERE IT IS!

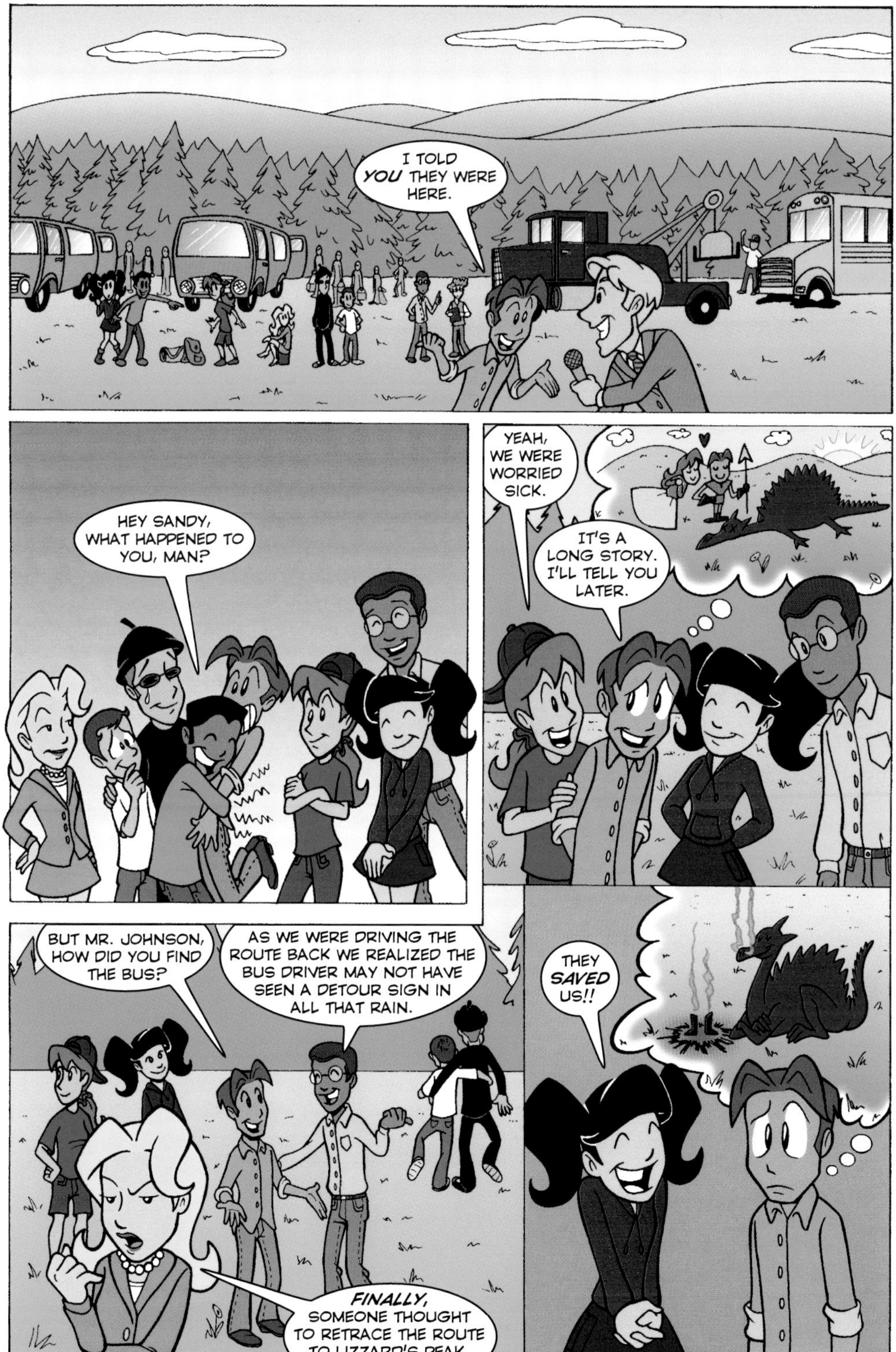
I TOLD *YOU* THEY WERE HERE.
HEY SANDY, WHAT HAPPENED TO YOU, MAN?
YEAH, WE WERE WORRIED SICK.
IT'S A LONG STORY. I'LL TELL YOU LATER.
BUT MR. JOHNSON, HOW DID YOU FIND THE BUS?
AS WE WERE DRIVING THE ROUTE BACK WE REALIZED THE BUS DRIVER MAY NOT HAVE SEEN A DETOUR SIGN IN ALL THAT RAIN.
FINALLY, SOMEONE THOUGHT TO RETRACE THE ROUTE TO LIZZARD'S PEAK.
THEY *SAVED* US!!

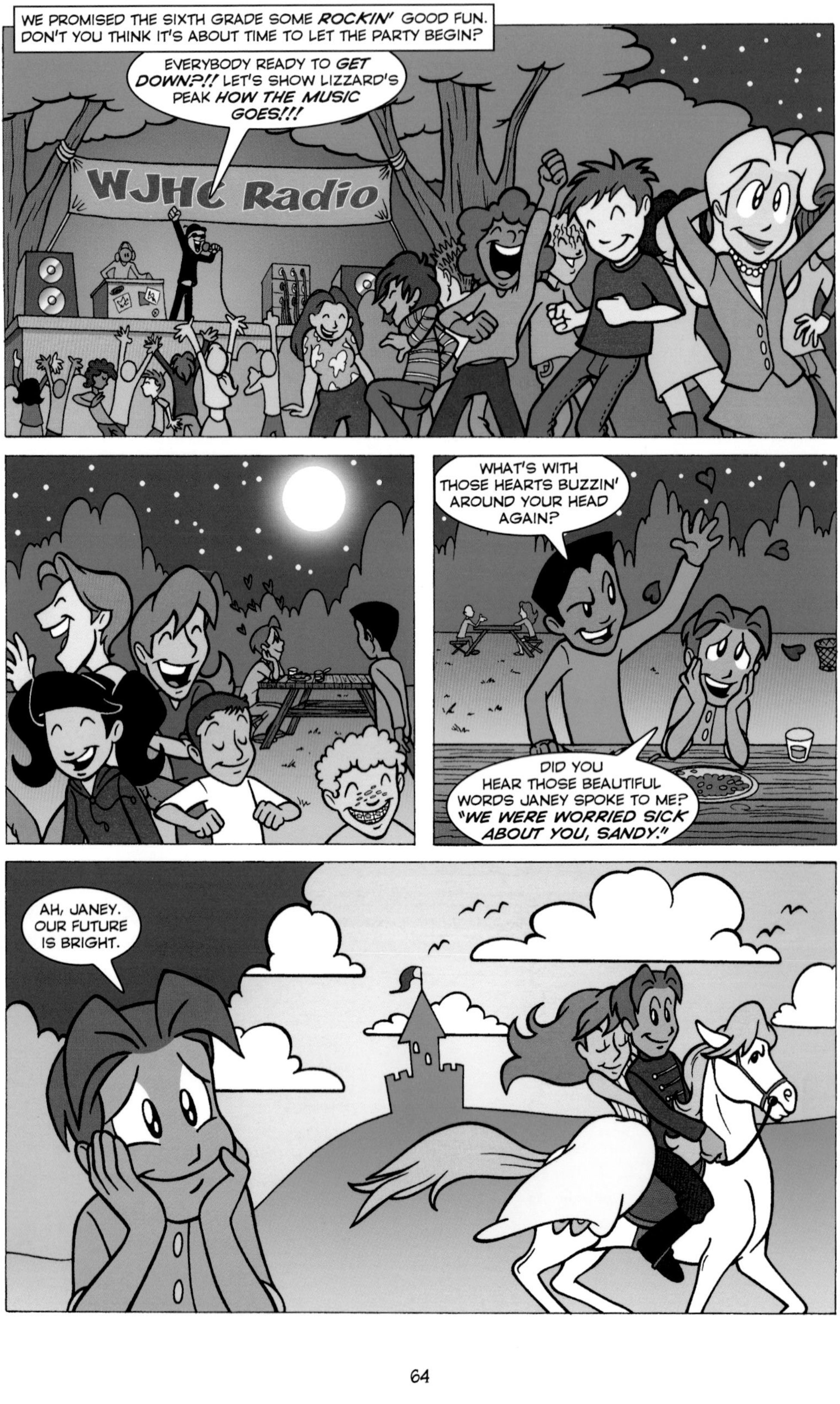
WE PROMISED THE SIXTH GRADE SOME *ROCKIN'* GOOD FUN. DON'T YOU THINK IT'S ABOUT TIME TO LET THE PARTY BEGIN?
EVERYBODY READY TO *GET DOWN?!!* LET'S SHOW LIZZARD'S PEAK *HOW THE MUSIC GOES!!!*
WJHC Radio
WHAT'S WITH THOSE HEARTS BUZZIN' AROUND YOUR HEAD AGAIN?
DID YOU HEAR THOSE BEAUTIFUL WORDS JANEY SPOKE TO ME? *"WE WERE WORRIED SICK ABOUT YOU, SANDY."*
AH, JANEY. OUR FUTURE IS BRIGHT.

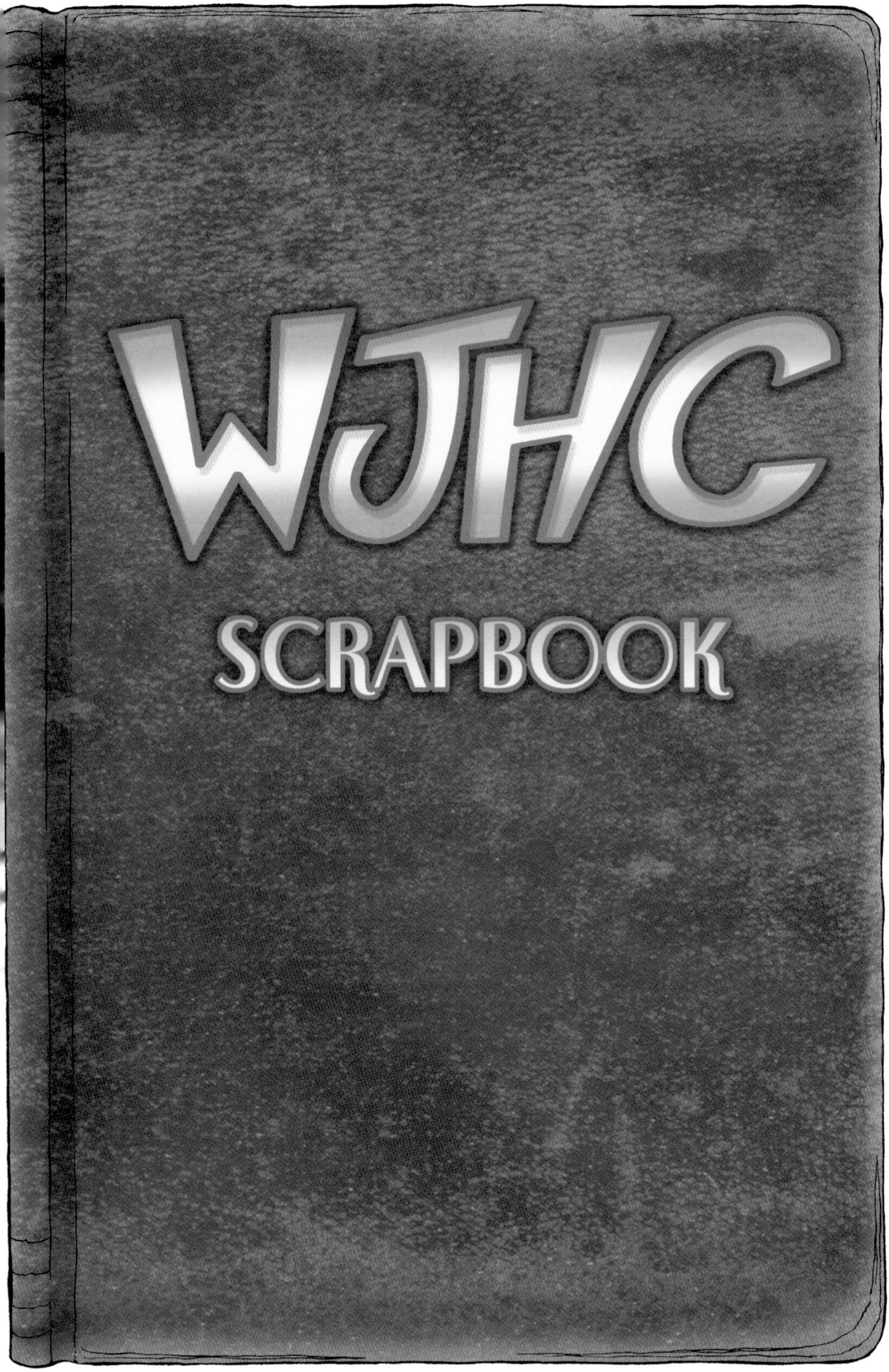
WJHC
SCRAPBOOK

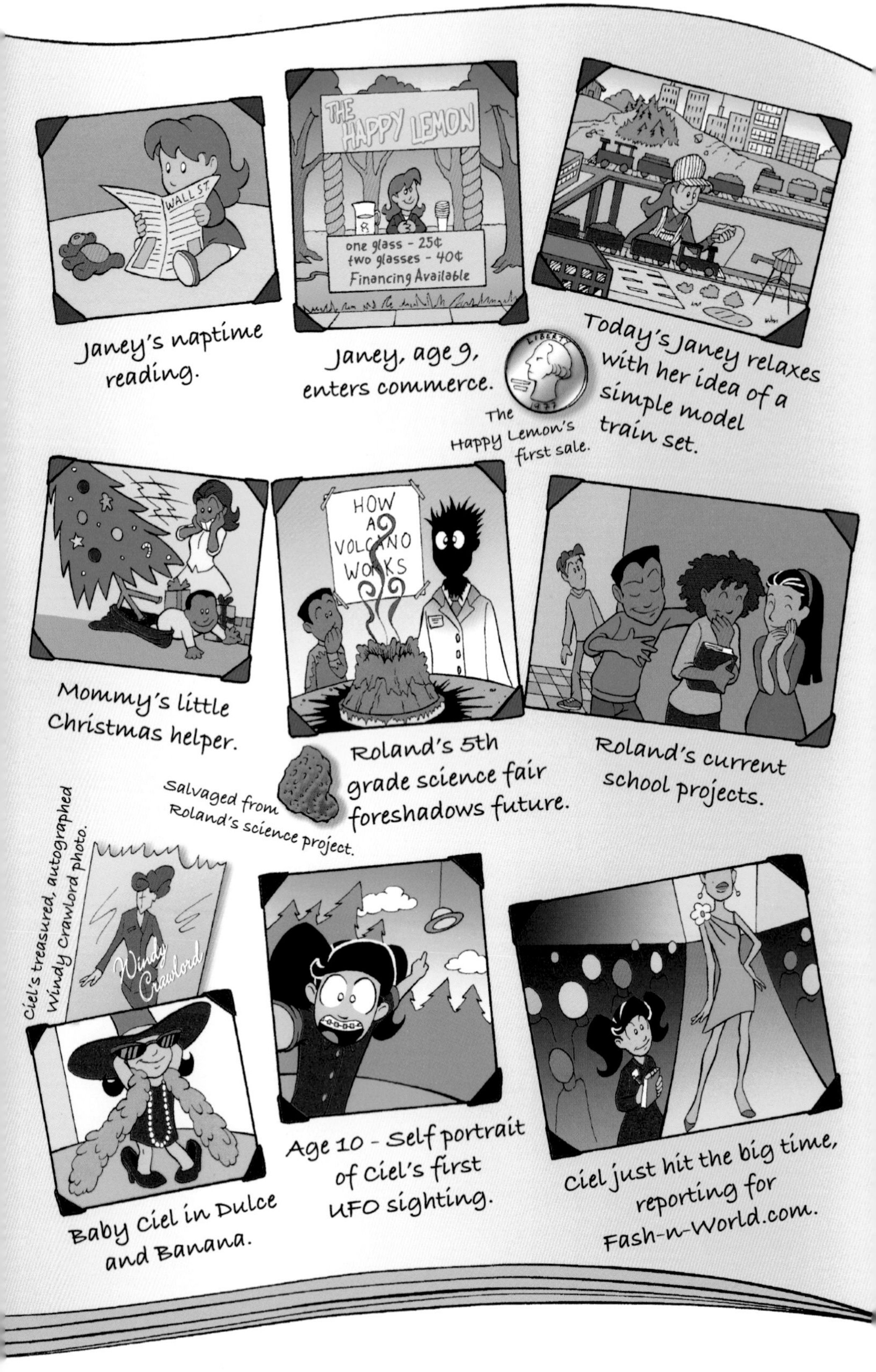
WALL ST.
Janey's naptime reading.
THE HAPPY LEMON
one glass - 25¢
two glasses - 40¢
Financing Available
Janey, age 9, enters commerce.
LIBERTY
The Happy Lemon's first sale.
Today's Janey relaxes with her idea of a simple model train set.
Mommy's little Christmas helper.
HOW A VOLCANO WORKS
Roland's 5th grade science fair foreshadows future.
Salvaged from Roland's science project.
Roland's current school projects.
Ciel's treasured, autographed Windy Crawlord photo.
Windy Crawlord
Baby Ciel in Dulce and Banana.
Age 10 - Self portrait of Ciel's first UFO sighting.
Ciel just hit the big time, reporting for Fash-n-World.com.

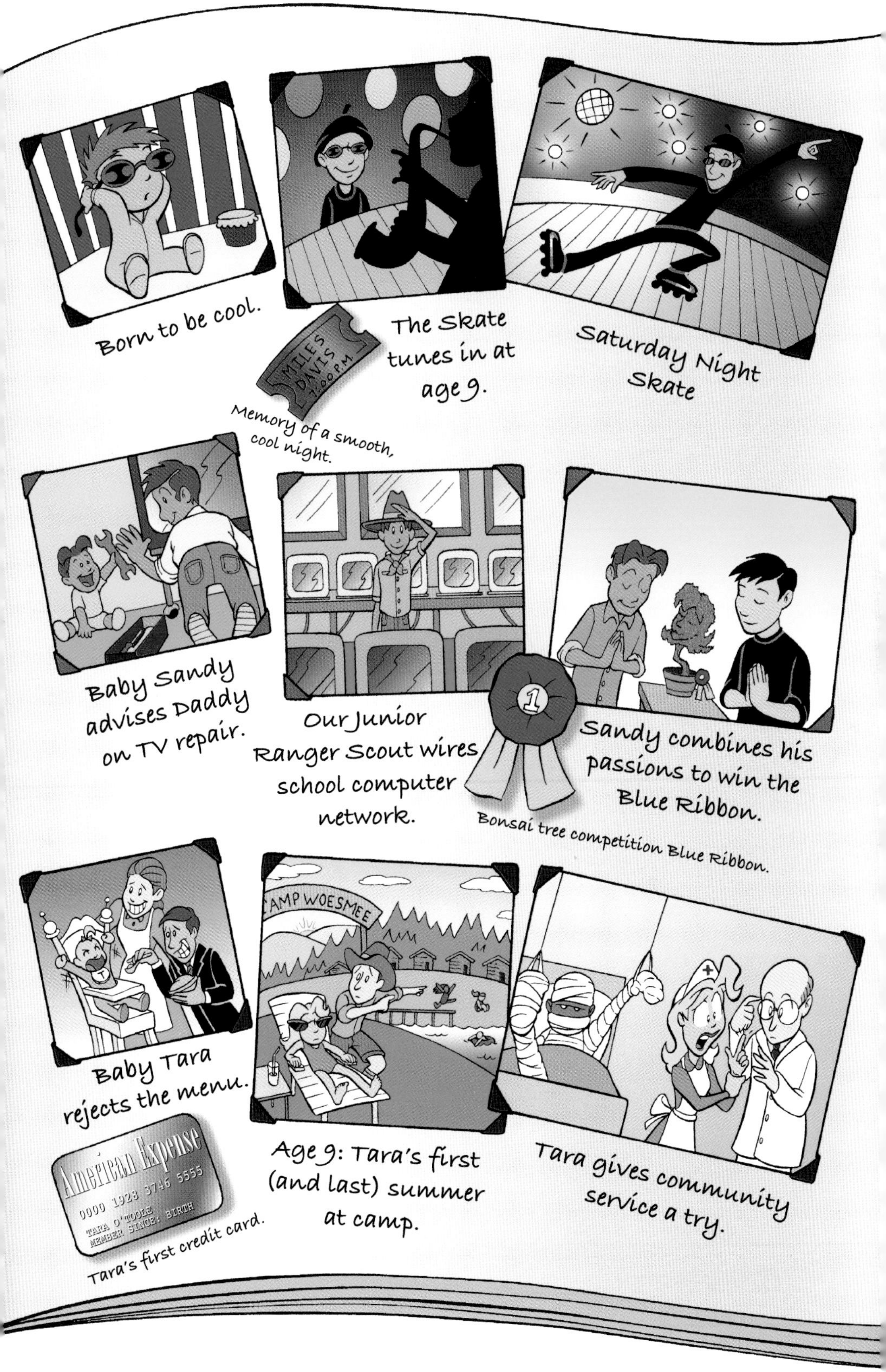

Born to be cool.
MILES DAVIS 7:00 P.M.
Memory of a smooth, cool night.
The Skate tunes in at age 9.
Saturday Night Skate
Baby Sandy advises Daddy on TV repair.
Our Junior Ranger Scout wires school computer network.
1
Sandy combines his passions to win the Blue Ribbon.
Bonsai tree competition Blue Ribbon.
Baby Tara rejects the menu.
CAMP WOESMEE
Age 9: Tara's first (and last) summer at camp.
Tara gives community service a try.
American Expense
0000 1928 3746 5555
TARA O'TOOLE
MEMBER SINCE: BIRTH
Tara's first credit card.

WJHC inside scoop!

Ciel

Check this out -- Ciel is a Spelling Bee champ. Yep, she's got a statewide first place trophy sitting proudly on her desk. Told you not to be fooled by her trendy girl looks.

Skate

You know those sunblocking, attitude rocking glasses the Skate wears? Well, there's more than good looks in those tinted babies. The Skate's as blind as a bat -- could barely tell Janey from Tara. Now that could lead to some scary stuff.

Roland

How 'bout this? Roland and his family volunteer at a homeless shelter. Yes, *Roland!* Turns out our *all about me* boy *is* capable of helping others. Course they keep him away from anything electronic.

Janey

Better sit down for this one. Miss all work and no play Janey is hooked on reality TV shows. Can you believe it? Next she'll want to be a contestant. Oooh, you might want to file away that piece of inside info.

Tara

Back to our own reality. Tara was the youngest American Expense charge card holder ever. Her parents felt she *needed* one at birth. Never know when a girl might have to purchase sodas or gum drops for everyone.

Sandy

Sandy "soft rock" Diaz recently took up the electric guitar. What do you suppose that's about? Better keep your eyes on this *WJHC* spitfire. Well, spitfire may be a little generous but there definitely *are* Sandy surprises in store.

WJHC
Note's Afloat!

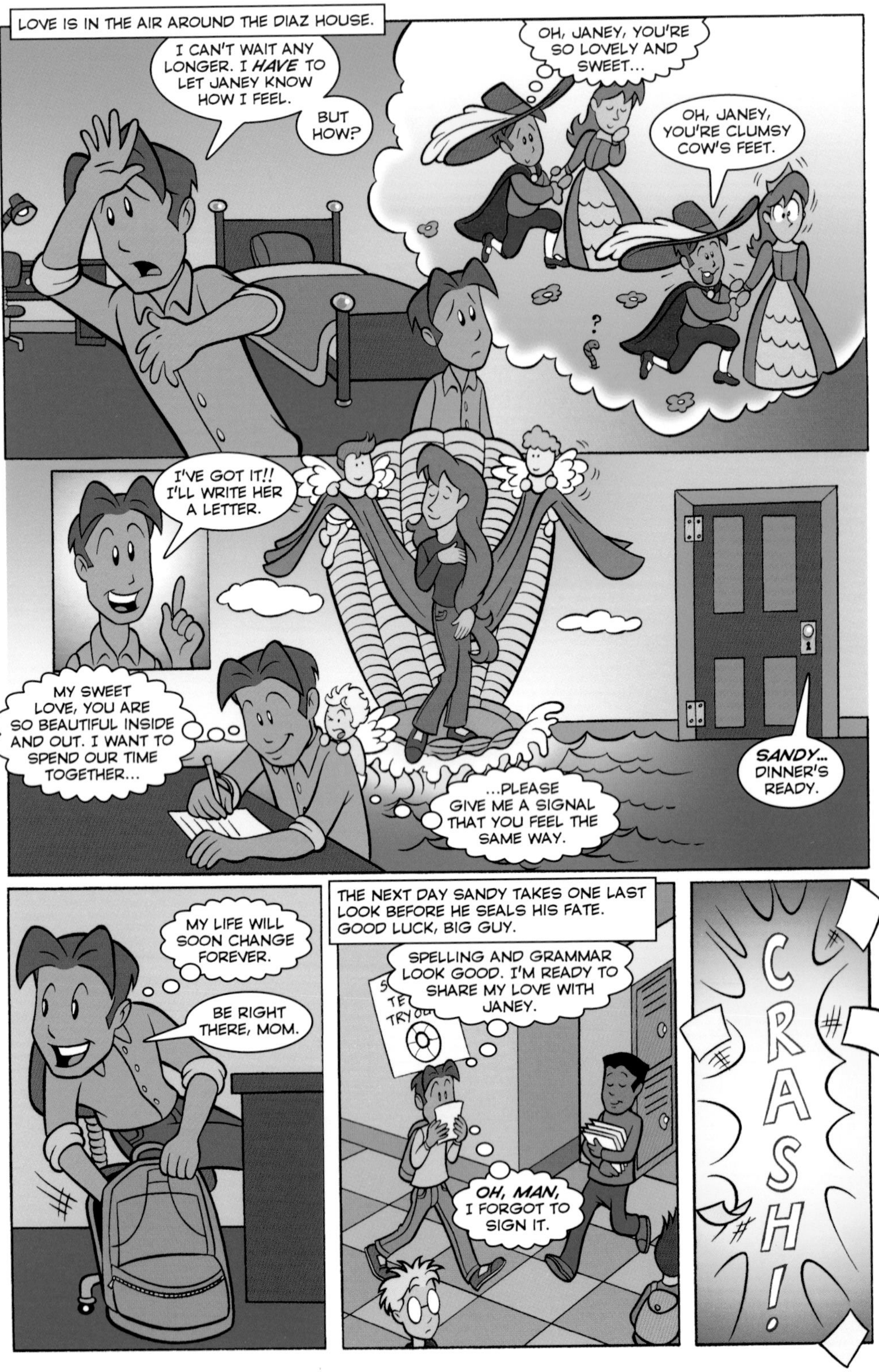

LOVE IS IN THE AIR AROUND THE DIAZ HOUSE.
I CAN'T WAIT ANY LONGER. I HAVE TO LET JANEY KNOW HOW I FEEL.
BUT HOW?
OH, JANEY, YOU'RE SO LOVELY AND SWEET...
OH, JANEY, YOU'RE CLUMSY COW'S FEET.
?
I'VE GOT IT!! I'LL WRITE HER A LETTER.
MY SWEET LOVE, YOU ARE SO BEAUTIFUL INSIDE AND OUT. I WANT TO SPEND OUR TIME TOGETHER...
...PLEASE GIVE ME A SIGNAL THAT YOU FEEL THE SAME WAY.
SANDY... DINNER'S READY.
MY LIFE WILL SOON CHANGE FOREVER.
BE RIGHT THERE, MOM.
THE NEXT DAY SANDY TAKES ONE LAST LOOK BEFORE HE SEALS HIS FATE. GOOD LUCK, BIG GUY.
SPELLING AND GRAMMAR LOOK GOOD. I'M READY TO SHARE MY LOVE WITH JANEY.
OH, MAN, I FORGOT TO SIGN IT.
CRASH!

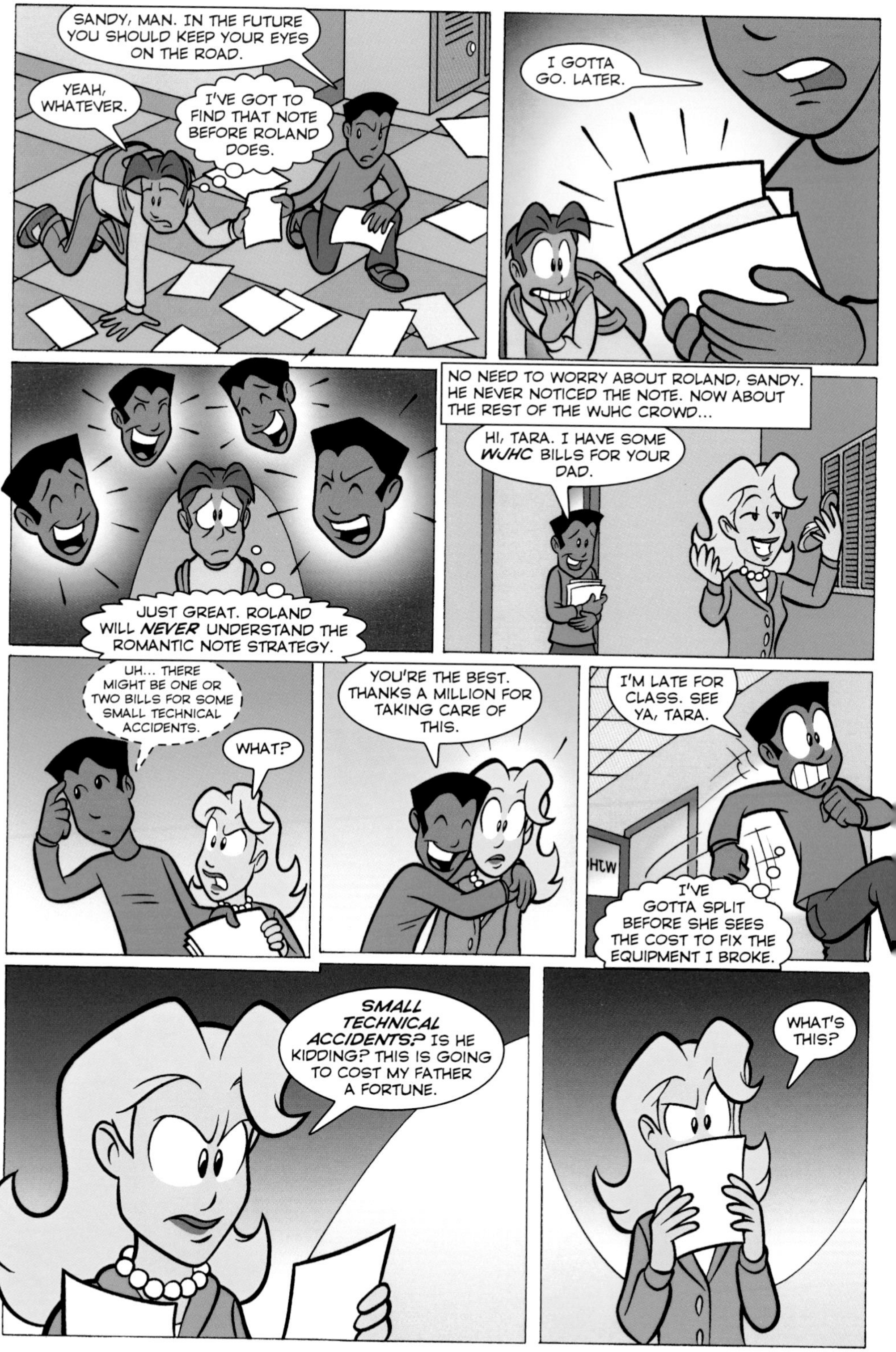
SANDY, MAN. IN THE FUTURE YOU SHOULD KEEP YOUR EYES ON THE ROAD.
YEAH, WHATEVER.
I'VE GOT TO FIND THAT NOTE BEFORE ROLAND DOES.
I GOTTA GO. LATER.
JUST GREAT. ROLAND WILL NEVER UNDERSTAND THE ROMANTIC NOTE STRATEGY.
NO NEED TO WORRY ABOUT ROLAND, SANDY. HE NEVER NOTICED THE NOTE. NOW ABOUT THE REST OF THE WJHC CROWD...
HI, TARA. I HAVE SOME WJHC BILLS FOR YOUR DAD.
UH... THERE MIGHT BE ONE OR TWO BILLS FOR SOME SMALL TECHNICAL ACCIDENTS.
WHAT?
YOU'RE THE BEST. THANKS A MILLION FOR TAKING CARE OF THIS.
I'M LATE FOR CLASS. SEE YA, TARA.
I'VE GOTTA SPLIT BEFORE SHE SEES THE COST TO FIX THE EQUIPMENT I BROKE.
SMALL TECHNICAL ACCIDENTS? IS HE KIDDING? THIS IS GOING TO COST MY FATHER A FORTUNE.
WHAT'S THIS?

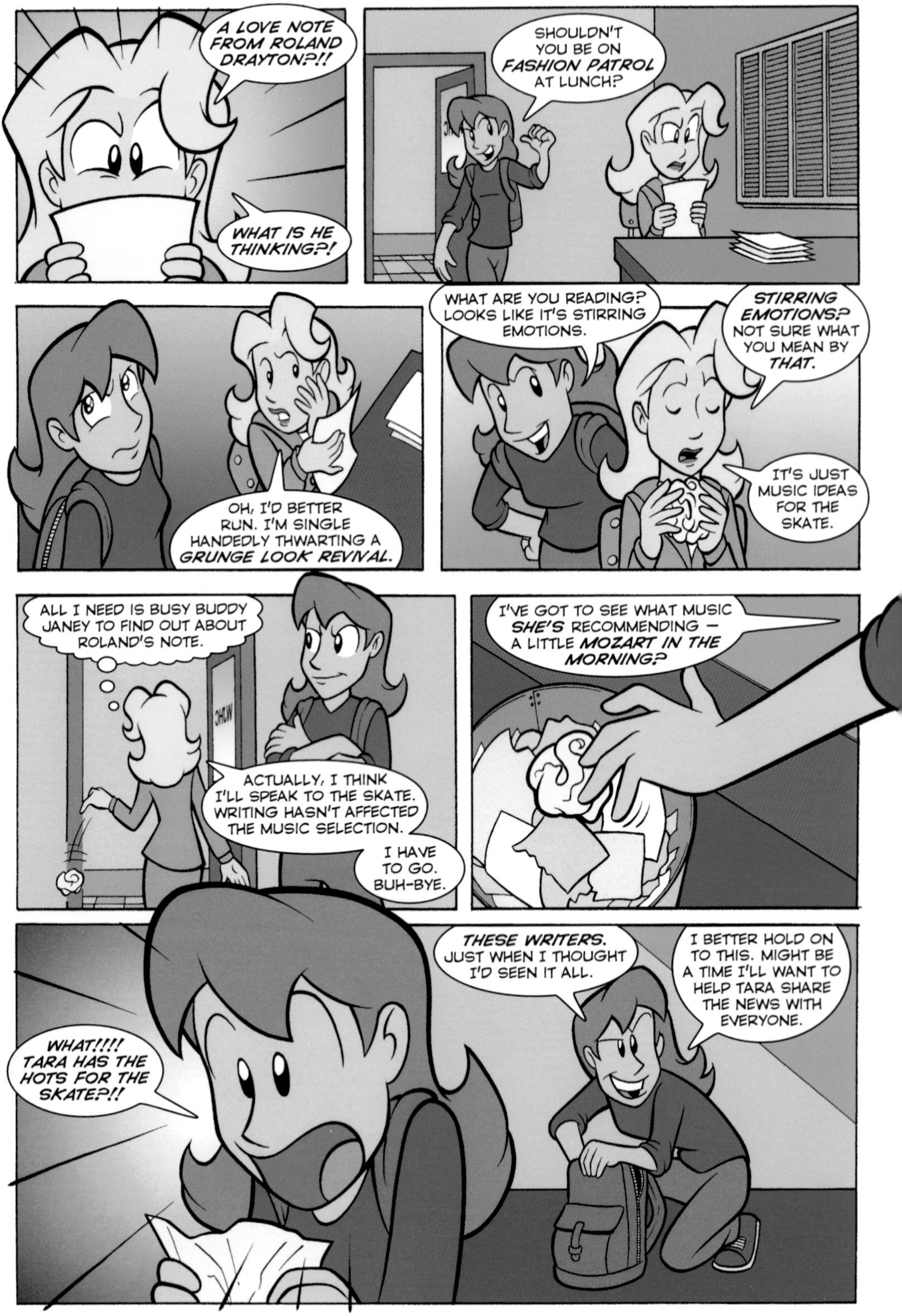

A LOVE NOTE FROM ROLAND DRAYTON?!!
WHAT IS HE THINKING?!
SHOULDN'T YOU BE ON FASHION PATROL AT LUNCH?
OH, I'D BETTER RUN. I'M SINGLE HANDEDLY THWARTING A GRUNGE LOOK REVIVAL.
WHAT ARE YOU READING? LOOKS LIKE IT'S STIRRING EMOTIONS.
STIRRING EMOTIONS? NOT SURE WHAT YOU MEAN BY THAT.
IT'S JUST MUSIC IDEAS FOR THE SKATE.
ALL I NEED IS BUSY BUDDY JANEY TO FIND OUT ABOUT ROLAND'S NOTE.
ACTUALLY, I THINK I'LL SPEAK TO THE SKATE. WRITING HASN'T AFFECTED THE MUSIC SELECTION.
I HAVE TO GO. BUH-BYE.
I'VE GOT TO SEE WHAT MUSIC SHE'S RECOMMENDING — A LITTLE MOZART IN THE MORNING?
WHAT!!!! TARA HAS THE HOTS FOR THE SKATE?!!
THESE WRITERS. JUST WHEN I THOUGHT I'D SEEN IT ALL.
I BETTER HOLD ON TO THIS. MIGHT BE A TIME I'LL WANT TO HELP TARA SHARE THE NEWS WITH EVERYONE.

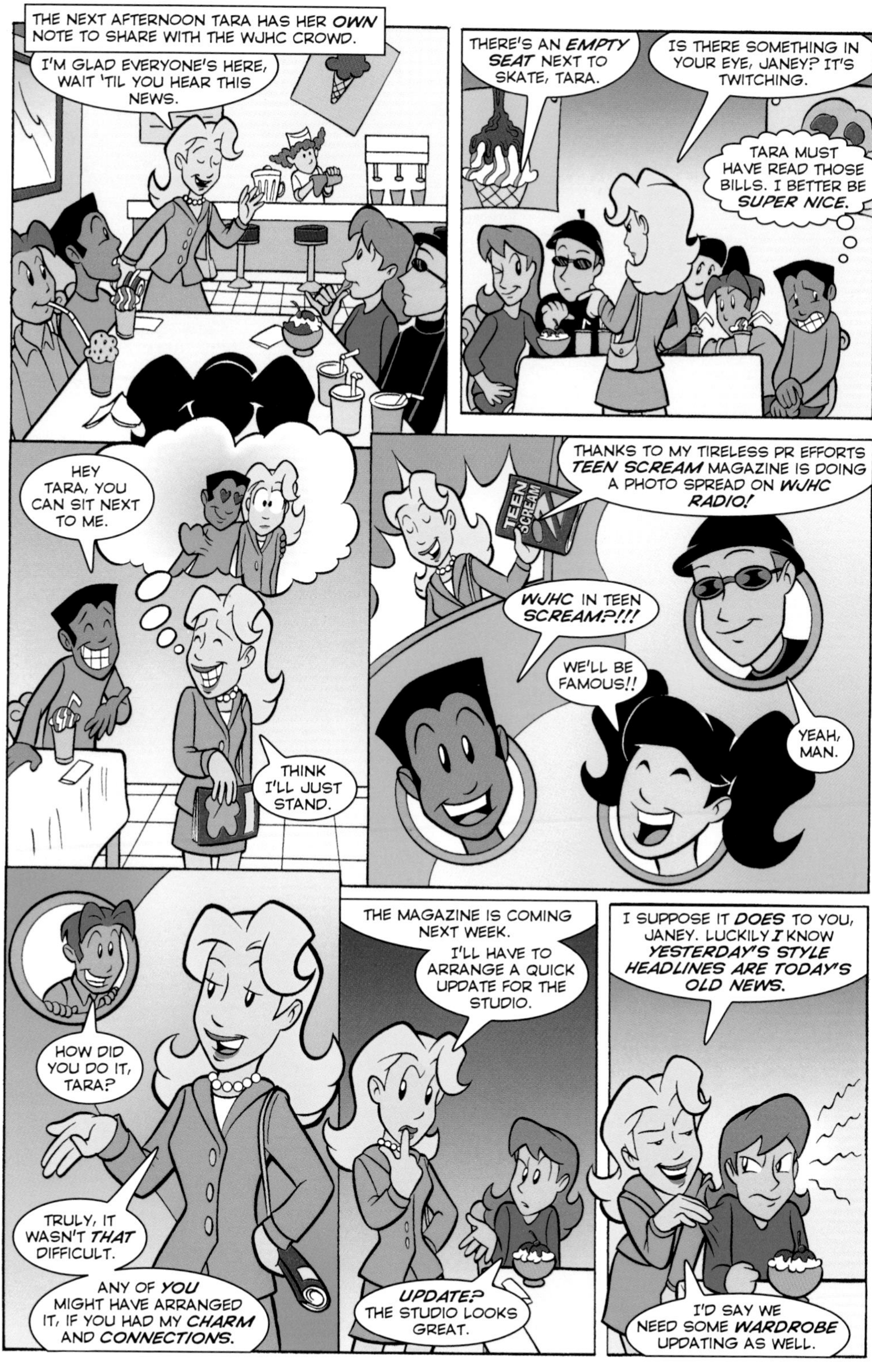
THE NEXT AFTERNOON TARA HAS HER *OWN* NOTE TO SHARE WITH THE WJHC CROWD.
I'M GLAD EVERYONE'S HERE, WAIT 'TIL YOU HEAR THIS NEWS.
THERE'S AN *EMPTY SEAT* NEXT TO SKATE, TARA.
IS THERE SOMETHING IN YOUR EYE, JANEY? IT'S TWITCHING.
TARA MUST HAVE READ THOSE BILLS. I BETTER BE *SUPER NICE.*
HEY TARA, YOU CAN SIT NEXT TO ME.
THINK I'LL JUST STAND.
THANKS TO MY TIRELESS PR EFFORTS *TEEN SCREAM* MAGAZINE IS DOING A PHOTO SPREAD ON *WJHC RADIO!*
TEEN SCREAM
WJHC IN TEEN *SCREAM?!!!*
WE'LL BE FAMOUS!!
YEAH, MAN.
HOW DID YOU DO IT, TARA?
TRULY, IT WASN'T *THAT* DIFFICULT.
ANY OF *YOU* MIGHT HAVE ARRANGED IT, IF YOU HAD MY *CHARM* AND *CONNECTIONS.*
THE MAGAZINE IS COMING NEXT WEEK.
I'LL HAVE TO ARRANGE A QUICK UPDATE FOR THE STUDIO.
UPDATE? THE STUDIO LOOKS GREAT.
I SUPPOSE IT *DOES* TO YOU, JANEY. LUCKILY *I* KNOW *YESTERDAY'S STYLE HEADLINES ARE TODAY'S OLD NEWS.*
I'D SAY WE NEED SOME *WARDROBE* UPDATING AS WELL.

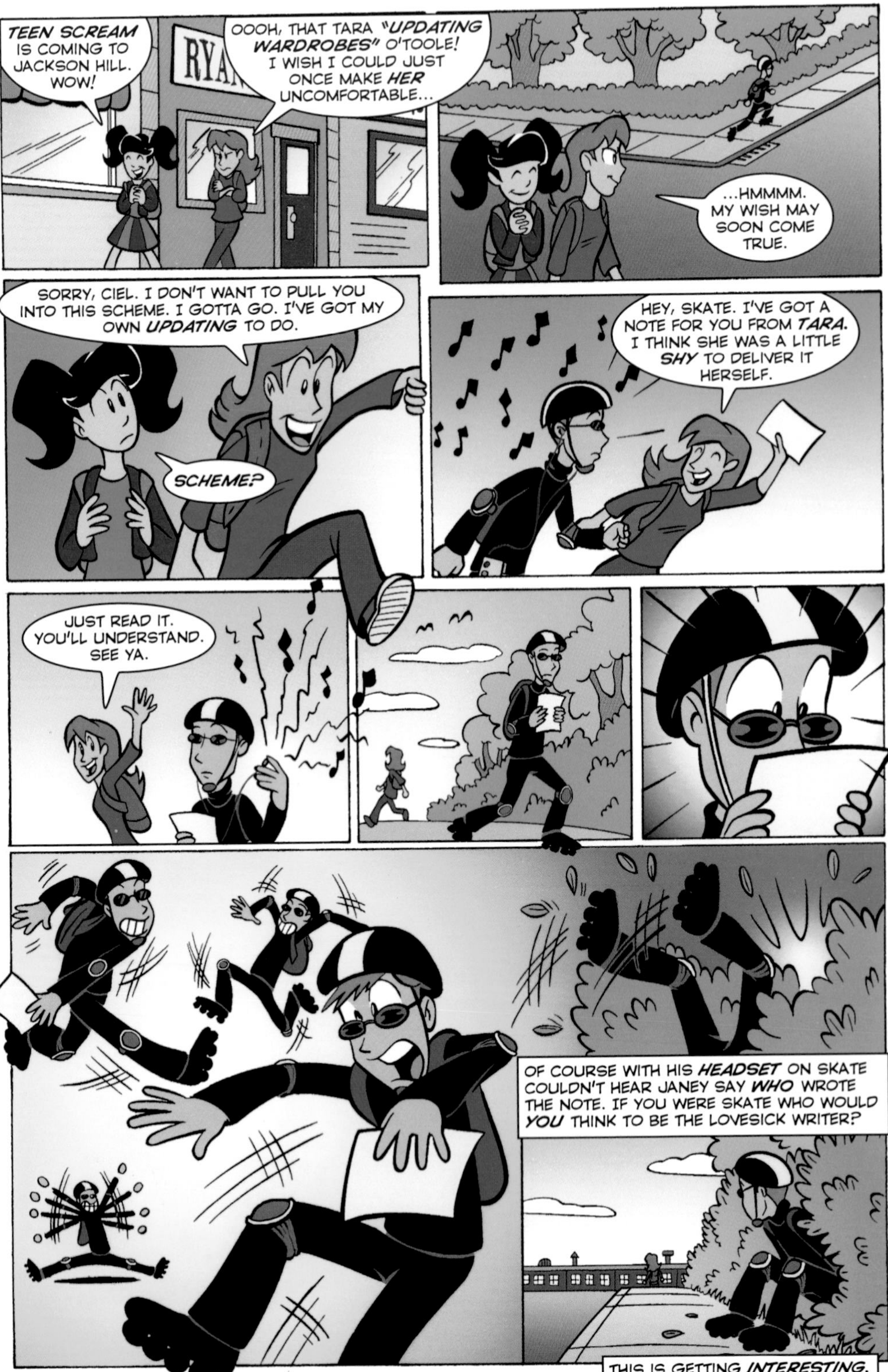

RYAN
TEEN SCREAM IS COMING TO JACKSON HILL. WOW!
OOOH, THAT TARA "UPDATING WARDROBES" O'TOOLE! I WISH I COULD JUST ONCE MAKE HER UNCOMFORTABLE...
...HMMMM. MY WISH MAY SOON COME TRUE.
SORRY, CIEL. I DON'T WANT TO PULL YOU INTO THIS SCHEME. I GOTTA GO. I'VE GOT MY OWN UPDATING TO DO.
SCHEME?
HEY, SKATE. I'VE GOT A NOTE FOR YOU FROM TARA. I THINK SHE WAS A LITTLE SHY TO DELIVER IT HERSELF.
JUST READ IT. YOU'LL UNDERSTAND. SEE YA.
OF COURSE WITH HIS HEADSET ON SKATE COULDN'T HEAR JANEY SAY WHO WROTE THE NOTE. IF YOU WERE SKATE WHO WOULD YOU THINK TO BE THE LOVESICK WRITER?
THIS IS GETTING INTERESTING.

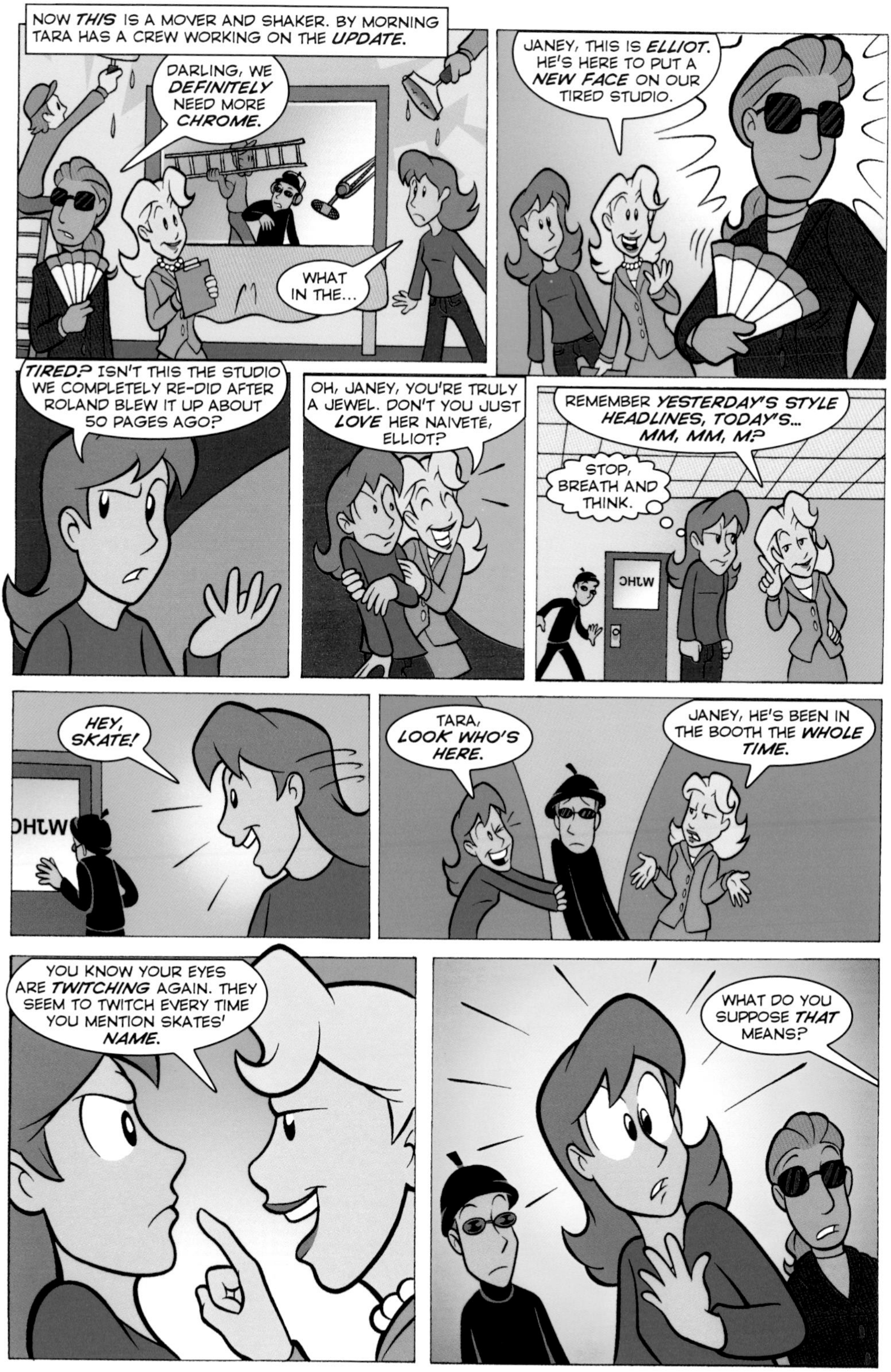
NOW THIS IS A MOVER AND SHAKER. BY MORNING TARA HAS A CREW WORKING ON THE UPDATE.
DARLING, WE DEFINITELY NEED MORE CHROME.
WHAT IN THE...
JANEY, THIS IS ELLIOT. HE'S HERE TO PUT A NEW FACE ON OUR TIRED STUDIO.
TIRED? ISN'T THIS THE STUDIO WE COMPLETELY RE-DID AFTER ROLAND BLEW IT UP ABOUT 50 PAGES AGO?
OH, JANEY, YOU'RE TRULY A JEWEL. DON'T YOU JUST LOVE HER NAIVETÉ, ELLIOT?
REMEMBER YESTERDAY'S STYLE HEADLINES, TODAY'S... MM, MM, M?
STOP, BREATH AND THINK.
WJHC
HEY, SKATE!
WJHC
TARA, LOOK WHO'S HERE.
JANEY, HE'S BEEN IN THE BOOTH THE WHOLE TIME.
YOU KNOW YOUR EYES ARE TWITCHING AGAIN. THEY SEEM TO TWITCH EVERY TIME YOU MENTION SKATES' NAME.
WHAT DO YOU SUPPOSE THAT MEANS?

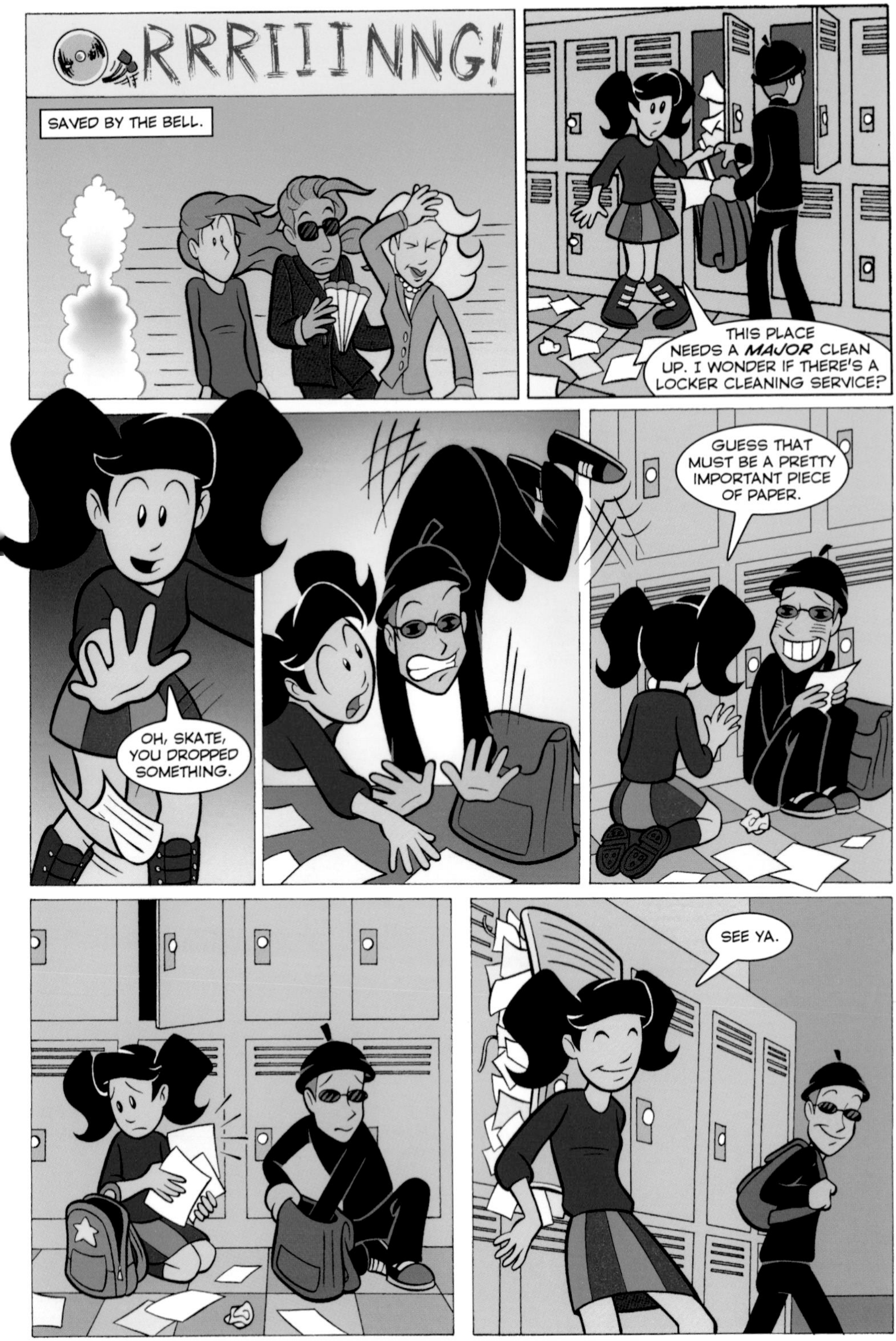
RRRIIINNG!
SAVED BY THE BELL.
THIS PLACE NEEDS A MAJOR CLEAN UP. I WONDER IF THERE'S A LOCKER CLEANING SERVICE?
OH, SKATE, YOU DROPPED SOMETHING.
GUESS THAT MUST BE A PRETTY IMPORTANT PIECE OF PAPER.
SEE YA.

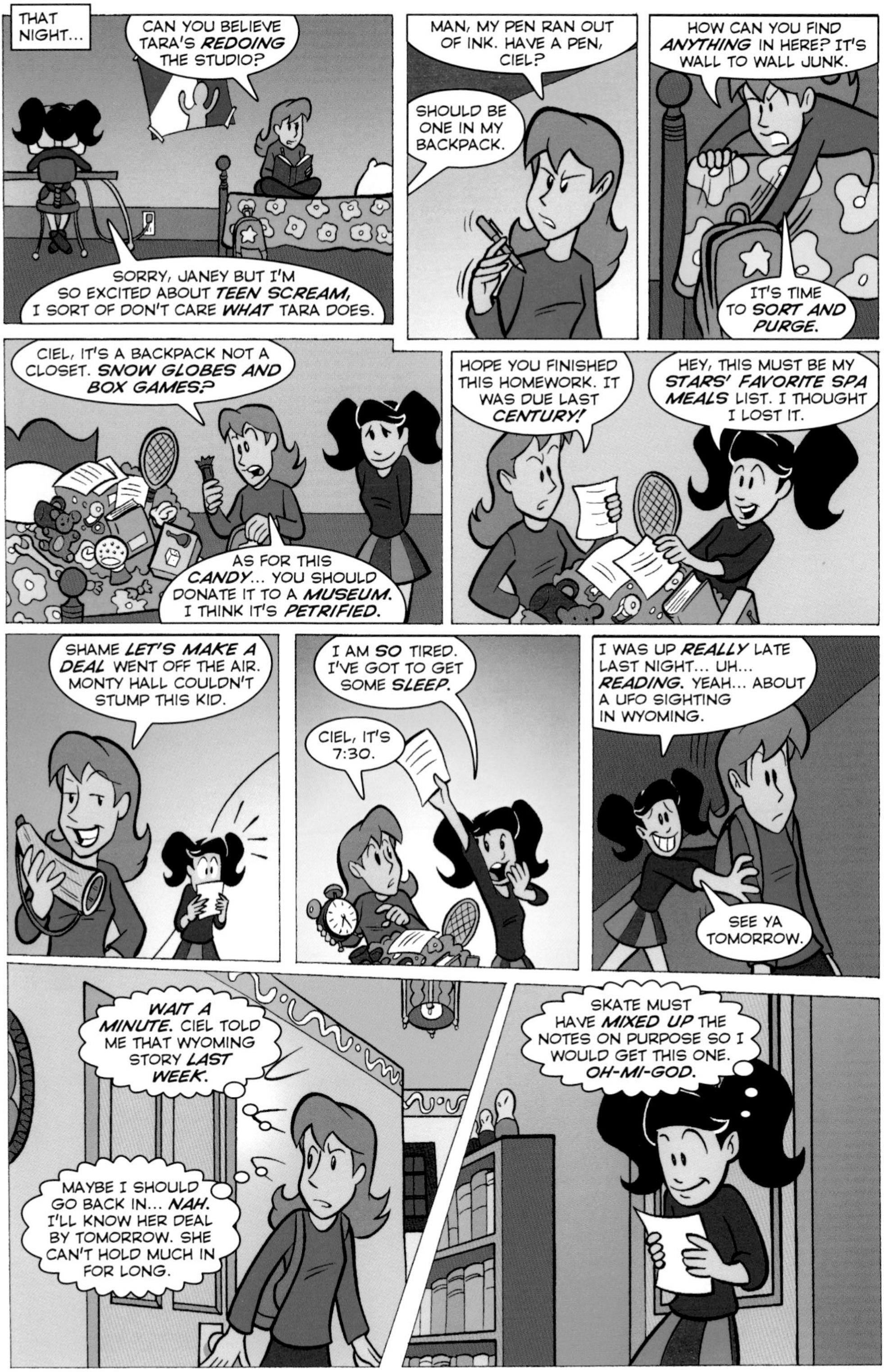
THAT NIGHT...
CAN YOU BELIEVE TARA'S REDOING THE STUDIO?
SORRY, JANEY BUT I'M SO EXCITED ABOUT TEEN SCREAM, I SORT OF DON'T CARE WHAT TARA DOES.
MAN, MY PEN RAN OUT OF INK. HAVE A PEN, CIEL?
SHOULD BE ONE IN MY BACKPACK.
HOW CAN YOU FIND ANYTHING IN HERE? IT'S WALL TO WALL JUNK.
IT'S TIME TO SORT AND PURGE.
CIEL, IT'S A BACKPACK NOT A CLOSET. SNOW GLOBES AND BOX GAMES?
AS FOR THIS CANDY... YOU SHOULD DONATE IT TO A MUSEUM. I THINK IT'S PETRIFIED.
HOPE YOU FINISHED THIS HOMEWORK. IT WAS DUE LAST CENTURY!
HEY, THIS MUST BE MY STARS' FAVORITE SPA MEALS LIST. I THOUGHT I LOST IT.
SHAME LET'S MAKE A DEAL WENT OFF THE AIR. MONTY HALL COULDN'T STUMP THIS KID.
I AM SO TIRED. I'VE GOT TO GET SOME SLEEP.
CIEL, IT'S 7:30.
I WAS UP REALLY LATE LAST NIGHT... UH... READING. YEAH... ABOUT A UFO SIGHTING IN WYOMING.
SEE YA TOMORROW.
WAIT A MINUTE. CIEL TOLD ME THAT WYOMING STORY LAST WEEK.
MAYBE I SHOULD GO BACK IN... NAH. I'LL KNOW HER DEAL BY TOMORROW. SHE CAN'T HOLD MUCH IN FOR LONG.
SKATE MUST HAVE MIXED UP THE NOTES ON PURPOSE SO I WOULD GET THIS ONE. OH-MI-GOD.

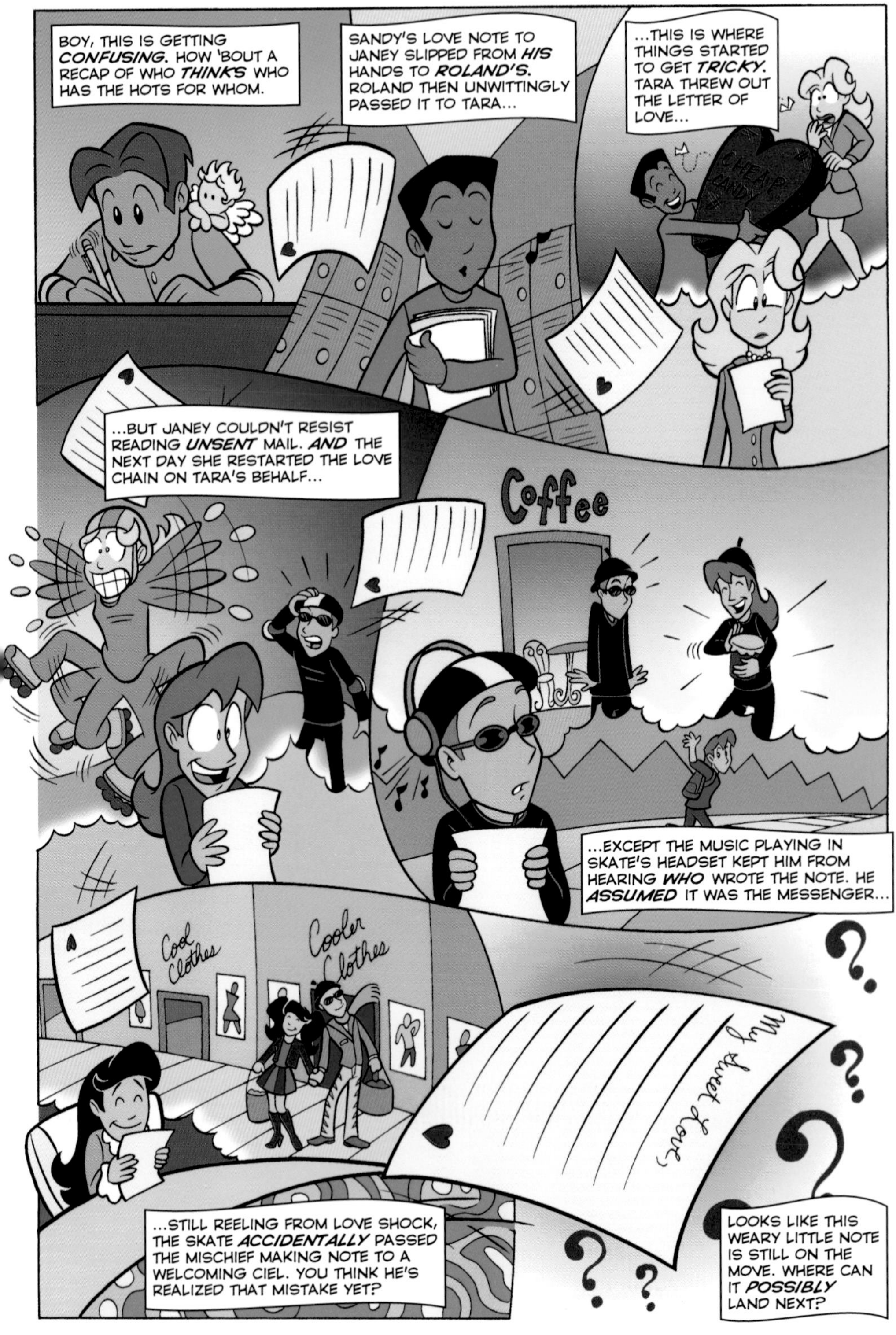
BOY, THIS IS GETTING CONFUSING. HOW 'BOUT A RECAP OF WHO THINKS WHO HAS THE HOTS FOR WHOM.
SANDY'S LOVE NOTE TO JANEY SLIPPED FROM HIS HANDS TO ROLAND'S. ROLAND THEN UNWITTINGLY PASSED IT TO TARA...
...THIS IS WHERE THINGS STARTED TO GET TRICKY. TARA THREW OUT THE LETTER OF LOVE...
CHEAP CANDY
...BUT JANEY COULDN'T RESIST READING UNSENT MAIL. AND THE NEXT DAY SHE RESTARTED THE LOVE CHAIN ON TARA'S BEHALF...
Coffee
...EXCEPT THE MUSIC PLAYING IN SKATE'S HEADSET KEPT HIM FROM HEARING WHO WROTE THE NOTE. HE ASSUMED IT WAS THE MESSENGER...
Cool Clothes
Cooler Clothes
My sweet love,
...STILL REELING FROM LOVE SHOCK, THE SKATE ACCIDENTALLY PASSED THE MISCHIEF MAKING NOTE TO A WELCOMING CIEL. YOU THINK HE'S REALIZED THAT MISTAKE YET?
LOOKS LIKE THIS WEARY LITTLE NOTE IS STILL ON THE MOVE. WHERE CAN IT POSSIBLY LAND NEXT?

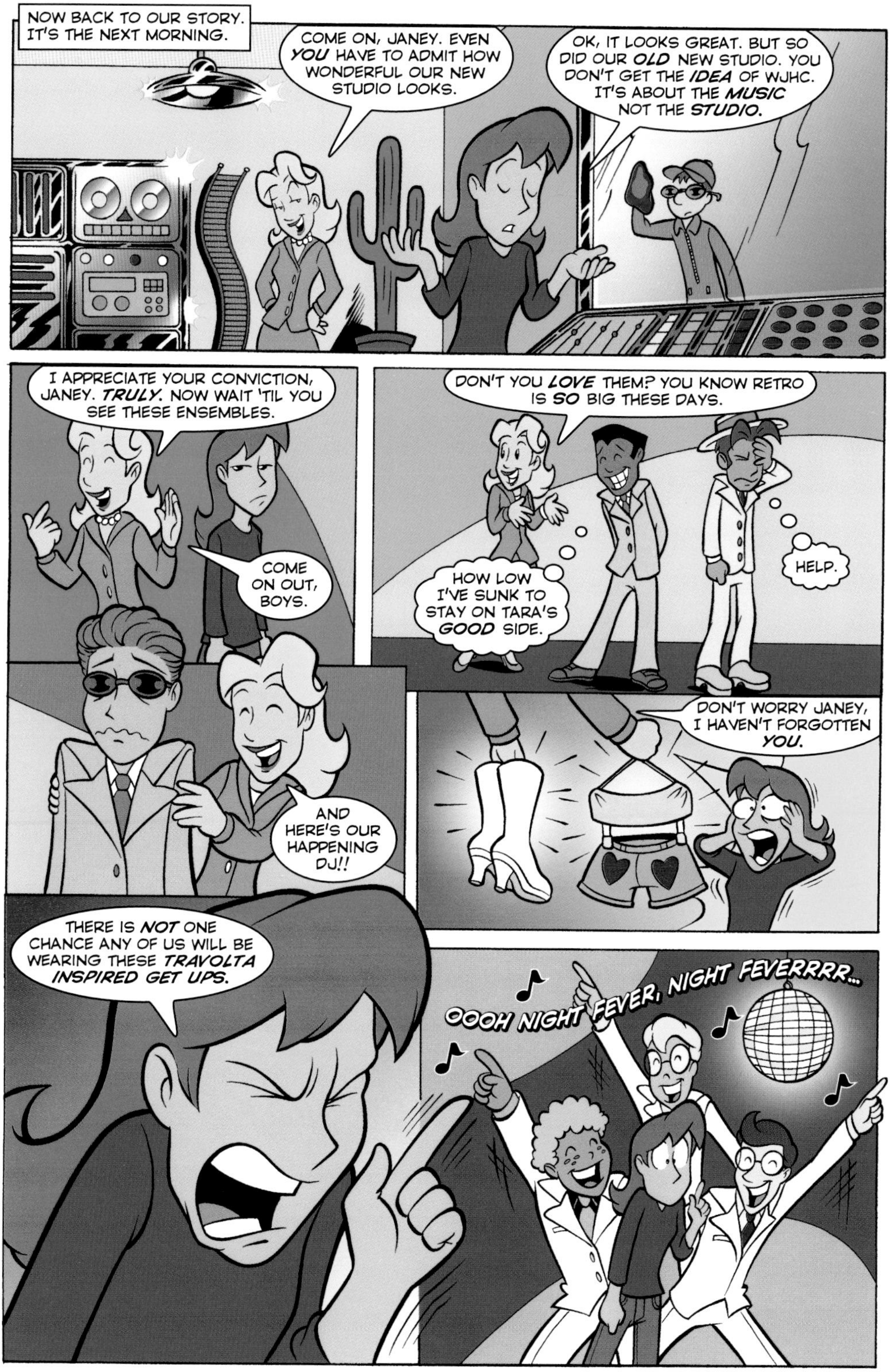
NOW BACK TO OUR STORY. IT'S THE NEXT MORNING.
COME ON, JANEY. EVEN *YOU* HAVE TO ADMIT HOW WONDERFUL OUR NEW STUDIO LOOKS.
OK, IT LOOKS GREAT. BUT SO DID OUR *OLD* NEW STUDIO. YOU DON'T GET THE *IDEA* OF WJHC. IT'S ABOUT THE *MUSIC* NOT THE *STUDIO*.
I APPRECIATE YOUR CONVICTION, JANEY. *TRULY*. NOW WAIT 'TIL YOU SEE THESE ENSEMBLES.
COME ON OUT, BOYS.
DON'T YOU *LOVE* THEM? YOU KNOW RETRO IS *SO* BIG THESE DAYS.
HOW LOW I'VE SUNK TO STAY ON TARA'S *GOOD* SIDE.
HELP.
AND HERE'S OUR HAPPENING DJ!!
DON'T WORRY JANEY, I HAVEN'T FORGOTTEN *YOU*.
THERE IS *NOT* ONE CHANCE ANY OF US WILL BE WEARING THESE *TRAVOLTA INSPIRED GET UPS*.
OOOH NIGHT FEVER, NIGHT FEVERRRR...

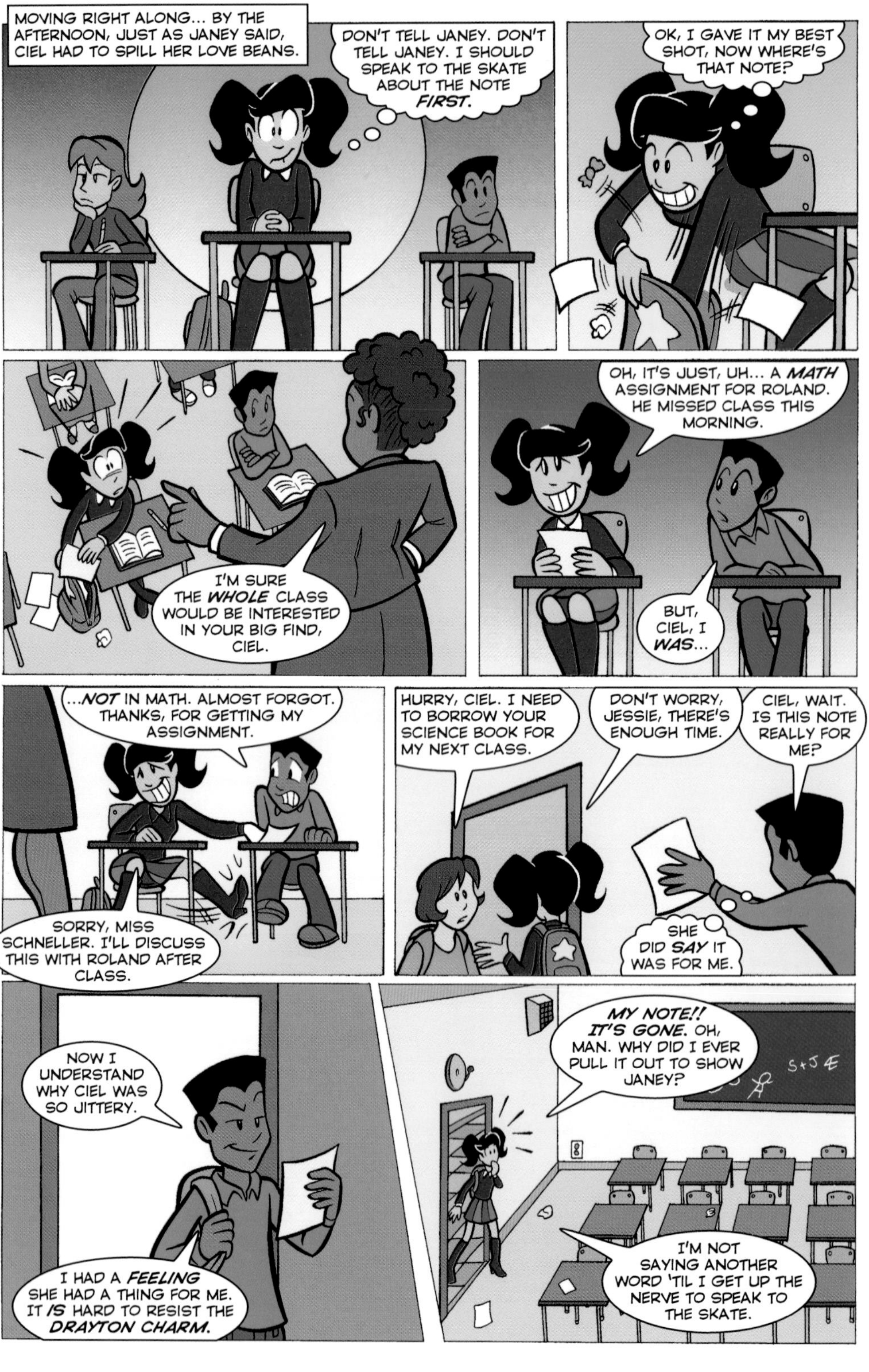
MOVING RIGHT ALONG... BY THE AFTERNOON, JUST AS JANEY SAID, CIEL HAD TO SPILL HER LOVE BEANS.
DON'T TELL JANEY. DON'T TELL JANEY. I SHOULD SPEAK TO THE SKATE ABOUT THE NOTE FIRST.
OK, I GAVE IT MY BEST SHOT, NOW WHERE'S THAT NOTE?
I'M SURE THE WHOLE CLASS WOULD BE INTERESTED IN YOUR BIG FIND, CIEL.
OH, IT'S JUST, UH... A MATH ASSIGNMENT FOR ROLAND. HE MISSED CLASS THIS MORNING.
BUT, CIEL, I WAS...
...NOT IN MATH. ALMOST FORGOT. THANKS, FOR GETTING MY ASSIGNMENT.
SORRY, MISS SCHNELLER. I'LL DISCUSS THIS WITH ROLAND AFTER CLASS.
HURRY, CIEL. I NEED TO BORROW YOUR SCIENCE BOOK FOR MY NEXT CLASS.
DON'T WORRY, JESSIE, THERE'S ENOUGH TIME.
CIEL, WAIT. IS THIS NOTE REALLY FOR ME?
SHE DID SAY IT WAS FOR ME.
NOW I UNDERSTAND WHY CIEL WAS SO JITTERY.
I HAD A FEELING SHE HAD A THING FOR ME. IT IS HARD TO RESIST THE DRAYTON CHARM.
MY NOTE!! IT'S GONE. OH, MAN. WHY DID I EVER PULL IT OUT TO SHOW JANEY?
S+J
I'M NOT SAYING ANOTHER WORD 'TIL I GET UP THE NERVE TO SPEAK TO THE SKATE.

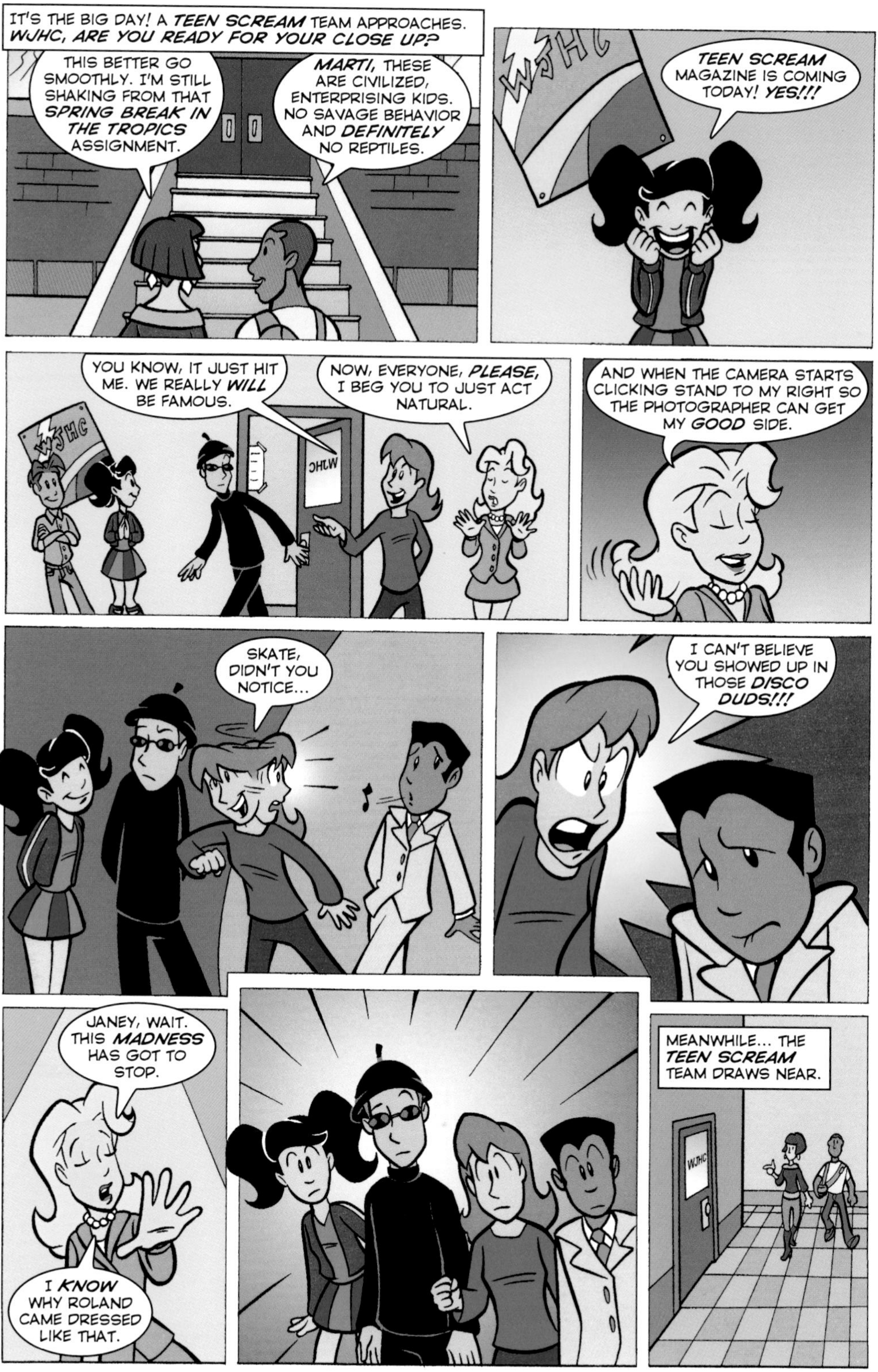
IT'S THE BIG DAY! A TEEN SCREAM TEAM APPROACHES. WJHC, ARE YOU READY FOR YOUR CLOSE UP?
THIS BETTER GO SMOOTHLY. I'M STILL SHAKING FROM THAT SPRING BREAK IN THE TROPICS ASSIGNMENT.
MARTI, THESE ARE CIVILIZED, ENTERPRISING KIDS. NO SAVAGE BEHAVIOR AND DEFINITELY NO REPTILES.
TEEN SCREAM MAGAZINE IS COMING TODAY! YES!!!
YOU KNOW, IT JUST HIT ME. WE REALLY WILL BE FAMOUS.
NOW, EVERYONE, PLEASE, I BEG YOU TO JUST ACT NATURAL.
AND WHEN THE CAMERA STARTS CLICKING STAND TO MY RIGHT SO THE PHOTOGRAPHER CAN GET MY GOOD SIDE.
SKATE, DIDN'T YOU NOTICE...
I CAN'T BELIEVE YOU SHOWED UP IN THOSE DISCO DUDS!!!
JANEY, WAIT. THIS MADNESS HAS GOT TO STOP.
I KNOW WHY ROLAND CAME DRESSED LIKE THAT.
MEANWHILE... THE TEEN SCREAM TEAM DRAWS NEAR.

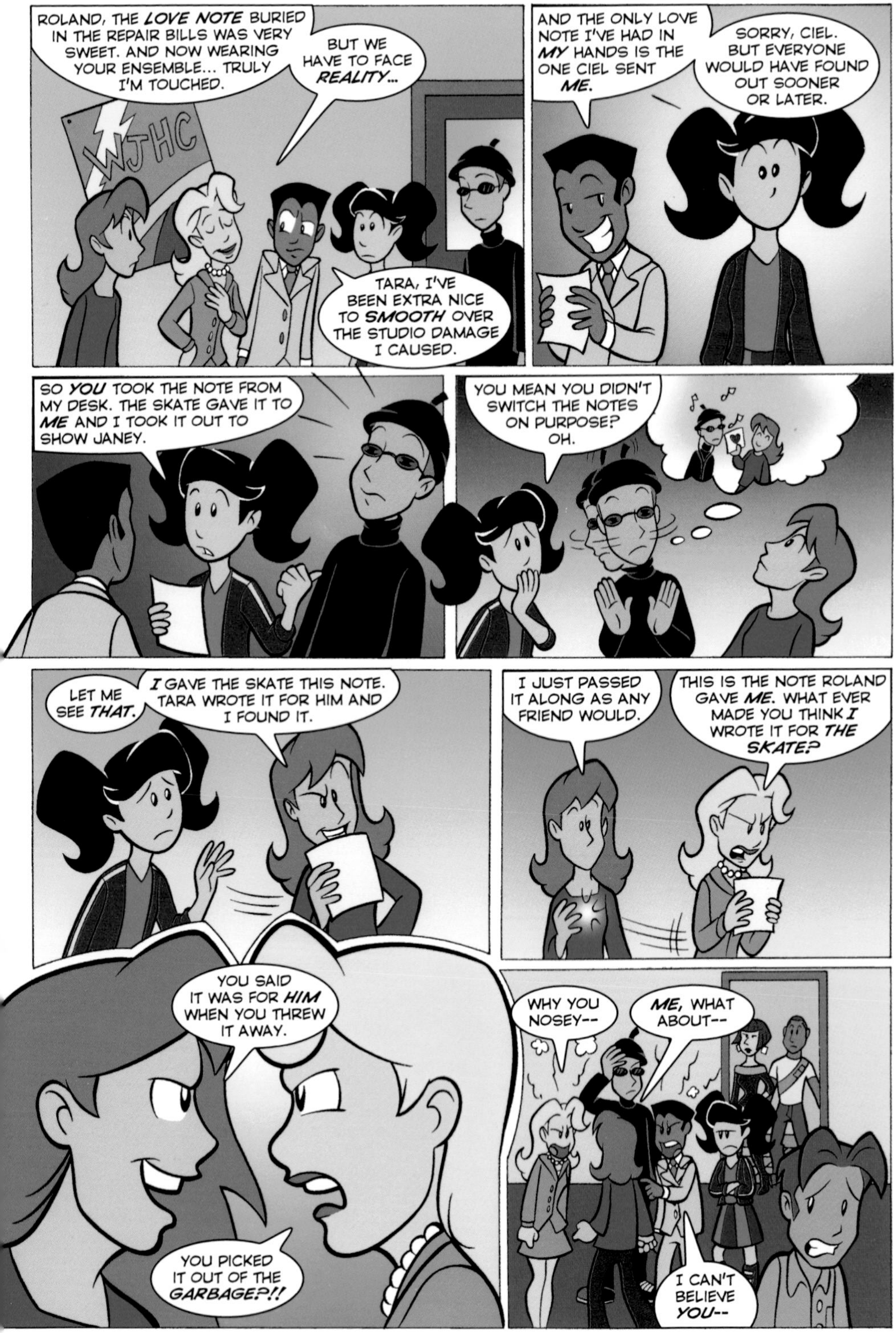
ROLAND, THE LOVE NOTE BURIED IN THE REPAIR BILLS WAS VERY SWEET. AND NOW WEARING YOUR ENSEMBLE... TRULY I'M TOUCHED.
BUT WE HAVE TO FACE REALITY...
WJHC
TARA, I'VE BEEN EXTRA NICE TO SMOOTH OVER THE STUDIO DAMAGE I CAUSED.
AND THE ONLY LOVE NOTE I'VE HAD IN MY HANDS IS THE ONE CIEL SENT ME.
SORRY, CIEL. BUT EVERYONE WOULD HAVE FOUND OUT SOONER OR LATER.
SO YOU TOOK THE NOTE FROM MY DESK. THE SKATE GAVE IT TO ME AND I TOOK IT OUT TO SHOW JANEY.
YOU MEAN YOU DIDN'T SWITCH THE NOTES ON PURPOSE? OH.
LET ME SEE THAT.
I GAVE THE SKATE THIS NOTE. TARA WROTE IT FOR HIM AND I FOUND IT.
I JUST PASSED IT ALONG AS ANY FRIEND WOULD.
THIS IS THE NOTE ROLAND GAVE ME. WHAT EVER MADE YOU THINK I WROTE IT FOR THE SKATE?
YOU SAID IT WAS FOR HIM WHEN YOU THREW IT AWAY.
YOU PICKED IT OUT OF THE GARBAGE?!!
WHY YOU NOSEY--
ME, WHAT ABOUT--
I CAN'T BELIEVE YOU--

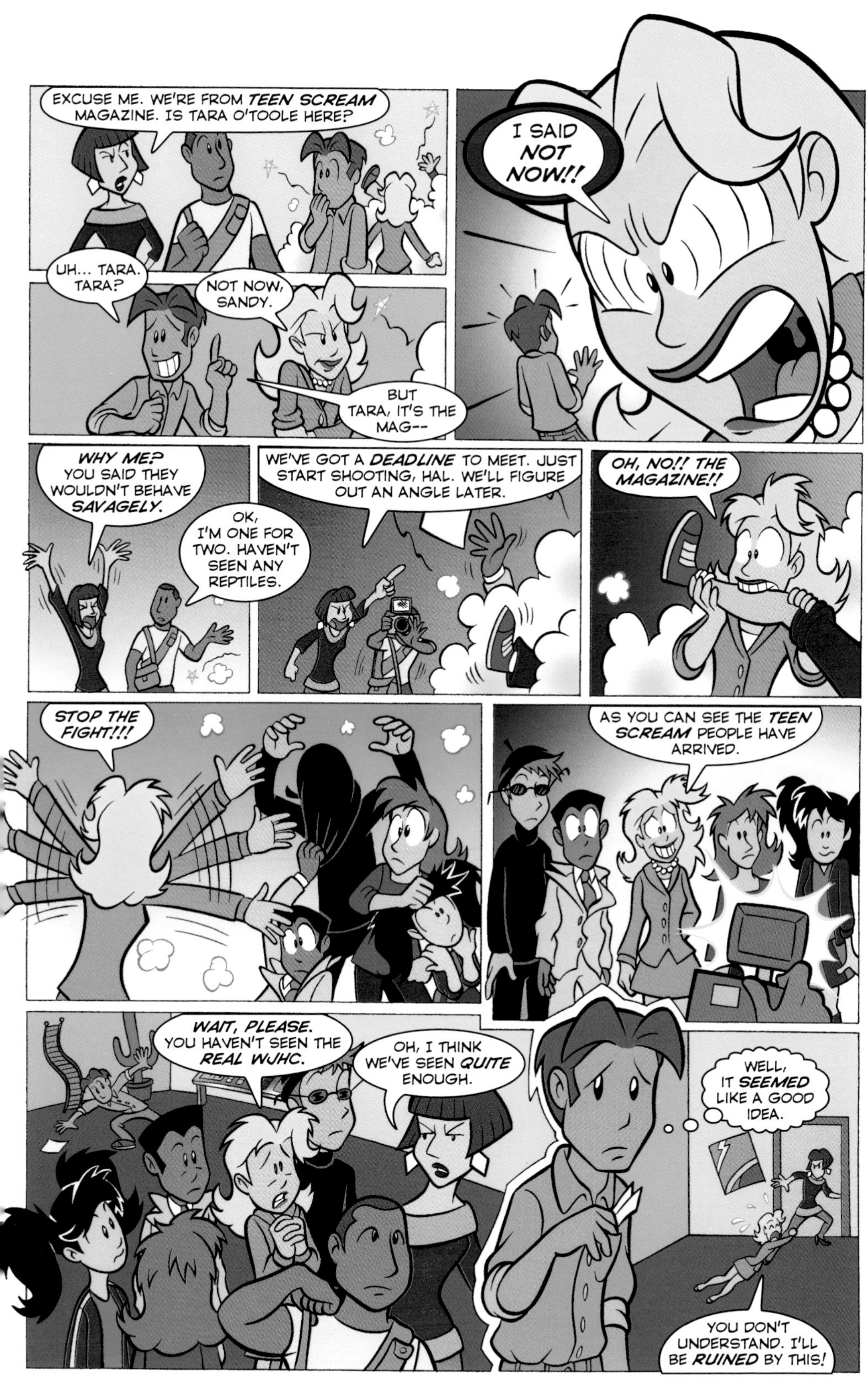
EXCUSE ME. WE'RE FROM TEEN SCREAM MAGAZINE. IS TARA O'TOOLE HERE?
UH... TARA. TARA?
NOT NOW, SANDY.
BUT TARA, IT'S THE MAG--
I SAID NOT NOW!!
WHY ME? YOU SAID THEY WOULDN'T BEHAVE SAVAGELY.
OK, I'M ONE FOR TWO. HAVEN'T SEEN ANY REPTILES.
WE'VE GOT A DEADLINE TO MEET. JUST START SHOOTING, HAL. WE'LL FIGURE OUT AN ANGLE LATER.
OH, NO!! THE MAGAZINE!!
STOP THE FIGHT!!!
AS YOU CAN SEE THE TEEN SCREAM PEOPLE HAVE ARRIVED.
WAIT, PLEASE. YOU HAVEN'T SEEN THE REAL WJHC.
OH, I THINK WE'VE SEEN QUITE ENOUGH.
WELL, IT SEEMED LIKE A GOOD IDEA.
YOU DON'T UNDERSTAND. I'LL BE RUINED BY THIS!

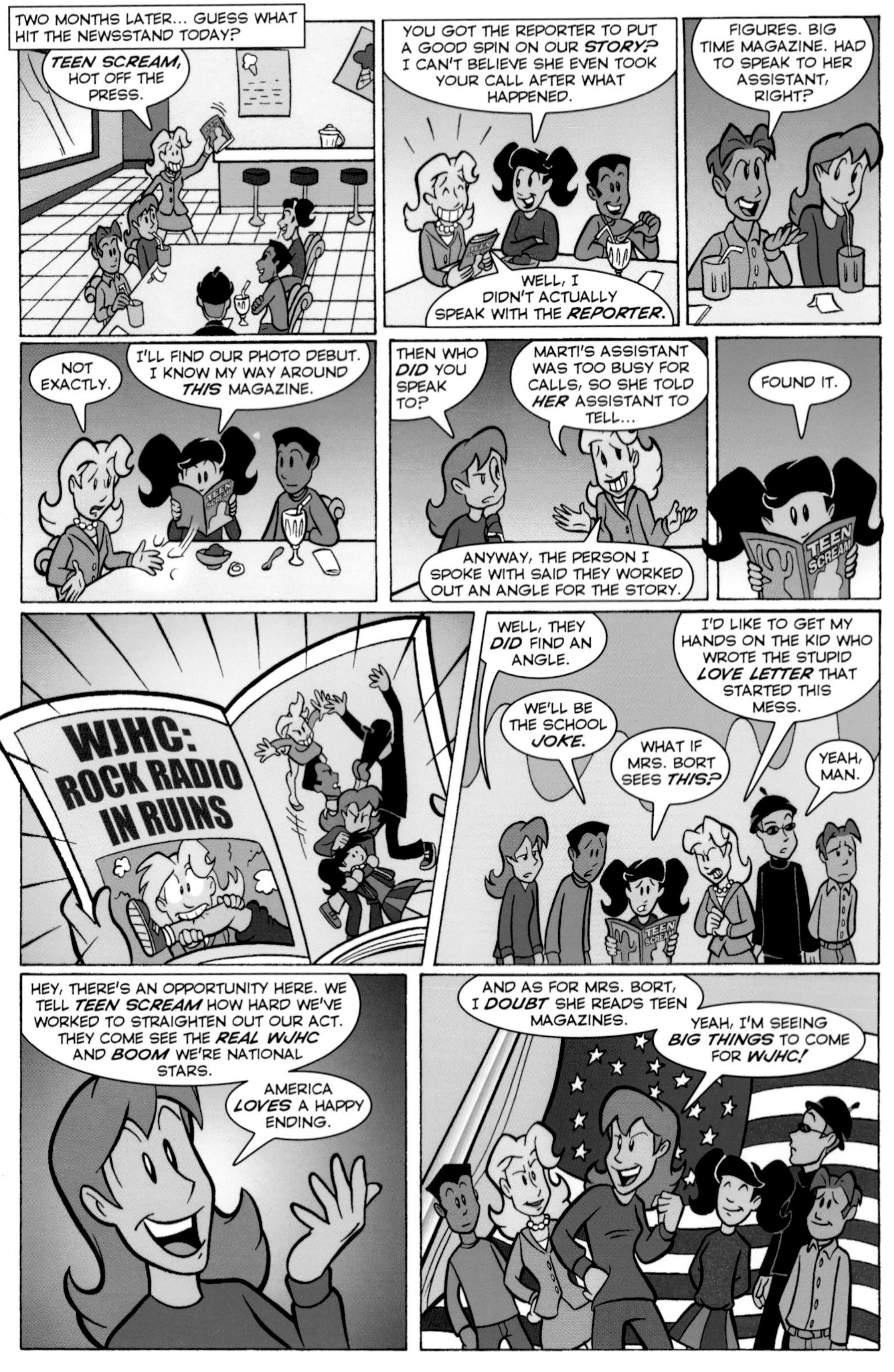
TWO MONTHS LATER... GUESS WHAT HIT THE NEWSSTAND TODAY?
TEEN SCREAM, HOT OFF THE PRESS.
YOU GOT THE REPORTER TO PUT A GOOD SPIN ON OUR STORY? I CAN'T BELIEVE SHE EVEN TOOK YOUR CALL AFTER WHAT HAPPENED.
WELL, I DIDN'T ACTUALLY SPEAK WITH THE REPORTER.
FIGURES. BIG TIME MAGAZINE. HAD TO SPEAK TO HER ASSISTANT, RIGHT?
NOT EXACTLY.
I'LL FIND OUR PHOTO DEBUT. I KNOW MY WAY AROUND THIS MAGAZINE.
TEEN SCREAM
THEN WHO DID YOU SPEAK TO?
MARTI'S ASSISTANT WAS TOO BUSY FOR CALLS, SO SHE TOLD HER ASSISTANT TO TELL...
ANYWAY, THE PERSON I SPOKE WITH SAID THEY WORKED OUT AN ANGLE FOR THE STORY.
FOUND IT.
TEEN SCREAM
WJHC: ROCK RADIO IN RUINS
WELL, THEY DID FIND AN ANGLE.
I'D LIKE TO GET MY HANDS ON THE KID WHO WROTE THE STUPID LOVE LETTER THAT STARTED THIS MESS.
WE'LL BE THE SCHOOL JOKE.
WHAT IF MRS. BORT SEES THIS?
YEAH, MAN.
TEEN SCREAM
HEY, THERE'S AN OPPORTUNITY HERE. WE TELL TEEN SCREAM HOW HARD WE'VE WORKED TO STRAIGHTEN OUT OUR ACT. THEY COME SEE THE REAL WJHC AND BOOM WE'RE NATIONAL STARS.
AMERICA LOVES A HAPPY ENDING.
AND AS FOR MRS. BORT, I DOUBT SHE READS TEEN MAGAZINES.
YEAH, I'M SEEING BIG THINGS TO COME FOR WJHC!

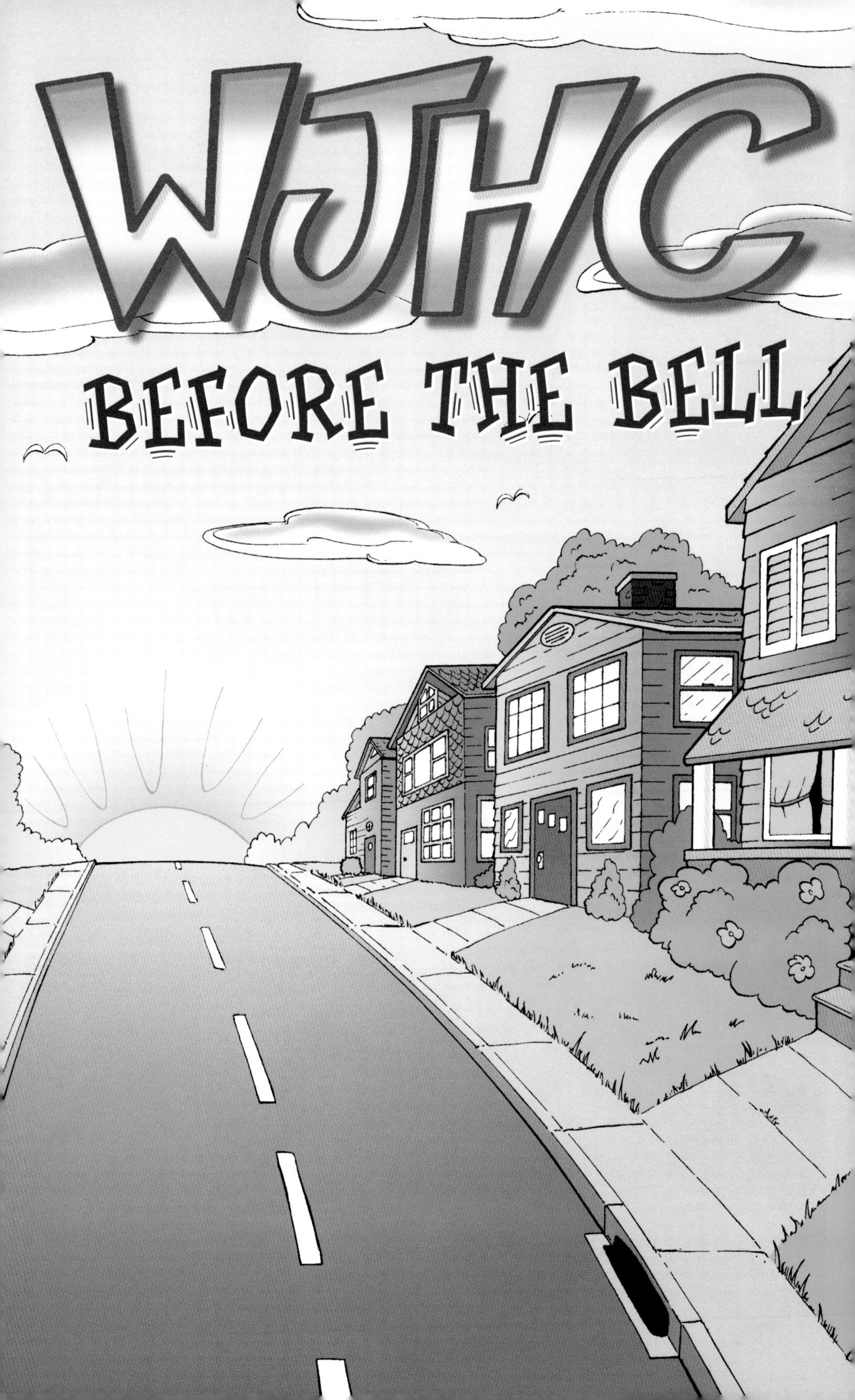
WJHC
BEFORE THE BELL

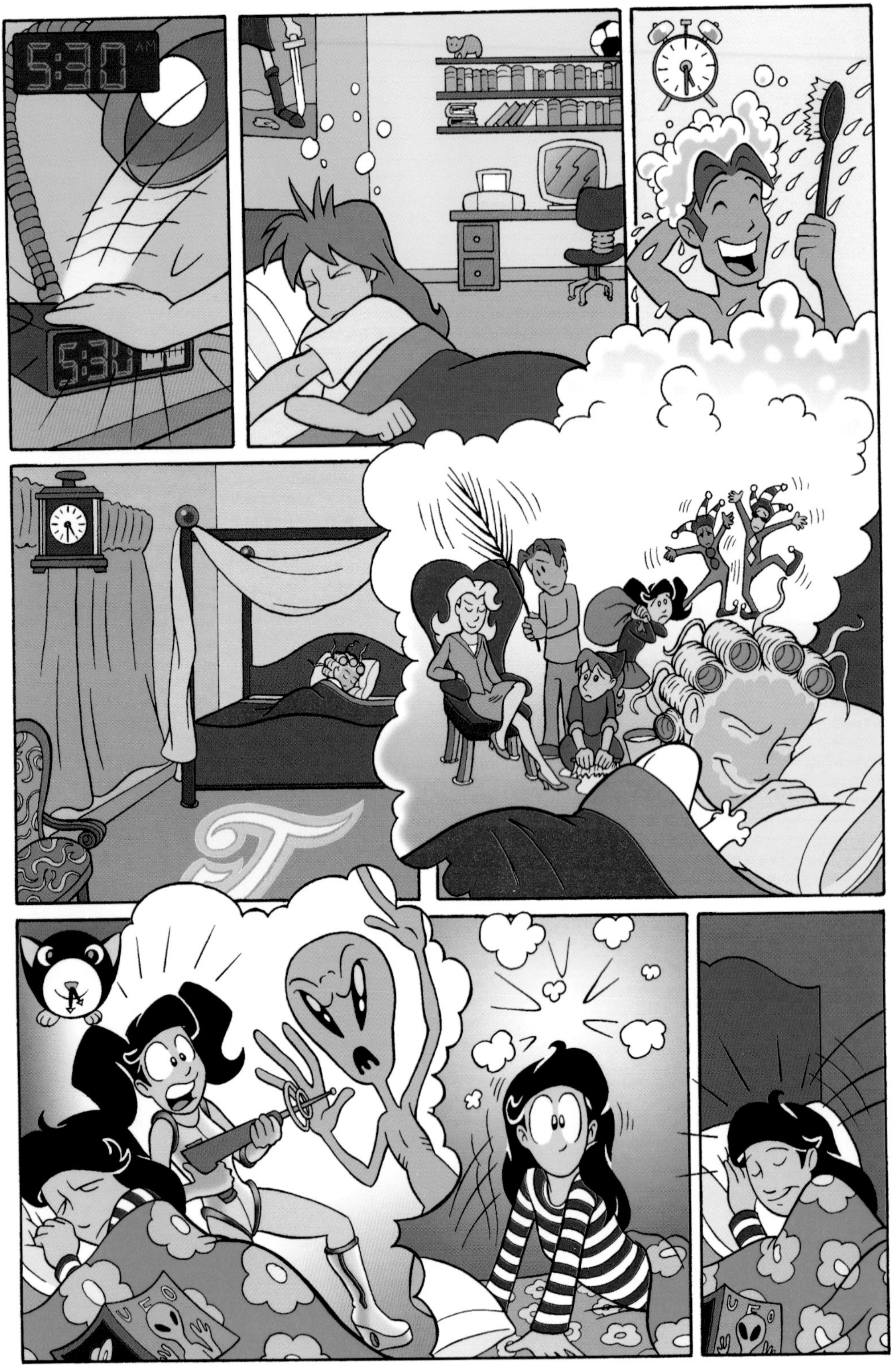
5:30 AM
UFO

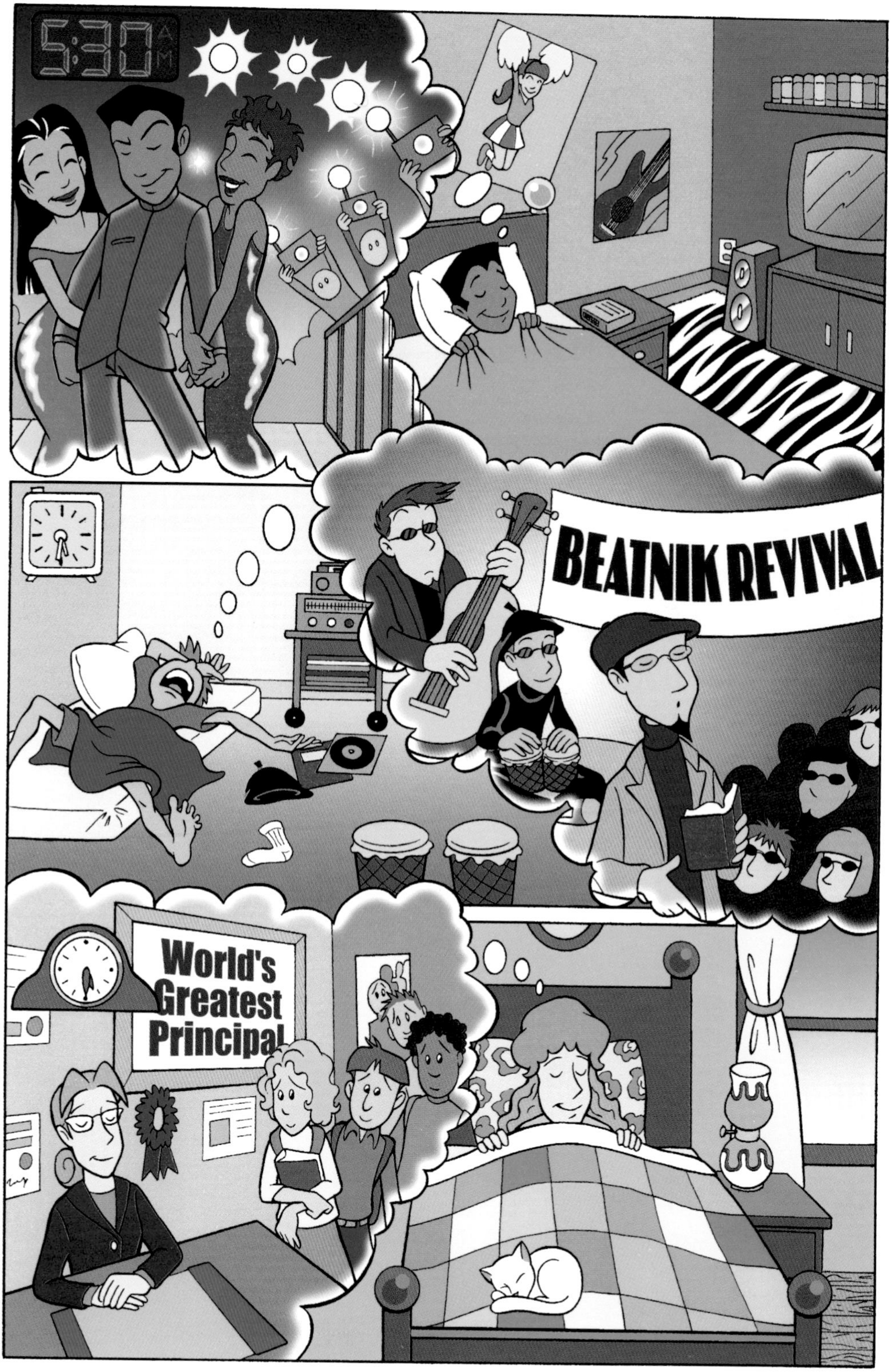
5:30 AM
BEATNIK REVIVAL
World's Greatest Principal

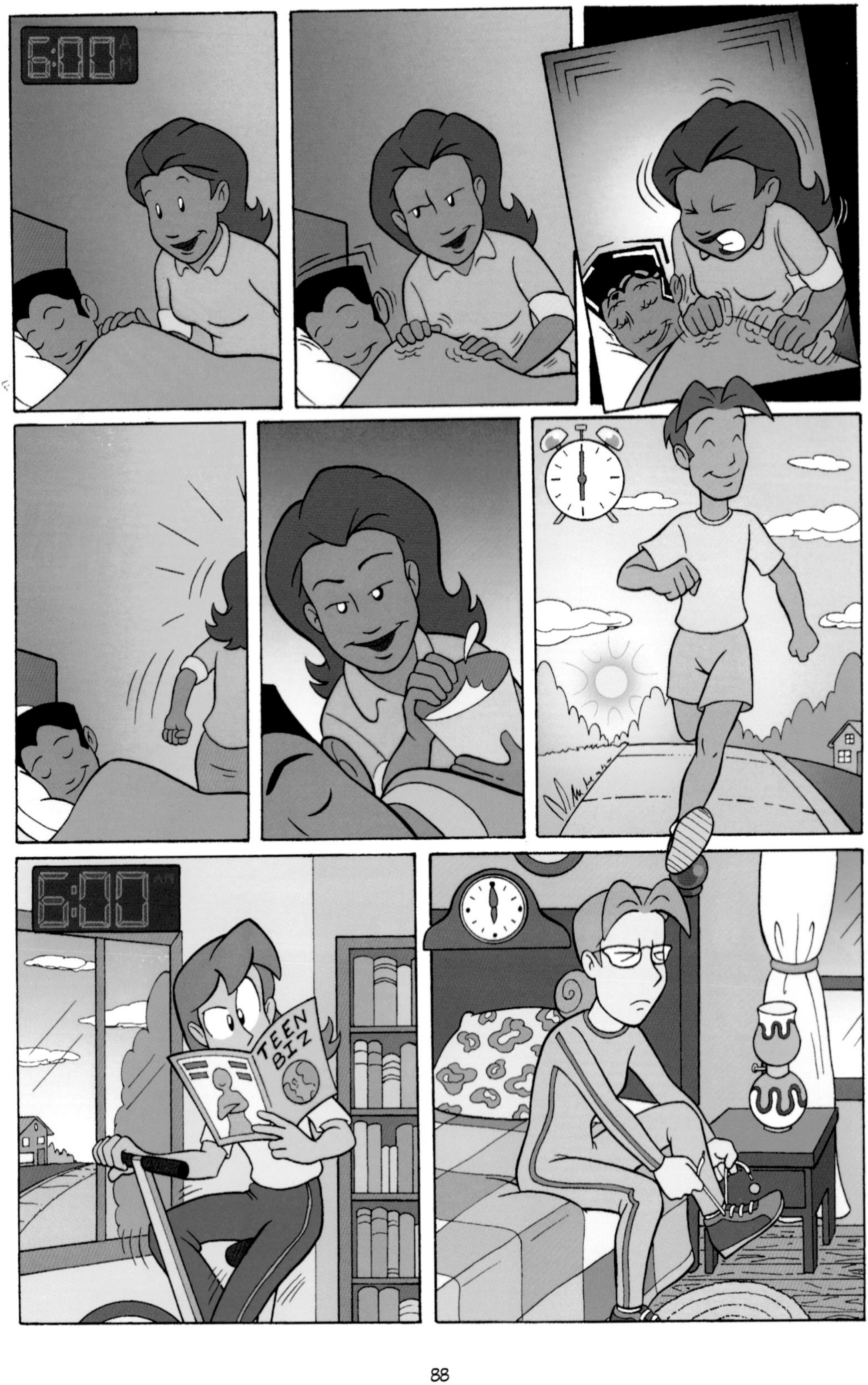
6:00 AM
TEEN BIZ
6:00 AM

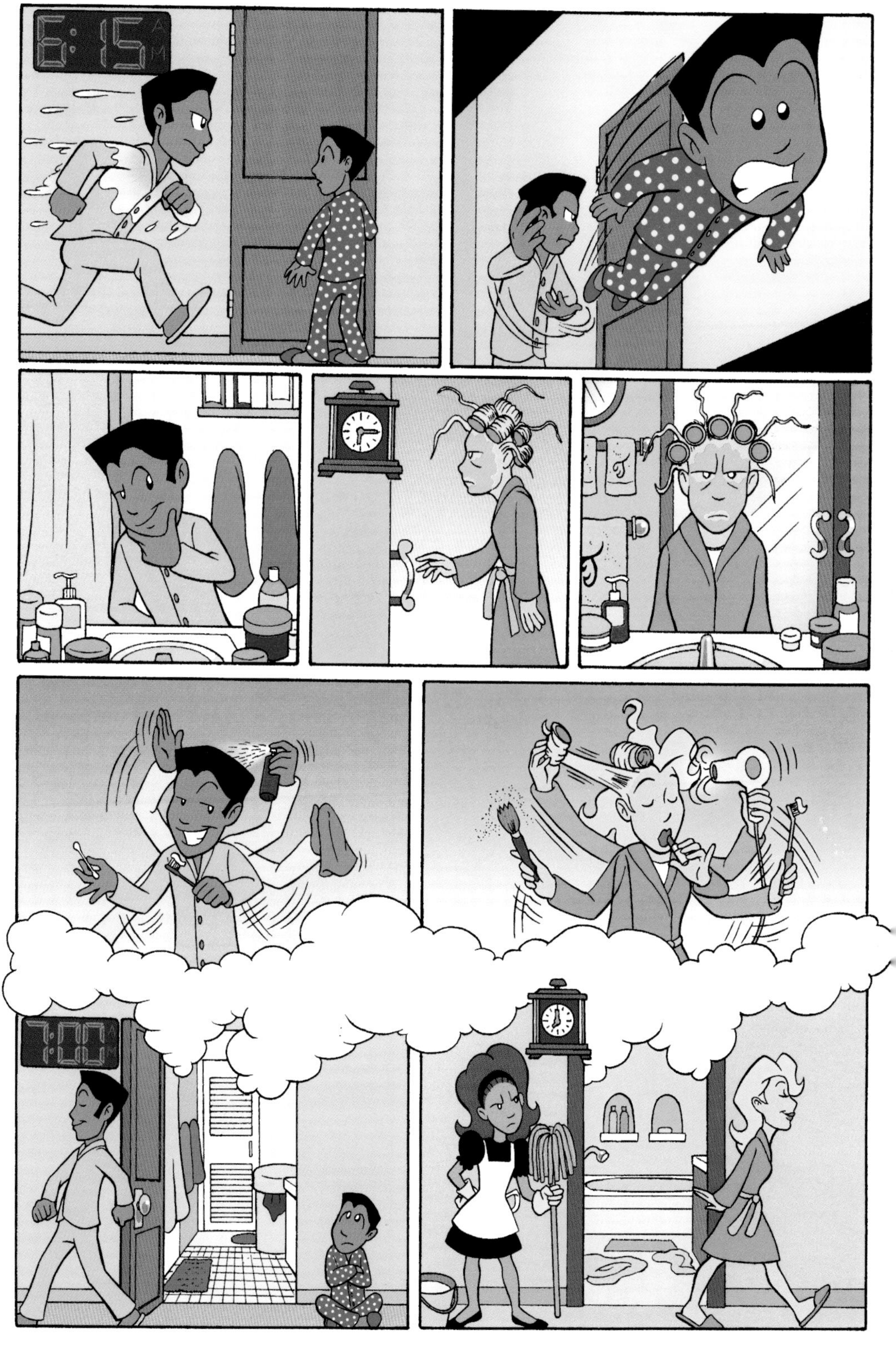
6:15 AM
7:00 AM

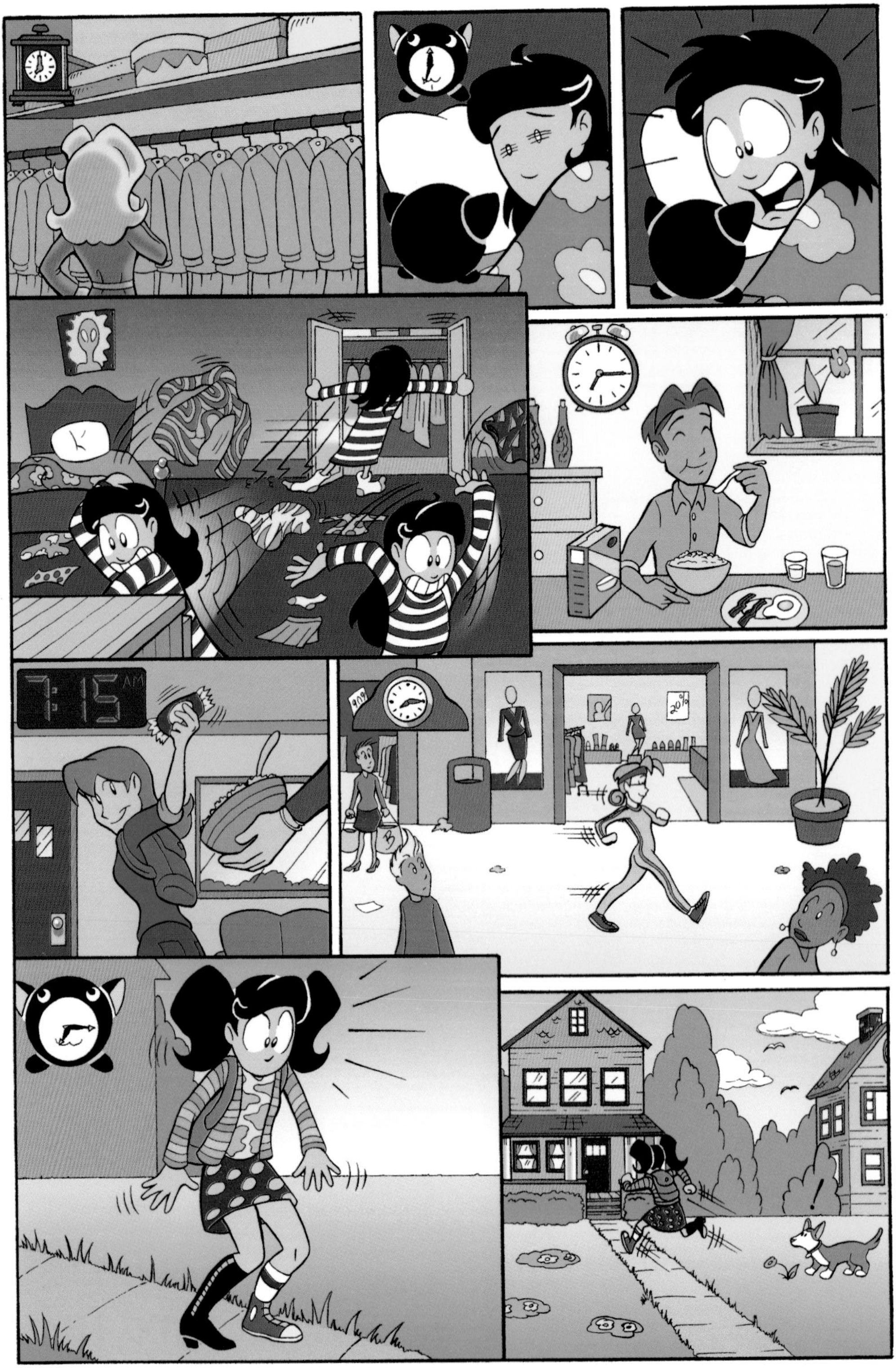
7:15 AM
20%

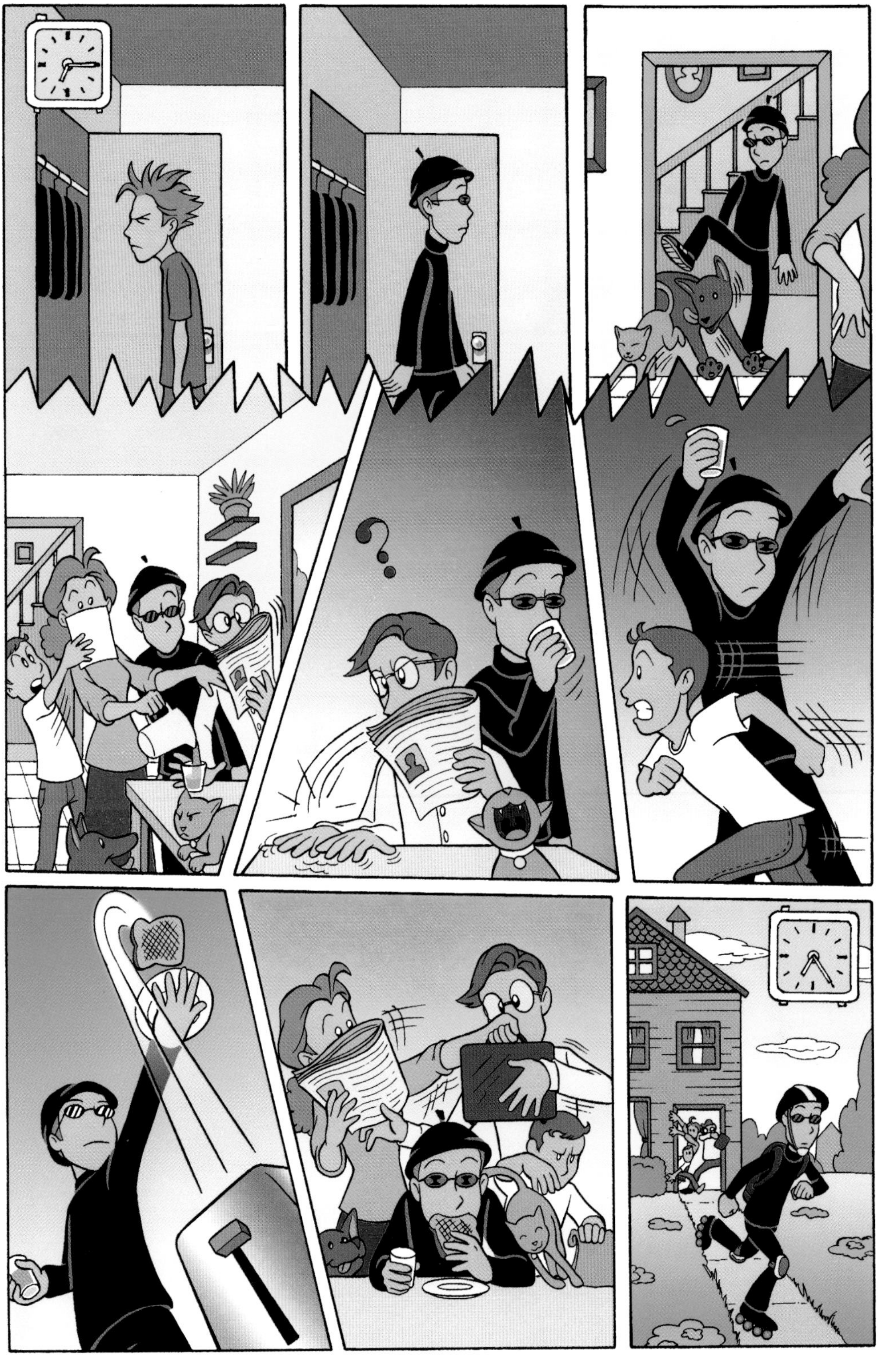

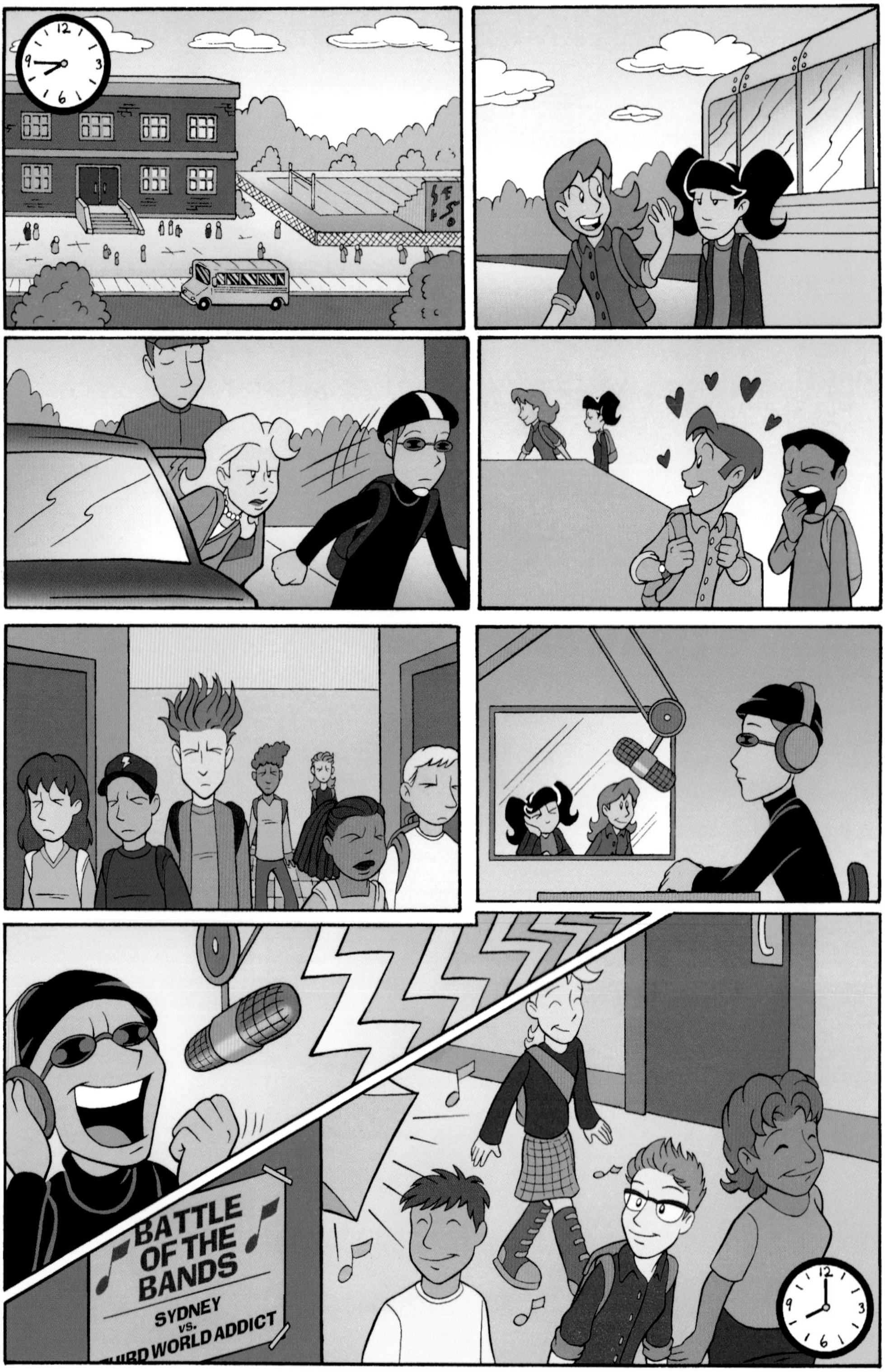
BATTLE OF THE BANDS
SYDNEY vs. THIRD WORLD ADDICT

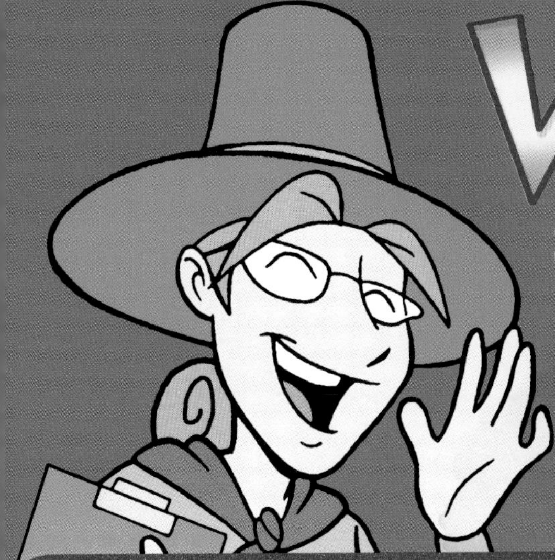

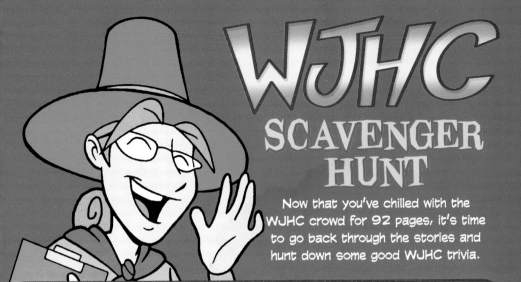

WJHC SCAVENGER HUNT

Now that you've chilled with the WJHC crowd for 92 pages, it's time to go back through the stories and hunt down some good WJHC trivia.

1. Radio station ***WJHC*** starts with a ***W*** because it's a typical prefix for U.S. radio stations east of the Mississippi River (West of the Mississippi they start with ***K***.) Search the pages to find what the ***J***, ***H*** and ***C*** stand for.

2. One of the DJ wannabees on page 14 plays a different cameo role in each story, except ***Before the Bell.*** Can you figure out which one he is?

3. Janey Wells has one busy schedule. How early does she wake up each morning to fit everything in?

4. Superstar Beatrix Lane is a globe-trotting jetsetter. Search to find the name of the hotel Beatrix stays in when she's in Jackson Hill.

5. Turns out Sandy Diaz, electronics whiz, has a creative side. What does Sandy do to express himself artistically?

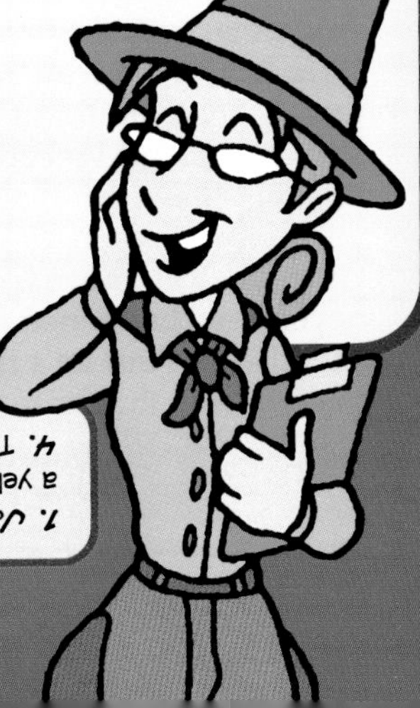

Turn the page upside-down for the answers!

1. *Jackson Hill Crowd* - page 21; ***2.*** The guy with the glasses wearing a yellow shirt and red suspenders - page 14; ***3.*** 5:30 am - page 86; ***4.*** The Jackson Hill Plaza - page 41; ***5.*** Bonsai tree sculpting - page 67

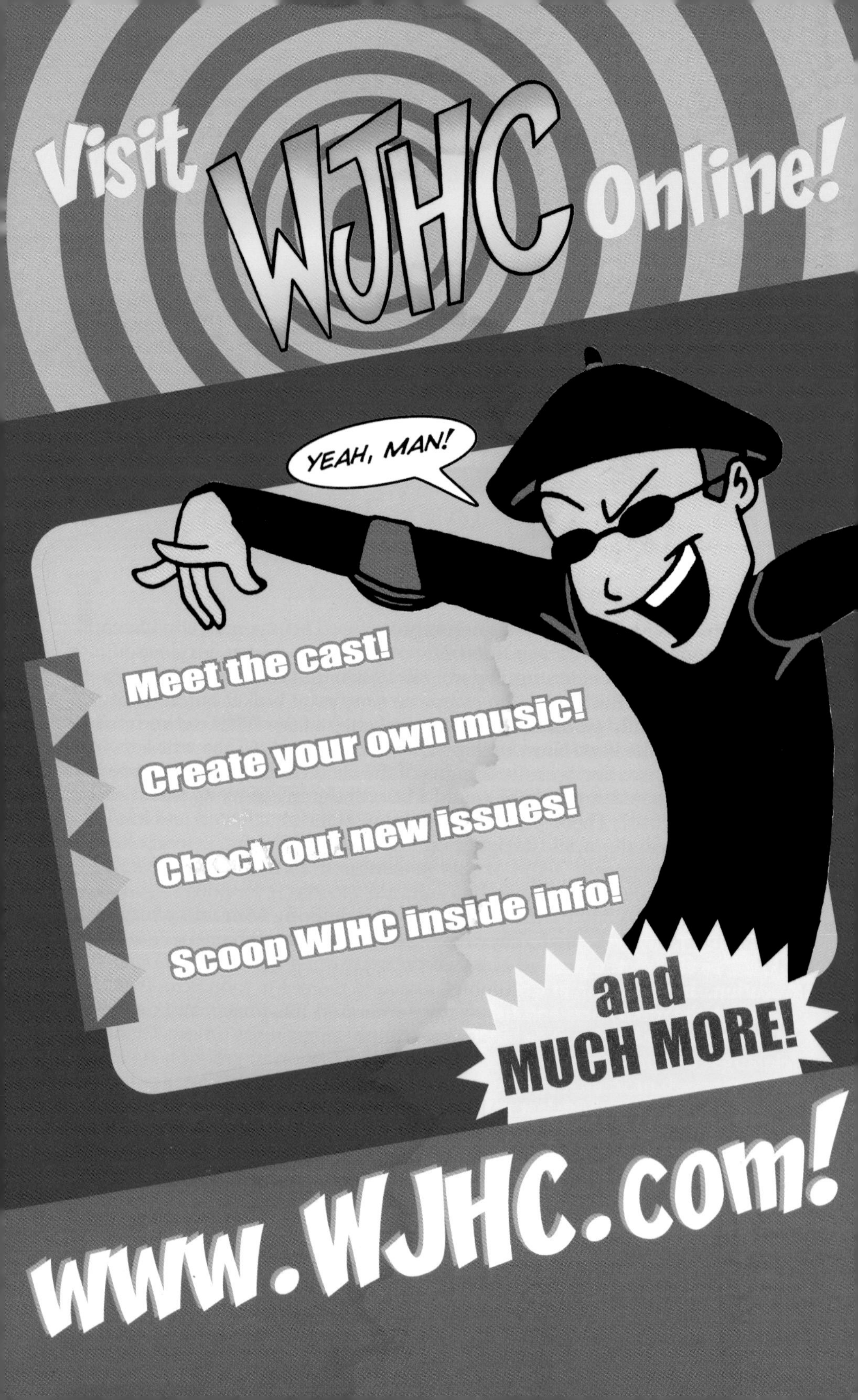
Visit WJHC Online!
YEAH, MAN!
Meet the cast!
Create your own music!
Check out new issues!
Scoop WJHC inside info!
and MUCH MORE!
www.WJHC.com!